Kage

A Becky Hawk Suspense Novel

KAGE

A BECKY HAWK SUSPENSE NOVEL

BY ROBBIE LANIER

Kage: A Becky Hawk Suspense Novel
First edition, April 2025

ISBN 979-8-9917627-1-7

Library of Congress Control Number: 2025905068

Printed in the United States of America

Cover photo by PinkBadger, iStock
Back cover photo: Releon8211, iStock

TESSELLATA BOOKS
Virginia, USA
editora@tessellata.org

To my wife, Sherri.

CHAPTER 1

The last rays of sunlight spread a red-orange shade over the valley and town below when he finished his climb and found a chalk scribbling above the dark, rocky crevice. It instructed him to come inside. He'd visited there before but never dared to enter, even when he'd been curious as a child and the opening hadn't looked as tight. Wiping sweat from his brow, he worked his way up the steep ground to it. Cool air met his face when he shined his flashlight in. He called out and listened to only his echo inside. This was a bad start. He didn't like surprises, especially when they involved his plans. And this plan had to go flawlessly.

He thought about it while staring in. As much as he feared it, the meeting had to be that day. He removed his hat and tie, summoning courage before he squeezed into the tight space. Almost immediately his body became stuck between the rocks, and he experienced moments of panic before pushing through to a section wide enough for him to snake along until he could stand again.

The inside of the cave cooled his sweat while he waited for his nerves to ease and his eyes to adjust. He dusted his shirt and pants while shining the light over glistening rock formations, grown thick over millions of years. Absent was graffiti and other evidence of human visitation. The size of the place surprised him. Dripping water sounds came from near and far.

He called out again and listened to the dripping and his echo. He took hesitant steps, stopping before the small hole of fading sunlight behind him disappeared entirely. The air had turned cooler, cold even. Moist limestone underfoot sloped downward into total darkness. He heard the squeaks of bats from it. Thoughts of becoming lost there entered his mind. Claustrophobia stirred with his other fears. He pulled a pistol with a silencer attached from his belt and slid in a clip before calling out once more.

A voice, faint and low, came from somewhere ahead. He listened while he walked and cursed and shook the flashlight when it dimmed and died. The weak batteries managed a low beam that steadily faded again.

"Come here," he yelled and heard his voice break. "Come to me. It's dark. I can't see."

He turned the other way, looking for light. He wanted to go back now, but the darkness had disoriented his sense of direction. "Help," he yelled. "Help me." He looked down and calmed a bit.

The faint light that showed below indicated the steepness of the slope he stood on. His dress shoes slipped on the limestone, and he struggled keeping his balance when he began his walk downward. It took only five steps before his feet slid from under him. The flashlight bounced from his hand. However, he managed to keep his grip on the pistol while he tumbled downward and crashed against the cave wall at the bottom. Different parts of his body ached on his slow rise to his feet, but the light was near now. It glowed from a jagged fissure in the wall. He trudged to it and peered in before stepping inside with his hands tight on the pistol grips and trembling in front of him.

The glow covered only a small portion of the alcove he stood in. He saw the source, a railroad lantern on the floor. He lowered his pistol to his side when he saw the outline of a human figure sitting and staring at him from behind the lantern. Hesitantly, he walked toward it.

"Why didn't you meet me outside like before?" he asked. The figure still stared. "I mean…I just wondered…why not." He looked around as far as the glow would allow. An iron pot hung over smoldering coals. Piles of books and newspapers lay around a rotted mattress and blanket. A harsh stench overpowered the earthy smell of the cave.

He removed his handkerchief and patted his face while walking closer to the lantern and the figure behind it. "Are we still in agreement to it all?"

There was a lengthy silence. "Yes."

"Good. I'm leaving early in the morning for my trip. They sleep late nowadays. They'll still be in bed. The back door will be unlocked." He took a few more steps closer. The very familiar facial features that were revealed then by the light had always disturbed him. A book with Japanese symbols on the cover lay beside the lantern. "Would you like for me to leave some more books for you in my room?"

Icy blue eyes glared through the black hair spilling over them. An unnaturally pale face contrasted the colors. "Yes, as it's my only way to learn about this world." Resentment dripped from the voice.

"I'm sorry. You deserved better than what they gave you. I hope you don't blame me in any way."

"It was their choice, and they gave me nothing."

He found the tone unsettling. "I know that, but now's your chance to even things." He showed the pistol and silencer. "It's a German, seven sixty-five Luger. I bought it from a contact in Knoxville. It's untraceable—quiet too. You won't have to worry about the neighbors hearing the shots. Just don't get caught with it. Silencers are illegal, you know." It was a forced joke that made him uneasy after he'd said it.

The eyes finally blinked. "Let me see." A white hand reached out.

"Have you ever fired a gun?"

"I can learn."

"Let me show you a few things first." He knelt beside the lantern. "Can we have more light?"

"I can see."

"Ok. This is the toggle. Use it to chamber a round. Safety here. Magazine catch here. It holds eight rounds. That should be more than enough. I brought another clip just in case." He removed it from his pocket with a thick roll of bills and handed everything over. "I left the safe door ajar. It's in the office. You need to leave one of them near it. I want it to look as if she was forced to open it. It has to look like a robbery." He watched hands roll out the bills. "That's all they had in the safe. You keep it. The rest is in the bank. It'll be best to not touch that until later."

"So, they're wealthy?"

"Yeah. You could say that. They hardly do business anymore, except for a few old friends on occasion, but they've invested, and they've saved. They travel a lot also, so nobody will think anything of it if they're not seen for a few days. That will give me time to come back from my trip before I report it to the police. It may take me a while to collect on the policies. I'll find you when I do. You'll get half. It'll be worth the wait. I promise."

"It's a lot?"

"Yes. As always, they were thinking of only each other when they bought their policies, now, if they die together..." He smiled and watched an understanding nod. The money went into a pocket. The hands then fumbled with the pistol mechanisms. "Can you handle this?"

"I can."

"Yeah. Sure, you can." He'd wondered for a while. Curiosity now got the better of him. "This won't be your first time, will it? The women they've found along the highway—they're yours?" He felt a chill when the eyes turned up with an emotionless stare. "Not that it matters to me. You know I don't care. You don't have to tell me anything. I only wondered."

"You wonder too much."

"Sorry. Didn't mean to pry. I just—"

"I won't have any trouble killing them. Is there anything else?"

"No. Nothing. Well, just one thing. Listen, I know how they treated you. I'd hate them too. But understand what we're doing here. Remember, make it look like a robbery, not revenge killings. Don't... don't torture them or anything."

Hands tinkered with the pistol mechanisms again.

"Looks like you're confused. Let me show you how that works. Is there anything we can use for a target?"

"I'm done with this book."

"That will work." He took it and walked to the other side of the room. "This is the summer you and I become rich, my friend. All our years of grief from them will be worth it, don't you think?" As he propped the book against the cave wall, the light behind him brightened until the entire alcove was lit. He heard the metallic sound of the Luger racking a round. He turned to face the silencer, his mouth working in a silent beg. Then, what he saw in the corner of the room on a slab of limestone forced a tight cry from him.

"Wrong," the voice said. "This is the summer people will learn my name."

"Plea—" The Luger spit a bullet between his eyes.

CHAPTER 2

Dan Bowman turned off the ignition and listened to his old pickup sputter while it tried restarting itself. There was much work the truck needed, more than Dan could afford, but he didn't care for now. He walked to the screen door of the house and knocked. Rylie Holbrook came out with a grin.

"You're starting early today," Rylie said, his grin spreading over his chubby, unshaven face. "Thought you'd be working."

Dan had learned to ignore the patronizing tone. There was no use lying. He could tell Rylie had guessed. He held out two dollars. "They fired me."

Rylie took it. "Sorry about that, old buddy. Just a minute." He returned with a pint canning jar.

Dan took it and swirled the clear liquid inside while watching the tiny bubble beads.

"You know mine's always good," Rylie said. "Why test it?"

"Habit, I guess."

Rylie chewed on the cut of tobacco in his jaw while he stepped onto the porch. He spit into the yard. "They smelled it on your breath again, I reckon."

Dan looked away and nodded. "Yeah. They'd been watching me pretty close lately."

"Well, we're both getting old," said Rylie. "Too damned old for highway work for sure. Any ideas about what you're going to do now?"

"Whatever I can find, if there's anything *to* find. That blasted interstate has taken everything away from here. The town is dried up. You wouldn't be needing a deliveryman, I guess."

"Nah. Brant will be doing that now that he's out of school. Wish I could help you, Dan. I really do. Maybe it's time your girl looked for a job, being that she's graduating too. Hell, you've done plenty to support her."

Dan took an absent look at the blue mountain ridges. His eyes settled for a moment on the giant, white rocks of Overlook Hang. He shoved away an unpleasant thought. "I was hoping she might go to college."

Rylie smirked and spit. "Yeah, Dan," he said with a pat to the back. "I'll keep my ears open in town for something, but, like you say, it's slim pickings. Maybe it's time to move. That damned highway must've taken the jobs somewhere."

"Yeah," Dan said. "Thanks." He walked back to his truck, knowing there were some things that would follow him wherever he went.

"Closed Until Further Notice," read the sign placed on the front door of the large house.

He'd showered and combed his hair. In an upstairs bedroom, he looked into a mirror and admired himself in a suit and tie. There'd been hats in the closet too. He tried on an Irish wool one but liked the black fedora. It matched the suit better. He took sunglasses and a watch from the nightstand, put them on, and smiled when he looked at himself again.

He checked his new watch. It showed three-fifteen, and it surprised him that his stay in the house had been that long. He went into the office once more, making sure it was all in the exact order he wished.

The van he'd found parked along the mountain road near the cave the day before was now packed with everything he'd found that might be useful. He'd left enough space in the back for sleeping. How soon he'd return depended on the success of his journey. He had the money and supplies to last for as long as it took. He lifted the two suitcases he'd found packed in the bedroom, took a few books from a shelf, and left through the back door, locking it behind.

It delighted him that he'd found a second walkie talkie in a desk drawer. The first had been inside the van. He could tell they were refurbished army surplus, probably used for business operations. There would be a use for them.

The van looked well maintained, the inside clean. The gauge showed a nearly full tank. He felt anxious to start and took a moment to go over a checklist in his head before placing the Luger into the glovebox with his handcuffs, parachute cord, and duct tape. He also tossed in the two handfuls of small flowers he'd plucked from a wreath in the house. He turned the ignition and drove to the front.

An old man walking his dog passed on the street and gave a warm wave with no suspicion on his face. He returned the wave with a smile. It was a smooth start to a day he'd long planned. His expectations were high. In addition to the two bodies in the house, he'd left a hidden note elsewhere. Only if destiny smiled on him would it ever be read. Finding the right person to send to it would be difficult. He controlled fate only so much.

However, there was a certain nurse just ten miles away whose fate he *would* determine that evening. She'd gained a week or so of fame in the local paper that spring when she'd saved the district's congressman from choking at a local restaurant.

Over time, he'd learned that patience was a virtue. Planning and organization meant everything. He'd watched and studied her for over a month, even walked past her in the hospital parking lot once and said hello. He'd found following her without raising her suspicions comically easy. She was pushing thirty but still single and lived alone. Her twelve-hour shift ended in just over an hour. She'd go by the post office, maybe the grocery store, and then home, where she'd shower, heat a frozen dinner, and eat in front of the television before early bed. Her back door was easy to enter, even when locked.

She'd be different from the others—the highway drifters and the prostitutes who worked the truck stops. A hero nurse would garner attention, at least statewide. The task force investigating his kills would surely work more aggressively. Moving to another area would be necessary. It was his decision, though, the news and shock of her death, or her continued existence in this world. He would decide the fate of Mary Louise Givings. He drove and pondered his judgment. This was his favorite part of the game.

CHAPTER 3

The driver of Linville County School bus number twelve had given up controlling the kids half an hour earlier. It was the last ride of the school year over the curvy mountain roads. Summer break had begun. Talking had turned to yelling and laughter. Water pistols, snuck inside lunch boxes and book bags, squirted streams into the air.

As with all other days, two seniors rode in the back. One seemed oblivious to the noise while she finished her page length signing of the other's yearbook.

"Better finish up, Shy," Cathy Conner said. "Your bus riding days are almost over."

The bus made a wide turn onto Old Mill Road, its tires spinning in a muddy spot before gaining traction.

Shiloh Bowman signed her name, sweeping a loop from her S around the other letters. She pushed heavy glasses up her nose and handed Cathy back her Cavalier.

"Guess this is it?" Cathy said. "We've sure logged some miles together on this bus. I've enjoyed the company. See you at graduation."

"Yeah. Maybe."

"What in the world do you mean, yeah maybe? Maybe you've enjoyed it, or maybe I'll see you at graduation?"

"I'll probably come, but Mr. Wilkes said he could mail my diploma if I wanted. Sometimes it's hard for me to get away."

"You're not serious. You can't be. You've already bought your cap and gown. Can't your dad drive you? Surely, he wants to see you get your diploma."

Shiloh looked out the window while the bus stopped. "Yeah. I'm sure he does. It's just that things can change with him from day to day. You know what I mean."

Cathy made an understanding frown. "Well, listen, my parents and I can pick you up. We'll come early so I can do your hair."

Shiloh smiled slightly. "Cathy, would it be Ok with your parents if I stayed with you some this summer?" She looked up the hill toward her house while waiting for an answer.

"Shiloh," the driver yelled.

"Sure. I'd love for you to come spend some time. It's only that we don't have a lot of room with my brothers and all. I don't think it could be for days or anything."

"I understand. See you around." Shiloh stood.

Cathy grabbed her hand. "So, you *are* talking about staying for days. You know I'll let you if my parents say you can. Hey, I'll come stay with you some too. We can go to some parties over the summer. It'll be great."

"Until you leave for college. Guess I won't see you much after that."

"I'll be coming home most weekends, silly."

Shiloh nodded. "Sure. That sounds good."

Cathy held her hand out. "We did it, Shy. To the class of sixty-five."

Shiloh latched her thumb against Cathy's and slid her palm over her friend's. She walked up the bus aisle, taking squirts of water from the laughing kids. She glanced at the wide-angle mirror at the front of the bus one last time. The excited first grader with a happy face and brown pigtails had grown into a skinny young woman with thick glasses who seemed to always look afraid. She turned away from the reflection.

"Shake a leg, Olive Oyl," a freckled-faced fourth grader with a red flattop said. He gave her a squirt from his pistol.

A distant explosion turned everyone's head. Brown dust made a cloud in the sky from where the new interstate ramps were going up.

"Hey, Shiloh," someone yelled. "I hate telling you, but someone lit a match next to your old man."

The driver turned and shouted reprimands over laughter. "Have a nice summer, Shiloh," she said. "Hope to see you around."

"Thanks, Mrs. Davis." Shiloh stepped out and began her walk up the driveway. Halfway there, she saw his old pickup parked in the drive. She turned as the bus drove away and then sat on the ground with her chin against her fists and an unpleasant feeling rolling in her stomach. It was half an hour later when she walked to the house.

He sat on his old recliner. A radio beside him played country music at low volume. His head was turned backward, his eyes closed. He held a nearly empty jar in his hand.

"Daddy?" She shook him.

His eyes half opened. He looked at her for a moment before burbling something. He tried to rise before falling back and spilling the remainder of the jar on his work pants. His eyes closed again.

She watched him adjust himself. The man was old now, much older than the fathers of her classmates. His white hair had thinned, enough to show his reddened scalp. His wrinkles had grown deeper recently. He was old but not as old as he looked. He'd been fired that day. She'd known it would happen sometime. She picked up his jar, turned off his radio, and walked to the kitchen.

Canned biscuits, sausage, and chicken salad were the only foods in the refrigerator. She ate a chicken salad sandwich and drank orange juice at the kitchen table. She'd promised herself not long before that she'd wait until school was over before doing it. By the time she'd finished her sandwich, she thought she might have the courage to.

In her bedroom, she emptied her book satchel on the bed. She packed a few clothes, her toothbrush, and glasses case. Her babysitting money in a cigar box went in also. She heard him cough and rustle, and she took a look out her bedroom door. He slept with his mouth open. A snore was rolling out. She knew it would be late, maybe morning, before he woke. She packed a few last things, went to her nightstand, and found paper and pen.

"Thank you for raising me," she wrote. "Get better, please. Please find a way. Love always, Shiloh." Then she lay down on her bed to think about it once more.

Mary Givings had found a boyfriend. He worked with her at the hospital. That was evident by the scrubs the guy had worn when they arrived at her house together.

He'd parked at a church nearby and watched for two hours. Pizza was delivered, and then the blinds of the bedroom were drawn. If the boyfriend hadn't moved in, he certainly had the intention of staying all night. Whatever the case, fate had smiled on Mary Givings that day.

He went to the back of the van, where he ate two pickles from a jar, drank water from a thermos, and urinated into a milk jug before driving away. His desire for another kill was strong. Mary Givings' good luck would be someone else's misfortune. That was the way with winds of fate.

He took back roads on his way to the highway. He'd go east, all the way to the coast maybe, finding the easiest marks along the way to satisfy his desires while searching for the perfect one for his final game. There was no need to rush. He felt powerful and in control. His journey was just beginning. The possibilities were endless.

He turned the van onto Old Mill Road.

CHAPTER 4

Shiloh considered going back while standing at the foot of the driveway. Maybe if she talked to him, told him what she'd planned. Maybe that would be the incentive he needed. No, she'd been through it too often. The older she'd become, the more she'd realized how much weight she'd carried. She would become an adult in six months. But six months was too long. He would be frustrated over losing his job, and a hard time would follow. She'd write to let him know she was safe and ask him not to look for her. One day she would visit him. This eased her conscience enough to begin walking.

She'd checked the bus schedule from Waynesville weeks earlier and knew there'd be time to make it. The sun was low behind her as she walked down the dirt road. It was only a short distance before she heard the roar of an engine approaching.

He stopped the van when a blue convertible sailed past in a dust cloud. Boys piled in it laughed at him. One of them threw an empty beer can that bounced off the van's windshield. He opened the glovebox and removed the Luger while the dust settled.

The sound of the engine was familiar to Shiloh. It could be heard each morning and afternoon during Brant Holbrook's trips to and from school. She heard it at night too, often late, when he returned from his father's deliveries. She tried ignoring it then but turned and jumped aside when the car slid to a stop feet behind her.

Four other seniors were with Brant. Shiloh knew them all, however they were classmates she'd avoided. She saw by the shine in their eyes that their celebration of the last day of school had already begun.

Brant was the only one whose hairstyle wasn't influenced by The Beatles. He had the same, slick-backed ducktail he'd worn through high school, along with the usual t-shirt with sleeves short enough to show off his snake and heart tattoos. "Hey, Shiloh, where you going?" he asked. "Ain't nothing that way except road. What's with the bookbag? We're done with that shit."

She turned. "Leave me alone, Brant," she said, and walked faster when the car rolled beside her.

Cliff Broose sat on the passenger side with a cigarette between his lips. "Hey, Shiloh," he said, "do me a favor and let me see those brown eyes unmagnified. I really don't think you'd be that bad if you lost the glasses. I mean it."

"Work on the ass and tits some too," Ricky Kuester said from the backseat. He smiled and slugged his beer back while the others laughed.

Brant turned back his beer and looked toward the sound of an engine. The black van he'd just dusted crept over a hill.

"Are you leaving your old man?" Cliff asked. "Finally getting the hell away from him? I don't blame you. What's your plans? I won't squeal."

Shiloh sped up her steps.

Brant turned his eyes from the van and caught up to her. "Want a ride, Shiloh? Come on. Celebrate with us. We've earned it. Get out, Cliff. Let her sit between us."

Cliff opened the door and stepped out. "Come on with us," he said. "We'll give you a beer or two. After watching you all those years in class, I'd love to see how you'd be loosened up some." He grabbed her arm. She jerked away and ran toward the woods with Cliff chasing while the other boys howled.

"Hey, where are you going?" Cliff yelled, closing distance. "I don't bite—most times." He chuckled and grabbed her from behind. She squealed before crashing into a mountain rhododendron bush, feeling a burn in her leg with the sound of her dress ripping. She managed to keep on her feet and ran into the woods while hearing the boys' shouts and laughs.

Only Brant wasn't laughing. He watched the van pull to the opposite side of the road. Its tires splashed through a puddle before it stopped. Brant flicked his cigarette, got out, and walked toward the man in a black hat and sunglasses staring at him from the window. "What do you want, jerk?" he yelled.

In his lap, he held his Luger while watching the boy come closer. He wondered if he should. It would be messy. He'd have to shoot all five boys if he shot one. Perhaps he should let it go. The girl was the one he really wanted, but the boy coming toward him was the one playing the game now. He was the one who'd determine his own fate.

"What are you staring at?" Brant yelled.

His finger went around the trigger. He put a hand on the window crank.

Cliff climbed back into the convertible. "Come on, Brant. Let's go get more beer. Don't worry about that fucker."

Brant took a long stare at the man. "I know you don't I?" He watched the window roll down and pointed at the man. "Yeah, I've seen you before, asshole, and I'll see you again. I'll give you something to stare at next time." He shot a middle finger and walked back to his car.

The man in the van smiled and waved when he drove past the boys.

She crashed through the woods without looking back. She was scared and desperate to get far away from the boys, but a dull pain in her leg from the rhododendron bush slowed her. Her book satchel had grown heavy also. She stopped to look back and then sat on the ground. There was blood on her leg under the tear in her dress. She spit on her hand, wiped at the cut, and looked at sun rays shining over the mountain ridges. It would be dark by the time she made it to Waynesville now. She'd most likely miss her bus. However, there was the sound of nearby traffic. The thought of hitchhiking scared her. There'd been horrible stories around school recently of girls found along the interstate, but Brant and his friends had sealed her decision to leave that town.

Five minutes later, she walked along the eastbound lane with her thumb out. A semi-truck stopped ahead of her. The door opened. She was careful approaching and kept her distance. The driver was an older man with a trusting smile.

"Where are you off to today?" he asked.

This one was a runaway. She'd hung her head, and her steps had been hesitant before the boys approached her. The stuffed satchel she'd carried and her direction toward the interstate were also tip-offs. He took pride in reading his targets. The only question was east or west. He chose the eastbound on-ramp.

Driving slower than the speed limit, he saw the semi stop and pick her up. He drove by and got a better look at her nervous expression as she climbed into the cab. Definitely a runaway, he thought before taking the next exit ramp, crossing over, and waiting until the truck passed. He fell in behind it.

Darkness was settling. The taillights of the truck came on and swirled down a steep, winding grade. He slowed down to keep his distance. In doing so, he repeatedly lost sight of the truck while more traffic entered the highway ahead of him. Soon, he lost it entirely. As disappointing as it was, the thrill of the hunt had invigorated him. There'd be others. He'd be patient and choose wisely.

He neared the place of a recent kill. She'd been a prostitute who'd approached him at a truck stop parking lot. She'd been barely twenty, he guessed, his youngest. Fear had paralyzed her and rendered her unable to speak or resist after she'd learned her fate. The kill had been as disappointing as the small article in the paper about her the next day, but none of the five he'd left on the highway had made the news in the way he'd wanted. The police were giving the papers only the basic information, either by design or gross incompetence. Regardless, his chosen name would be known soon enough. He'd see to that.

He passed the exit where he'd left the prostitute. Then, several miles more, he entered the foothills. This was the farthest east he'd ever ventured. The flattening landscape was new to him. He stopped to stretch and buy a soda, and he considered the friendly, redheaded cashier, however ten minutes of observation showed him the little store was too busy. He decided the risk would not be worth her, and he continued on his journey.

He felt fortunate to possess total recall and often used it to re-experience his kills. He sipped his soda while driving, cleared his head, and zoned back to that morning. He saw the first one again, cooking breakfast and unaware of him just behind her. He saw her blood splatter on the wall and smelled burnt gunpowder while she fell against the stove then backward with a thud that shook the floor. But, it was the second he replayed over and over again, her face turning a bluish hue, wide eyes that reddened from blood vessels bursting under pressure. The croaks she'd made while he turned the garrote tighter, he would remember forever. His memory of it took him into a trance-like state.

He hardly noticed the lights of two large cities he passed or his merger onto another highway that took him to even flatter country with wide tobacco and soybean fields. Traffic became scarce. When he drifted out of his trance, a road sign told him Wilmington was fifty miles away and a place called Black Lake was five. Far ahead, he saw taillights. He leaned toward the windshield while pressing the accelerator. The lights were the semi's. A smile spread.

Black Lake. The name flashed in his mind again. He'd read about it. The town had been in the papers, one or maybe two years earlier. He pushed himself to remember. It came gradually. It was a tiny town. A woman solved some crimes there. Yes, that was it. She'd solved crimes—some murders. One had been her own husband's. She'd become a police officer afterward. No, a police chief, the first or one of the first female chiefs in the state. How had he forgotten? It had been big news for a short time. Excitement surged in him. Could he be so lucky this early in his hunt? He pressed his memory for more. A vague picture of the woman came. Dark hair and eyes. A round and rather pleasant face.

He found himself squeezing the steering wheel and driving twenty over the speed limit. The semi was close. Its headlights illuminated the Black Lake exit sign ahead, his new destination. He would allow the young runaway to go her merry way. There was a bigger fish in the pond now. Then, the right turn signal of the semi flashed, and his pulse quickened more.

CHAPTER 5

Chris Heath would've been considered nimble even among other seventeen year olds. Enough so that he easily jumped and gripped the frame of the window he'd just smashed out at the back of Jimmy's Lakefront Grocery. He pulled up, wriggled his body through, and dropped to the floor. Keeping low, he took a quick glance around before going to the beverages and slipping five bottles of wine into his burlap bag. Mini's Brunswick stew was his next stop. He cleaned the shelf of it and then did a crouched shuffle toward the cigarettes behind the counter.

The sound of tires rolling into the lot made him freeze. He peeped around the aisle and jerked back when a flashlight shined in. The front door shook. He'd had close calls with cops before, this female one more than once. On his knees, he watched her shine her light through the windows before she walked back to her car and drove away. From experience, Chris kept still. He knew cops would sometimes drive away after checking a building, kill their lights, and come back to catch the crook slipping from his hiding place. So, he waited. A semi rumbled up and braked at the phone booth across the street. A girl with a bag climbed out. She had a short conversation with the driver before the door closed and the semi geared away. The girl appeared unsure of herself as she glanced around while walking into the phone booth.

Things were getting too busy there for his comfort. Chris watched the windows while he shuffled to the back of the building, unlocked the door there, and slipped out. He took one step toward the lake and froze to the sound of yet another vehicle approaching. He heard it roll into the parking lot, absent a headlight shine, and stop at the corner of the building. "Shit," Chris whispered. The woman cop had seen something and circled back. He crouched in a dark spot and pressed against the wall. A door opened then closed softly. He heard walking and was a second away from sprinting toward the lake when a man in a suit and hat cut around the corner and strode past. Chris watched him from behind while backing away with his bag.

Becky Hawk finished her night patrol by checking the doors of businesses on the waterfront, happy it was Friday and looking forward to a weekend with friends. A soft lake breeze blew white smoke mingled with the smell of burning hickory and cooking barbecue around her. She grinned while rattling one last door before driving her patrol car to Jabber's Grill. Jabber, as she'd guessed, was slow-cooking pork shoulders for the next day. He sat on a lawn chair outside the cinderblock cookhouse, wearing his stained apron and a cigarette glowing between his fingers. A baseball broadcast came from a transistor radio on his lap.

"Well, how ya doing, Chief?" he said with his sly, crooked grin and bright, expressive blue eyes. "I was just wondering if you'd drop by tonight. Any mischief happening?" He reached inside the cookhouse and brought out another chair.

"None that I saw. Thank you." She sat. "Who's winning?" She'd never been a baseball fan until meeting the man. He talked baseball, and fishing, and told great stories. She knew how he'd gotten his nickname without ever asking.

"Yankees. Mantle hit a homer. He ain't what he used to be but he can still knock the tar out of 'em. Ford's pitching a shutout."

"That barbecue smell is your best advertisement. It's making me hungry."

"Want me to fix you up a sandwich with slaw?"

"Not now. Company is coming tomorrow, though. I think chopped plates with your hushpuppies and slaw for dinner just might make everyone happy."

"Bring 'em all down."

"Wouldn't have coffee made, would you?"

"Why, you've known me long enough to not ask that. Keep up with the game for me. Be right back."

He held his parachute cord and watched her from the corner of the building. Phone booth lights illuminated the girl thumbing through a directory. His eyes scanned vacant streets while the sound of the semi faded. He watched the girl studying the directory. This was the moment he felt most alive. The anticipation. Life or death was his decision. Occasionally, he allowed life but not tonight. He made a loop with his cord and stepped from the corner.

Billy Bryan of the Athletics had just broken up Ford's shutout when Jabber walked back out with two cups. "You're still drinking it black ain't you?"

"Yes. Thanks." Becky reached for it, ready to fill Jabber in on the game, but her hand froze when a wavering scream broke from somewhere.

Jabber looked toward the street. "What in tarnation?"

Becky stood and grabbed her keys from her belt. "Where did it come from?"

"I don't know. Sound bounces off the buildings here. The water plays tricks with it too." He took the cup back. "Want me to go with you?"

She got into her patrol car while noting the time on her watch. "No. Finish cooking the barbecue. Call me if you see or hear anything else." She gunned the car down the street.

Chris Heath heard the scream when he loaded the bag into his rowboat. He hesitated before getting in and shoving off. It was the girl, he thought. The man he'd seen had done something to her. He stopped rowing and looked in the direction of the store, feeling torn. Going back would probably ruin everything. There was much for him to lose. How could he help anyway? Maybe it wasn't what it seemed. He listened for more sounds but heard only the frogs croaking from the bank. A spotlight waved at the waterfront. He felt relieved. The woman cop would handle it. There would be no need to risk his plans. He rowed more, stopped, and looked back again.

Becky drove through the waterfront, shining her spotlight on every dark alley and crevice. She checked for boats on the water, and radioed the Bolton County sheriff's dispatch, requesting they notify their lake patrol of the situation. She turned the spotlight back on and roamed it while she drove through the lumber yard. The night watchman waved with his flashlight and approached. He smiled and leaned into the window when she stopped.

"What's going on, Becky?"

"Cletus, have you heard a woman scream?"

His grin made his plump cheeks dimple. "Some more than others."

Becky rolled her eyes. "Thanks anyway."

"Didn't hear anything. Been inside the plant," he called while she drove away.

She crossed the tracks and drove through the village of small homes near the shoreline that the lumber plant workers inhabited. No one stirred. Most house lights were out. As with every other night in Black Lake, all was quiet.

Nevertheless, the scream stayed in her mind. Her uneasy feeling grew stronger as she drove slowly, looked, and listened. Across from Jimmy's Grocery, she noticed a receiver hanging in the phone booth. She stopped to check it and found on the floor a pair of horn-rimmed glasses with thick lenses. She gave her ponytail a tug before beginning an inspection of the surrounding area with her flashlight.

Chris turned the boat and glided along the cattails and reeds of the shoreline. He paddled softly while listening. It was quiet. The frogs had stopped croaking in his presence. The moon provided enough light for him to barely see a narrow, dirt road running along the shoreline. He followed it until the banks became too steep to see over.

Time to go back, he thought. Nothing else I can do.

But he couldn't forget the scream. The person who made it had definitely been in trouble. He sat and listened a few minutes more. The slam of a car door on the bank above him made him jerk. He sat still in the boat while an engine cranked and tires rolled. He rowed slowly toward the level part of the bank and was startled again, this time by a goose that broke from her nest when he passed.

Becky heard the engine sound before she saw the vehicle turn from a back road with its lights off. It drove toward the highway. She ran to her patrol car and spun the tires leaving. Taillights lit far ahead of her. She flipped on her blue light and siren. The vehicle down the road instantly surged ahead and continued accelerating. Becky wasn't comfortable with speed, but she pushed her patrol car near eighty down a straight section of road, grabbing her radio mic and announcing the situation when she saw the vehicle would make the highway before she got close.

"What's the vehicle description?" The transmission came from a deputy who sounded as if his late-night snooze had been interrupted.

"Not close enough to see," Becky said into the mic. "He's not stopping for me."

"What's your reason for stopping him?" This deputy sounded more awake although with no more sense of urgency.

"Help me get him stopped and I can tell you then." She cringed, dropped the mic, and put both hands on the wheel when she came upon a sharp curve. Tires squalled. She felt the back of the car slide, while she fought to recover control. The car spun around and screeched toward a guardrail. Dirt flew onto the windshield. A bang jarred Becky and sent the car bouncing down the shoulder of the road as she fought with the wheel, softly tapping the brakes until gaining control. Her attempt to accelerate again brought a grinding sound that made the car shake. The siren blared into her ears when she got out long enough to see the fender tangled against the back left tire. She reached into the car, found the mic, and killed the siren. "I've been involved in a minor accident. Any deputy close by, check Highway four-twenty-one. The taillights looked like a Chevy's."

"Want us to check all the Chevys on the highway, Chief?" came the sarcastic-laced reply. "Everybody, get ready for some good overtime pay."

Becky slapped the dash and gave her reply without keying the mic.

He drove while looking into the rearview mirror. His hands trembled on the wheel, not from fear but the rush of adrenaline that always came after his kills. The girl had put up a fight with strength that belied her lank frame. He'd managed to get a hand over her mouth after her first scream and struggled with her inside the phone booth. She'd calmed some when he'd promised not to hurt her, and he'd even persuaded her to bring her bag, while he walked her to the van. It was there where he drew his cord tight on her neck, constricting her sounds as he watched her eyes flutter from terror to acceptance of her destiny. He'd impressed himself with his proficiency. His kills were becoming easier, not as messy and drawn out as the first were.

He looked behind him again. The officer who'd come after him and wrecked was an added treat. He wanted to know if it was her, but he needed food and a place to sleep. There'd be time to learn more about the lady chief of police of Black Lake before his return there.

CHAPTER 6

It was against a tree beside a dirt road where Shiloh lay. A purplish ligature wound ran a perfect circle around her neck. Her face bore a hint of its final contortion. Her hands rested together on her lap with a small flower and a slip of paper between her fingers. The night had quietened until a goose broke from the bank near her and flew away honking.

Ever so slightly, Shiloh's head twitched. Her blue hued lips moved a little and then spit out frothy saliva. She sucked in a lungful of air as her eyes sprung open, wide and red, and she clawed at her fuzzy visions. In a moment, she stood and stumbled in terrified confusion. A hoarse cry rattled in her throat when she fell off the bank.

Chris heard the splash near his boat and saw her sink when he looked back. He breathed a profanity while checking his pockets and tossing his knife onto the floor of the boat before diving in.

Panic made her sink quickly. It was she who found him ten feet under, when her thrashing arms touched his leg. Her hands latched to him and pulled him down more while he blindly fought to take control. The struggle tired him fast. He gagged for air when he broke the surface with her clinging tightly. The bank was too steep and high to return her to it. Through no small miracle, the boat still floated nearby, and he was able to make a few strokes and grab it before he and she sank again.

She lay on the floor of the bow, weeping while he rowed. Her cries came out raspy and tight. He attempted a calming voice while talking to her. A lake patrol boat cruised a hundred yards away. He nearly hailed it but thought better and turned their course away from the light of the town. He turned his head to the sound of a distant siren. "Christ, I don't need this," he muttered while struggling for a plan.

The girl quietened for a while but still trembled. When they were far out on the water, shrieks broke from her again before another fit of hysteria seized her. The boat rocked and nearly tipped before he was able to calm her.

"Get away from me," she spluttered, holding her arms up defensively. "Leave me alone." Her scratchy words tailed into a begging whine.

"It's Ok. You're safe."

She wiped wet hair strands from her face.

"What's your name?" Chris asked.

She squinted through her swimmy vision. The voice was different from the man's. "Let me see you. Let me see your face." She realized only then how different her own voice sounded.

He brought himself close. Dripping, sandy-blonde hair hung over blue eyes, not icy blue like those of the man but deep blue and benevolent. He smiled. "Not too hideous, huh?"

She looked a moment longer. "Who are you?"

"Chris Heath. No reason to be afraid of me. I'm just trying to help out."

She detected a northern accent. Other than from television and movies, it was the first time she'd heard one "I'm Shiloh. Did you bring my glasses?"

"No. Sorry. Nice name."

"Where are we going?"

"Well, I can take you anywhere you want, but I know some people that can probably help you. They're good folks. There's a woman there. She's not a doctor but almost as good as one. And you'll be safe with them."

Shiloh touched her neck and felt her wound. Each breath burned her throat.

"Did you know that man?" he asked. "Was he after you for some reason?"

"No. What did I do? Why was he hurting me that way?" She felt herself breaking down again.

He placed his hands on her shoulders. "I don't know but relax. I promise you, I'll keep you safe. Are you a runaway?"

Her eyes turned up. "How do you know that?"

"Lucky guess. I saw you when you got out of the truck. You just had that look."

Shiloh slid back and shielded herself with her hands. "You were watching me?"

"No. Nothing like that. I just happened to be in the neighborhood. I know runaways when I see them."

"How?"

"Well, probably because I'm one myself. You were trying to call your folks back there, right? Having second thoughts?"

"No."

"Then who were you calling? You don't have to say if you don't want to."

Shiloh found his voice soothing. Her trembling eased, and her mind cleared some. "Someone I don't really know."

"Are you really running away? Or are you just getting away for a while?"

"I don't know. I think I'm really running away."

"Then be careful about who you talk to. It's easy to get sent back. People will act all nice but call the cops as quick as they get a chance. Cops don't care about why you left. It's only their job to send you back. I didn't get from Jersey to here without learning a few things."

"That's where you're from?"

"Yeah. Camden, Fairview Village. I left about six months ago. Had to get away from my mom. Been train hopping most of the way, because thumbing is the quickest way to get sent home. Listen, I won't ask questions. But I think it would be good if you let me take you to these people I know. Your neck looks pretty bad, and I'll bet you could use some hot food. Sound good to you?"

Shiloh nodded while listening to the oars slosh.

Cooking smells wafted through the camp and brought a crowd around the main fire. Smaller fires burned near the huts and tents. It was the hobos' favorite time, a time to socialize over food and drink in celebration of the end of another working week before a long rest in their cots.

Flynt stirred a large pot of stew. Clay lit his pipe. Byron and Red whittled sticks and shared a bottle. Andi, still damp from her sponge bath, joined them.

"New perfume tonight, Andi?" Flynt asked.

"It's soap. Ever heard of it?" She gave Flynt's white beard a playful pull.

Clay leaned over with a grin and smelled. "Nah. Essence of Paris, for sure."

"She's on the prowl tonight, boys," Flynt said. "I guess the priest will be working overtime at the confessional booth tomorrow."

Andi gave his beard a harder pull and got a yell from him "A lady can't even clean up without being razzed by ya hooligans."

The crowd grew. Sticks and grilling hooks with meats and vegetables on the ends went over the fire. Conversation came easy with jokes and chuckles. A more raucous noise was rising from a fire on the other side of the tracks, but the hobos were used to it and paid it no mind.

"How old are you?" Chris asked. They stood at the edge of the woods, just past the light of the fires.

Shiloh saw only flickering clouds of orange. The voices carrying from them made her nervous. "Eighteen in December."

"North Carolina law says you're an adult at eighteen, so, if they ask, you turned eighteen last December. These are good folks. They don't want the cops showing up, but if you tell them what really happened to your neck, they'll go get them for sure. Tell them your boyfriend back home did it, and you caught a bus here to get away from him." He held her arm and guided her into the camp.

He drove over fifty miles before searching for a place to rest. The New Hanover Memorial Hospital parking lot was his pick. He'd learned that he drew less attention in large, public areas where vehicles were parked round the clock. The van would blend in there while he slept.

He changed into comfortable clothes then walked across the street to a cafe and returned with a burger and Nehi grape. He sat in the back of the van and ate while replaying the details of his latest kill. He saw her face and eyes again and heard her sounds. He felt a connection with her soul now, as he did with all his victims. She was undoubtedly his youngest. He looked forward to reading the news and learning more about her. It had been a good day. He felt satisfied while he ate.

When he was through with his burger, he went through the girl's bag. Under her clothes, he found a cigar box containing a little money. He dumped it out and dug more through the bag. There were two photographs at the bottom. The first was the girl when she was maybe three years younger. She posed in a chair with a white-haired man standing behind her with his hands on her shoulders. They were dressed up. "First Presbyterian Church." It was printed in gold lettering on the corner of the photograph. The second was an 8X10 graduation picture. The girl's hair had been done. It flowed past her shoulders. Her dark bangs hung across her forehead from under her cap. She made a proud smile. Her made-up appearance would've fooled him if not for the glasses. He laid back on his mattress and studied the pictures more with his flashlight. He had a thought, closed his eyes, and concentrated. The female officer's picture from the paper came to him. He pressed his mind to bring out the facial details. "No," he whispered. "Luck is not that kind to me."

CHAPTER 7

Black Lake had changed much in two years. The new mayor and commissioners understood the potential of the sprawling lake the town was named after. They'd worked with the county to pass zoning ordinances that, while slowing the lumbering business, preserved the lake's natural beauty. The town's dark past was fading. "Discover Your Adventure at Black Lake," was the slogan used in an aggressive marketing campaign. And it was working. The summer before had been the best ever for local merchants.

That summer promised to be even better with wide interest shown in the second annual Blackberry Festival, an event permanently scheduled for the second weekend of June, so as not to coincide with other towns' Fourth of July and Memorial Day celebrations.

For Becky Hawk, the increased revenue meant both a raise and the addition of a part-time officer's position to the previously one-woman department. Curt Nickles, a young, single man who needed extra cash to pay for his new Mustang was the applicant she'd chosen. He'd proven to be a competent officer, who was always willing to put in overtime when it didn't interfere with his regular job of operating a forklift at the lumber company. He sported a fresh flattop haircut and wore his uniform neatly pressed when he entered the police station, showing surprise that Becky was still on duty. He sat and listened to her recounting of the events that led to her wreck.

"Could you tell me anything else about it? Shape? Color?" he asked.

"No. It was too far away. I turned on the blue light too soon. He saw me coming and kicked it. There's no doubt he was avoiding me for some reason. Sorry you'll have to patrol in the old car today. I'll get the other one to the shop Monday."

"No problem. I'm just happy you weren't hurt. Did this all happen right after you heard the scream?"

"Yes. I saw the vehicle just after I found that in the phone booth." She pointed to the glasses sealed in an evidence bag.

Curt lifted them from the desk and whistled. "Damn, somebody sure can't see this morning."

"You would think not. It seems whoever lost those would know it right away. That's what bothers me. Nobody showed up looking for them."

"Maybe the eye doctor could tell us whose they are."

Becky nodded. "Why don't you take them by there today." She sipped her coffee. "And be on your toes to anything out of the ordinary. I have a bad feeling about all this."

"What do you think happened, Chief?"

The phone rang. It was Jimmy Rogers reporting a break-in to his grocery store.

"Other than wine and Brunswick stew, there's nothing else I see missing," Jimmy said while Curt filled out his report at the front counter.

Becky checked the aisles once more. She then stepped outside to wait on the crime scene specialist she'd requested from the sheriff's office. She felt sleepy and worried when she knelt to again inspect the tire tread marks she'd found in the sand at the corner of the building. She looked up when Bolton County Sheriff Leroy Newton drove into the lot. He carried his revolver in a shoulder harness over a plaid shirt and wore jeans. Dark stubble on his face showed he hadn't taken time to shave.

"Hi, Becky. What have you got here today?"

"Break-in, Sheriff. Thanks for coming in off-duty. Someone knocked out a back window with a rock then managed to shimmy in. I've got some decent tread marks here. It looks like he drove down the dirt road in the back when he left."

"Take much?"

"Stew and wine are all."

Newton snickered. "And you need a crime scene deputy for this? Good grief, Becky, I assumed you had something serious when I heard the call."

Becky took a breath. She knew Newton and realized she would have to explain it all. "I would like to see if there are any good fingerprints in the store and on the receiver of the phone booth across the street. It would also be nice to have these tread marks photographed with a good camera."

"Black Lake can't afford you a camera?"

"All I have is a cheap one. It doesn't get good detail."

"And why dust the phone receiver?"

Becky stood to face him. "There could be more to this, Leroy. I heard a woman's scream late last night. Then I found a pair of glasses on the floor of the phone booth. The receiver was off the hook. There's a possibility we have an abduction. It would be nice if I had the prints of the person who used the phone."

"Petty larceny and kidnapping aren't normally accompanying crimes, Chief."

"Yeah, but a scream and a victim's belongings left behind quite often accompany a kidnapping."

"Ok, so you heard a scream, and you found a pair of glasses. Has anybody been reported missing? In the summer there's people on the lake day and night. All kinds of whoops and yells carry over the water. You've lived here long enough to know that. And you can't request lake patrol every time you hear something. I'll have to pay my boatman overtime now just because someone screamed and someone lost their glasses."

Becky felt heat on her neck. She pulled her pad from her pocket, knelt again, and began a rough sketch of the treads. "I heard the scream myself. It was from someone in trouble. The glasses I found are a strong prescription. The person who owns them isn't going to accidentally leave them behind. There's more to this than a break-in. That's why I'd like a crime scene specialist."

"Do you have any idea how many people touch a pay phone in one day? Any prints from that would be worthless."

"How do we know if we don't try?"

"Listen, Chief," Newton said, kneeling beside her. "I know you take your job as seriously as I do mine, but we have to use judgment and prioritize. I can't send my crime scene guys out for every break-in or for every time you suspect something. If we make something big out of each little thing we won't have time for the serious stuff. Thank God you weren't hurt in your wreck last night. High speed pursuit takes experience behind the wheel, by the way."

Becky bit her lip while she drew. "Thanks for the concern, but it was only a fender bender."

"Could've been a lot worse from what I hear. I'm just trying to give you good advice, Becky. I also want us to have a good working relationship, but I have a whole county to serve. I only have so many resources." Newton stood and walked toward his car.

"Understood," Becky said, adding a few last details to her sketch. She felt tired and grumpy and wasn't in the mood to keep things on her chest. "Sheriff?"

Newton turned. "Yeah, Chief?"

"Are you normally this condescending to other officers or only the ones who happen to be women?"

CHAPTER 8

"Who did this to you, dear?" Andi asked while changing the cloth wrap around Shiloh's neck. She looked down with concern, her long, silver hair hanging beside her tanned face.

It had been daybreak when Shiloh fell fully asleep on a cot inside the woman's plywood and sheet metal hut. Each time she'd drifted off, the man's icy blue eyes had burned into hers again. Her hoarse cries had scorched her throat and brought Andi to her side.

"My boyfriend." Shiloh thought of a frog when she said it. She looked up while Andi's sun-spotted hands patted the wrap down firmly. She could see the woman's face well enough to detect the doubt in her eyes.

"So, he gets mad on occasion?"

"Yeah. And he hurts me. I had to take a bus and come here because of that."

Andi took a small bottle from her apron and dripped a sharp smelling liquid onto the wrap. "You're not being truthful, child. You don't lie naturally. I've been around a tad." Andi stepped to a small wood stove and brought back a steaming cup. "Drink this down. It will help the pain."

"What is it?"

"Willow bark tea."

Shiloh tasted it and made a face. "Where's Chris?" she asked.

"About camp somewhere. Drink the rest down."

Shiloh took another sip and handed the cup back. "I really don't want it now. I'm very tired."

Andi nodded and patted the wrap once more. "Very well. But first I wanna know what you're keeping from me. Are you in trouble? Tell me. It'll be our secret if you like."

"I'd like to sleep now."

"Yes, do that. But tell me this first. Did Chris do this to you? Be honest now."

"No. Chris didn't do it."

Andi smiled. "That's all I need to know. For now, anyways. You sleep and call me if you need me."

Cotton was the leader of the tramps. He wasn't skinny like the rest. His droopy face and eyes were suggestive of a basset hound's. He had a belly that hung well over his pants and biceps thick as hams. Both were on display when he stepped from his tent in a stained, white tank top.

"Brought your things," Chris said, holding up the burlap bag. His eyes darted to the others who'd gathered around. He knew to keep on guard while in their camp.

"Take it from him, Simon," Cotton said.

A skinny, rat of a man showed a snaggletooth maw when he grinned and took the bag. Others came from the tents and gathered around. A pot was placed on a grate over a low burning fire. Simon opened the bag and giggled while spilling the contents. The others swarmed to it. In seconds, the wine bottles were open and passed around. The Brunswick stew containers were torn open and poured into the pot.

"No smokes?" Simon asked with a twisted scowl.

"I had to leave in a hurry," Chris said. "A cop was shaking doors."

"Alright," Cotton said. "See ya then." He turned and walked.

"Hold on." Chris went toward him. Three tramps stood and blocked his way.

Cotton turned. "You want something, Sonny?"

"Where's my money?" Chris eyed the ones around him, judging which to slug first if need be. Those squatted around the pot with plastic spoons and paper bowls peered up at him while throwing back wine.

Cotton stepped past the three men in front of Chris. "The deal was five cartons of smokes also." His fat finger poked Chris' chest. "If you get it right next time, you'll get paid."

"You can dock me a couple bucks for not getting the smokes, but I want my money."

Cotton smirked and ran his hand through his slicked hair. "You either get the order right or there is no money for you. So not another word about it, road boy, unless you want to go back all busted up." He turned and walked toward his tent. "Bring me a bottle of wine and a bowl of stew, Simon," he said.

Chris took a step, and the three acting as Cotton's guards moved close. A few around the fire stood.

"Time to leave," the tramp directly in front of Chris said. He'd brought brass knuckles from his pocket.

Chris nodded. "Ok, sure," He turned and walked. "Sorry about the smokes, fellas," he said toward the assemblage of stringy beards on thin faces around the fire. "I'll do better next time." He took three more steps before turning and making a charge toward the fire. He jumped with his legs drawn back and sailed between two of the sitting men. Simon, spooning stew into a bowl, watched with wide eyes and opened mouth. Chris kicked the pot and sent hot stew sailing over the men on the other side. The maneuver stunned the tramps enough to give him time to bounce from the grate and make distance between them. In a second, he heard curses and feet falling behind him.

The hobos had seen it and were gathering on the other side of the tracks with sticks and other makeshift weapons.

"Got one behind you, Chris!" Clay yelled.

Chris was halfway across the tracks when he felt the hand on his shoulder. He turned and sent the tramp down with a fist to his jaw. He made it to the line of hobos and turned around in a boxing stance.

The tramps formed their own line and waited for Cotton to make it there. He carried a lead pipe and panted when he arrived.

"We're only here for him," Cotton said, pointing the pipe toward Chris. "No need for the rest of you getting pulled into his shit."

Shiloh stepped from the hut and joined Andi outside. "What's going on?"

Andi put her arm around her. "Only Chris stirring up trouble again. Flynt and the others will handle it."

"You and your men can go back to your camp, Cotton," Flynt said. He held a baseball bat on his shoulder. "The boy will stay away from you for now on. I'll see to it."

"That punk's a hoodoo," Cotton said. "He'll never bring nothing but trouble to your camp. Hand him over to us and we'll solve your problem right now."

"I'll deal with him," said Flynt. "He'll not bother you again."

Cotton looked over the hobo camp. His gaze fell on Shiloh. He raised his eyebrows and cut a vindictive grin toward Chris. "Who's the Angelina? I saw you bringing her here last night. She's yours?" He made a bold display of running his tongue over his lips.

Chris brought his butterfly knife from his pocket. With a click, a razor-sharp blade appeared to spin out on its own. "Listen to me, fat boy. You'd be surprised that a person could even think up the things I do to assholes like you with this knife. Touch her and you'll find out firsthand."

"This is over, Cotton," said Flynt.

Cotton shook his head. "Nah. Nah, it ain't over. You can bet it ain't." He swished the heavy pipe through the air as if it were a wand, slung it over his shoulder, and cut Chris a threatening grin. With his hand motion, the other tramps followed him toward the tracks.

Chris walked to Andi and Shiloh. "Don't worry about him," he said. "He's just a blowhard."

Andi watched the group walking away. "Don't underestimate any of 'em. I've seen a few in camps before. They're bad people, especially Cotton."

Flynt grabbed Chris' shoulder. For the first time, Chris saw an angry face behind the white beard. "You want to act like them?" Flynt asked. "Then go to their camp and stay. I've told you the difference between them and us." He looked at Shiloh. "We ride the rails to find work. They ride to steal and leech off people. I won't have crooks in this camp."

"I'm sorry, Flynt. It won't happen again," said Chris.

"I'm an easy captain to get along with, boy. But that doesn't mean I won't put my foot down. Any more problems, and you're gone."

"Yes sir."

Shiloh was close enough to Chris to see him smile at her when Flynt walked away. As she smiled back, something new smoldered in her, a hint of something wonderful.

CHAPTER 9

The ranch-style house was built the year before, with three bedrooms, two baths, and bay windows that provided a broad view of the lake from the den. There was a pier and a boathouse with guest quarters above it. It was all Bobby's. Becky had reminded him of that often until she realized it was only to appease her own conscience. Some remarks around town had floated back to her. How lucky for her, they'd said, that she'd been awarded conservatorship over the young man and now controlled his large inheritance. Gossip, she'd learned, had a sharp edge. To hell with those who did it, she'd finally decided and was glad she did.

Bobby's mental recovery had become of the utmost importance to her. It was nearly two years since the death of James Billings, the previous owner of the Black Lake Lumber Company. The passing of his uncle had been enough to plunge Bobby into a deeply depressed state. But his false imprisonment on a murder charge by a corrupt sheriff and local businessmen had pushed him to an emotional breakdown, one that Becky at first feared he may never recover from. She felt proud of the courage he'd shown and understood the dragon he'd fought, because she'd fought her own. That's why worry hit her when she returned home from her night shift and found Sharon McDowell, their seventy-year-old neighbor, sitting at the kitchen table with a coffee and somber expression. A pillow and blanket lay on the sofa.

"I'm sorry," Sharon said. "He found out the news and took it kind of hard."

Becky rubbed her eyes and sat down. "You should've called me. I would've come home earlier." She saw the Friday edition of The Bolton Record on the table and unfolded it.

Sharon frowned. "I saw it at the end of your driveway when I came over to check on things and brought it in. I had no idea that was in it."

"It's Ok. He'd have found out sooner or later. I don't blame you. Is he asleep?"

"Yes. We stayed up until midnight. I thought about calling you, but he seemed like he just needed company. I talked with him until he went to bed, then I slept on the couch."

"Thank you, Sharon. Bobby and I both appreciate all you do. I'll fix us both some breakfast."

"No. I have to get home and feed the cats. Call me if you need anything else. There's fresh coffee on the stove."

"Thanks again." Becky watched out the window while Sharon walked down the path in the woods to her home. She then poured a cup of coffee and took the newspaper to the sofa.

"Competency Hearing for Police Chief's Accused Killer Scheduled," the front page read. Becky looked at the picture. The withered face of Harrison Tolly stirred her disdain as much as ever.

Curt Nickles drank his coffee at the police department while he caught up on the latest edition of Popular Mechanics. He laid the magazine aside when the desk phone rang for the first time that day. "Black Lake Police Department."

"Good morning, sir. Any news from your fair town that you'd like to share today?" The voice had the friendly, professional tone of a reporter fishing for stories.

Curt took his report from the basket. "Our only thing is a B and E and L at Jimmy's Lakefront Grocery. Perpetrator or perpetrators broke a back window and entered the store sometime between nine last night and seven this morning. Merchandise valued at thirty-five dollars was removed." He tossed the report back and flipped open his magazine.

"So, I'm going to logically conclude that B and E and L is police jargon for breaking and entering and larceny, correct?"

"Yes. And that's all I have for you today." Curt waited for a thank you. "Anything else I can help you with?"

"The store you mentioned, it's the little business on the main street into town. There's a phone booth near it?"

"Yes."

"Any suspects?"

"No. None yet."

"And you're unsure of the exact time this happened."

"Correct."

"How long have you been on the force, Officer?"

"I'm new. Part-time only. Curt Nickles. And you are?"

"Nice to speak with you, Curt. I normally talk to your chief. Her name is, uh… Oh, my goodness."

"Chief Hawk. Becky Hawk."

"Yes. Thank you. You know, I've been reluctant to talk to her about how she came to be your chief. I understand there's a tragic story behind it. Maybe you can help. Her husband was murdered, am I right?"

"Yes, Chief Ed Hawk, about two years ago. Becky was mainly responsible for uncovering the crime ring involved. Lots of the town's big shots were in it. The town council thought enough of it to give her the chief's job."

"Very impressive. She must be quite a woman. I'm sure she does a fine service to your little town."

"Yes, she does."

"Was your brave and righteous chief on duty last night by chance?"

Something about the voice had changed and made Curt uneasy. "I haven't caught your name yet."

"I haven't told you. Was your Chief Hawk the unit on duty around twenty-two thirty hours, the one who lost control of her cruiser in her attempt to get a read on an unsub's vehicle?" There came a malevolent laugh. "You see, Officer Nickles, the jargon you boys in blue use to make yourselves sound important is easy, even to a layman. All anyone has to do is read a few Hard-Boiled Detectives magazines." Cackling followed.

Curt picked up pen and paper and noted the time. "Who is this?"

"It's not who but what. I could try to explain that to you, simple man, however you could never understand it. I'm more of a demon spirit than a man. The winds of destiny have blown me to your little town."

"You sound like a nutjob to me. Were you in town last night?"

"Oh, absolutely."

"Did you hurt anyone?"

"Search along the dirt road behind the location of your B and E and L. There's a sweet, young lady resting beneath a tree there who will answer that. She has a flower for you and a note for your Chief Hawk. I'm sure, with you and your Chief's vast forensic knowledge, you will quickly conclude my favorite method of disposal."

Curt's mind spun. In his three months as an officer, he'd only taken reports and written a few tickets. He wrote fast, trying to record verbatim what he heard. "So…So you *did* hurt someone? You killed someone? Who?"

"You sound rather agitated, Officer Nickles. I'm sorry I ruined your morning. I'll bet you were counting on another quiet day of small-town policing. Yes, I did kill someone. No, I doubt it hurt much. Experienced hands can render death faster than you'd expect. Take it from me, the line between this realm and the next is razor thin. So, there's your useful information for the day."

Curt held the receiver away this time to avoid the laugh. He sought tactful words and a tone that might reveal more. "Who did you kill?" was all that came.

"I'm sure the very capable Black Lake police force can identify the deceased. Tell Chief Hawk hello for me. Let her know that I look forward to meeting her—and we certainly will."

"Tell me who you are, creep."

"I'm an aberration. I have no human name. But, when you find the girl, you will learn what to call me for future reference. Goodbye, Officer Nickles. I'm happy you can now tell your friends that you spoke to a real killer today." A dial tone came.

CHAPTER 10

"Did you read the whole article?" Becky asked. She and Bobby stood on the pier and watched the first boats of the day buzz across the lake.

"Yeah, I read it. You should've told me. I'm thirty-two now. I'm a man. I don't like you keeping things from me."

"I'm sorry. I just didn't want to remind you of him. I didn't see any need in talking about it." She studied his face. It wasn't as easy to read as it once had been. Something in him had changed in the time he'd been with her. He was more confident and in control of his emotions. Becky was happy about it, but always worried there'd be a setback. The Manticores, the secret club that once controlled Black Lake, had left deep scars on Bobby's psyche. He'd healed but not entirely.

It wasn't the only bad hand Bobby had been dealt. The first had come while he was still in his mother's womb, defenseless against the alcohol and drugs she abused both their bodies with. His slightly irregular face and small build were merely the physical results, not the true challenges. "Is Papa Tolly going to get out?" he asked.

"No. He'll never get out." Becky removed her shoes, sat down, and dangled her feet in the water. Bobby joined her.

"The water is warming up," he said. "Do you want to take the boat out when they get here?"

"It's your boat, Bobby. We will if you want."

"I've told you before, everything is ours together, boat and all. You're my family now. Don't pay attention to what some people say." He looked toward the house. "The phone is ringing."

Becky didn't want to leave him. "Don't worry about it. They'll call back if it's important. I'm glad you think of me that way. I feel the same about you. We've been through a lot together. We've been good for each other."

"Yeah, we have. I'd probably be in prison now if it hadn't been for you. I know I've said it before but thank you."

"Why don't you and I just not think about all that anymore? Let's move on from it."

"I don't think about most of it. Except for Aunt Cynthia and Uncle Jimmy."

Becky saw his bottom lip quiver while he stared over the lake. "What's bothering you about them, Bobby?"

He shrugged. "W-when I s-saw..." He took a breath.

Becky put her arm on his shoulder. It had been a long time since he'd stuttered. "Take your time," she said.

"When I saw the paper, it reminded me of some things. It reminded me that Uncle Jimmy di-died thinking I killed Shannon and her mom. He never knew the truth."

Unpleasant memories returned to Becky as well. "Your Uncle Jimmy never believed you did that," she said, wishing she could sound more convincing. "He only gave them what he had to protect you from them. He knew how powerful they were in this town."

"I hope that's true, but they even made me believe I killed Shan-Shannon and her mom. I can't help but think that if Uncle Jimmy thought different, he'd have told me. If I wa-wasn't the way I am, if I was smart, he might've known the truth."

It was those sorts of comments from him that bothered Becky the most. "You are smart. You're brave too. I admire you for all you've overcome."

"There's still a lot I'm trying to get over," Bobby said, "like not hating Aunt Cynthia. She and Uncle Jimmy were my family before you. Most times she was good to me. I really think she loved me. But, for some reason, I can only think about the ba-bad things she did."

"I know you've heard the Cherokee story about the two wolves inside us," Becky said. "One wants good for you. The other is vicious."

"Yeah. They're fighting for my spirit, and the one I feed is the one who wins. I think about that story a lot. The phone is ringing again."

Becky stood. "Let's go inside. Maybe it *is* important. I need to clean up some anyway. They'll be here soon." A hand pushed her shoulder, and she turned.

"This soon enough?" Wendy Powers asked, her eyes dancing. She stood with her newlywed husband, and recent graduate of the State Bureau of Investigation academy, Aaron.

He wore a baseball cap and reading glasses when he left the phone booth and walked a block to the Wilmington Public Library. An assistant there helped him with the Bolton Record microforms from the past two years. There was much to read in them about Becky Hawk and the criminal organization she'd uncovered.

He became engrossed and lost himself, flicking through the articles, ingraining the details and pictures to his memory. There were also some historical details there about the Manticores, the secret group founded during the Civil War that practiced espionage for the Confederacy before turning into a ruthless gang of criminals. He'd read of them before, but there was some information in the papers he didn't know. The group survived and grew after the war. Under Harrison (Papa) Tolly's leadership, they'd left a trail of murders that went back to the early nineteen hundreds. Harrison himself pulled the trigger on Police Chief Edward Hawk when he got too close to the group's secrets. How many they'd killed would never be known.

The only member who'd cooperated with the authorities was Bud Sweeney. He'd turned state's witness and testified in the murders of a young girl named Shannon Monet and her mother. The killings were part of the Manticores' plan to frame the nephew of wealthy business owner, James Billings, for extortion purposes. Soon after his testimony, Sweeney was found in the main yard of Central Prison with his throat sliced. The final chapter of the Manticores had apparently been written.

He'd learned enough by then to know beyond a doubt that he'd found the perfect one. His dance of death with Becky Hawk had begun without her yet knowing it. He walked to the library's news racks and found the current Bolton Record, not really expecting the young runaway to have made the headlines yet. She hadn't, but the front page article made him forget that. He read the whole thing while standing. The town of Black Lake had indeed been a lucky find. An idea kindled in him and quickly grew into a flame.

Maybe the final chapter of the Manticores hadn't been written. Maybe there was room for one more in this dance. His idea, though dangerous and risky, seemed possible enough that he couldn't let it go. He left the library, walked back to the phone booth, and asked the operator to place a call.

"North Carolina Central Prison. How may I direct your call?"

He chose a mild, easy voice. "Yes, ma'am. I would like to speak to someone about scheduling a visit with an inmate by the name of Harrison Tolly."

CHAPTER 11

Aaron and Wendy's wedding had been in Raleigh the previous September, just before Aaron started his training at the academy. That was the last time Becky and Bobby had seen their friends. Aaron was assigned to the district office in Hickory after his graduation. Wendy took a teaching position at an elementary school there. The week-long visit had been planned for months. Conversation and laughter came easy at the dining room table over Styrofoam boxes of Jabber's chopped barbecue, hushpuppies, and slaw.

"See you're still going to that same, freaking hairdresser," Wendy said. "I'm sure the fashion world would go into shock if you took that ponytail down."

"It's my anxiety reliever," Becky said. "The fashion world will just have to accept it."

"Don't count on it." Wendy made a scissoring motion with her fingers. "Sleep well tonight."

"Think you can tolerate this crazy blonde for a week, Bob?" Aaron asked.

"If you can live with her, I can stand a week."

Wendy squealed a laugh. "Well, somebody has been taking smart-aleck lessons from somebody else." She ruffled Bobby's hair. "Guys, I've been looking forward to this visit for so long. It's going to be a great week. What're our plans before the big festival?"

"We'll just take it as it comes," said Becky. "Bobby talked about a boat ride today"

"I brought my fishing rod," Aaron said. "What's biting on the lake, Bob?"

"Just tell me what you want to catch, and I'll take you where they're biting."

Becky watched Bobby smile and felt happy the visit was today. The company would be good for them both. "Oh, I forgot," she said. "Be right back." She went to the kitchen and brought back a bottle and glasses. "Nothing goes with the smoky taste of barbecue like my homemade muscadine wine."

Wendy shook her head. "Nothing I'd like better than a big glass of rotgut, Dolly, but I'm going to have to pass on it."

Becky cast her a suspicious look. "You've never turned it down before."

"I'll try it," said Aaron.

"Sorry, Aaron," Wendy said. "You have to be at least thirty-five to drink that."

Becky poured him a taste.

Aaron swigged it, made a face, and slapped the table. "Good Lord, Becky, you drink that?"

Becky giggled with Wendy. "It's an acquired taste."

"How long does it take to acquire it?"

"Decades," Wendy said. "At least you'll never have worms now."

Becky took Wendy's arm. "Let me show you the rest of the house."

"I'm not done eating." Wendy grinned. "For some reason, I've had a heck of an appetite lately."

"Come on anyway." Becky pulled her up and through the living room, trapping her in the hall. "I wasn't going to say it before, but I will now. You're gaining some weight, aren't you?"

"Probably some." Wendy bit her lip, watched Becky's face, and then smiled wide. "I was wondering when your powers of deduction would kick in."

"Congratulations! How far along?"

The phone rang in the den.

"About sixteen weeks. Keep it a secret from Bobby. I want to tell him."

Becky hugged her.

"Easy on Junior there, honey."

"Becky," Bobby called. "Curt's on the phone. It sounds important."

A red light flashed on the dashboard as Aaron's black Chrysler sped through town. Becky had thrown on her duty belt and guided him toward their destination while filling him in on the details of the previous night. A knot in her stomach was growing.

"And this all happened at what time?" Aaron asked.

"Ten thirty-two is when I heard the scream. I was talking to Jabber behind the grill. I've still got the glasses I found. The phone booth is coming up. Turn left on the dirt road just past it."

Curt stood on the dirt road, waving his hands. They parked behind his patrol car and trotted to him. "I looked around the best I could, Chief," he said. "Haven't found anything."

Becky scanned the area. "Are you sure this is where he was talking about?"

"He said along the road behind our break-in. This has to be it. I tried calling you before I came and searched from the store to here. There's nothing."

"Did you let the sheriff's department know?" Aaron asked.

"No. Who are you?"

"Sorry, Aaron Powers of the SBI. I once worked for the Bolton County sheriff's office."

Curt gave him a suspicious look. "Under Scotland or Newton?"

"Scotland," Becky said. "But don't worry. Aaron's a good man. He helped me find Scotland and the Tollys when they were on the run."

"Nice meeting you then," said Curt.

"Same. Maybe we should get a deputy or two out here to help."

Becky didn't feel up to explaining herself to Sheriff Newton again. "No. Not yet," she said. "Let's go back to the store, spread out, and walk this way. If you see something, Curt, yell. Don't touch anything."

They moved slowly, fifty feet apart, Aaron on the road, Becky and Curt on the sides. They'd walked a distance from the store when Aaron called out, "You probably just have some jerk playing games with you, Becky."

Becky would have agreed if not for all that happened the night before. "Keep looking," she said. "Check for tire marks on the road." She looked back to see how far they'd walked. "Did you say he said she was under a tree?"

"Yep," Curt said. "Behind the store somewhere."

Aaron bent down. "Got tread marks here. Looks like somebody pulled off the road and into the grass."

He was crouched over them when Becky got to him. "They're the same as from the break-in," she said, kneeling. "Can you tell me anything about them?"

"I'm not an expert on tread marks, but these look wide, maybe a truck. Kind of a strange tread design, just rectangles in rows. I have a camera in the trunk. Be right back."

"Becky," Curt called from the lakeside of the road. "Come here."

His tone told her he'd found something. She ran, breaking through the brush, until she found him. "Put it down," she said. "You'll leave your prints on it."

Curt dropped the sheet of paper he held. A breeze caught it and sent him and Becky chasing. "There's writing on it, Chief. I think it's a note to us."

Another breeze took it toward the steep bank. It teetered on the edge long enough for Becky to make a frantic dive and snare it. On her belly, she read and forgot about fingerprints.

They arrived back at the lake house after dark. Wendy and Bobby shared popcorn on the sofa and watched TV. Wendy started to make a wise crack but stopped when she saw their faces. "Everything all right?" she asked. "We'd about given up on you guys."

Aaron plopped down on the sofa beside her. "Just somebody playing games, I think. We had to make sure there really wasn't a body."

"Sorry about missing the boat ride, Bobby," said Becky. "We'll do it tomorrow for sure."

"It's fine. We've been watching some shows and talking. Wendy told me the news. Congratulations, Aaron."

"Thanks, Bob."

Becky smiled and sat. "It's wonderful news. Have you been thinking about names?"

"A few," Wendy said. "Samuel is the front-runner if it's a boy. That's Aaron's dad's name. Possibly Rebecca if it's a girl."

"Get out of here," Becky said, grabbing a handful of popcorn. The happy moment helped her to momentarily forget the words in the note.

Aaron kissed Wendy.

None of them heard the dark van slip into the far end of the driveway.

CHAPTER 12

"She was walking down the road with a bag Friday afternoon," Brant Holbrook said, after being called to the front porch by his father.

Dan Bowman's eyes were tired and red. "Did you talk to her, Brant?"

"Might've said hey. She won't have much to do with me or my friends. She only hangs around with Cathy Conner. That's who you should talk to."

"I have," said Dan. "She hasn't seen her since she got off the bus Friday."

"Well, I can't help you more than that. Like I say, she doesn't have many friends. It looked like she might've been headed to the highway."

"Thanks," Dan said.

"No problem. Gotta run. See ya, Pop."

"Remember the Asheville run tonight," Rylie said. "Be back early enough to make it."

"Sure enough."

They watched Brant drive to the road, gun the convertible, and sling dust.

Rylie chuckled. "He really is feeling his oats these days. Reminds me of myself when I was his age." He pulled up an extra chair before taking a seat in a rocker. "Sit down and rest, Dan." He pulled a tobacco plug and knife from his pocket. "Want a chew?"

Dan shook his head and sat. "I don't know where the hell she might've took off to," he said. "She never went anywhere before."

Rylie spit into a tin can at his feet and rocked. "Told the county boys?"

"Yeah, but they're useless. All they said was they'd check around. I doubt they've spent five minutes looking for her."

"Kids grow up and go their own ways. Your girl probably needed a taste of being out on her own anyway. She'll be back when she runs out of money. Shit, don't worry about it."

"It's not that easy."

"Why ain't it?"

"Because she's not just running away from home. She's running away from me."

Rylie shrugged. "Well, you raised her. You got her through school. As I see it, you've done your part. Listen, you need to accept the facts. You're passed sixty. She's a teenager with all kinds of ideas about what she wants to be and do. Top that off with the fact that you're a... Well, you're a drinking man. Nothing wrong with that. I'm a drinking man. Lots of us are. It don't mean nothing. But an older drinking man and a teenage girl ain't a good fit anytime. And she ain't going to be happy until she takes off and gets a taste of the real world. So just let her have it and stop fretting while I break out a jar. No charge today. You look like you could use it mightily."

"I need to go. I want to check around town some more and...and..." Dan leaned forward and stared at his shaking hands. "Oh, dear Lord."

"Aw, hell, nothing wrong with wanting a drink to settle your nerves. Be right back."

For the first time since he could remember, a tear rolled from Dan's eye.

CHAPTER 13

Ed Hawk's old fingerprint kit had rarely been used. That Monday morning it lay on newspapers spread atop the police station desk. Becky adjusted her desk lamp and concentrated on a powder-dusted sheet of paper. She worked a square of clear tape over the ridges she'd found. Her teeth clenched, and she made a grunt of frustration when she pulled the tape up without the results she'd wanted. The door opening caused her to sit up straight.

Wendy carried shopping bags when she walked in. She took a second to look and laugh. "Bad makeup day, Dolly?"

Becky blushed and reached for the damp rag she'd kept handy. "Why are you out so early?"

Wendy sat and handed over her compact mirror. "Been checking out some of your new shops. Look." She dangled tiny, pink pajamas. "Pretty cute, huh?"

"Yeah, they're cute as a button," Becky drawled, looking into the mirror and wiping her face.

Wendy returned the pajamas to the bag. "You know, Black Lake has really grown since I was here last. It could actually pass as a town now. I've never seen so many people here."

"Summers have been this way the last couple of years. Wait until the festival. That's when you'll really see the crowds." Becky checked her face again before closing the compact and handing it back. "What are Aaron and Bobby doing today?"

"Out on the fishing boat again. Maybe Aaron can land a few today. I think his feelings got hurt a little when Bobby showed him up yesterday."

Becky smiled for the first time that day. "Bobby's learned every good fishing spot on the lake since he got that boat. It's nice seeing him enjoy his inheritance after all he went through."

"He's changed a lot since the last time I saw him," said Wendy. "He seems so much happier. You should give yourself a pat on the back for some of that."

"Well, I don't know who should get credit, but it's nice seeing him smile more."

"You could take some pointers. I haven't seen many smiles from you since Saturday. What's up? Something about that note?"

Becky nodded. "Something happened Friday night. I can't get my mind away from the thought that someone's in danger."

"How can you know that for sure? All you have is a note from some jackleg that you don't even know. There's no body, no missing person, nothing but a note."

"And a pair of women's glasses in a phone booth and a scream from someone in trouble. You can ask Jabber. He heard it too."

"You know I believe you. But you're doing all you can. Come on, Beck, lighten up. We've planned this visit too long for you to be so bummed out."

"I'm sorry. It's just with the hearing coming up and now this." She sighed. "There's a lot on my mind."

"Yeah, I've been keeping up with the news about Harrison. I'm figuring he's putting on an act. What do you think?"

"That miserable old man is as competent as we are. It's just another of his schemes. He and his lawyer have been playing games with the courts for the past two years."

"Is he the last of those Manticore jerks to be tried?"

"Yeah. Cynthia got fifteen years. Quincy is on death row. Bud cut a deal and got thirty, but it turned out to be a death sentence for him too. These last couple of years have been an eternity. I want it to finally be over."

"It'll be over before you know it. So, cheer up for my sake, please."

Becky forced her best smile. "I will."

"Mind if I read that? Just curious."

Becky turned the note around. Wendy leaned over and read through the fingerprint dust:

> You will not catch me. You will not see me until the time I decide to appear to you. But, as the ether that surrounds you, I'll be there. There will soon be more like this girl. Only I know who they will be. I'll choose to my liking and pick my times, unhindered by your flimsy attempts to stop me. It will be futile for you to look for clues, because clues will not connect you to me. I do not exist as a human being. I am a demon from the depths of the earth. The winds of destiny have blown me to your little town. So be prepared for your mettle to be tested. I have plans for you.

If you fail, I will enter your mind and be the worst spirit in your reality or fantasy.

Kage.

Wendy looked up and stared straight-faced at Becky. "Well," she said after a moment, "it sure looks like somebody's self-esteem counseling sessions went horribly wrong. Kage?"

"It's a surname from Germany, but I'm guessing that's from the Japanese meaning—shadow."

"Either you're smarter than I thought, Beck, or you've had some help."

"I called Duke and talked to some people in the languages department this morning."

"So, you're *really* taking this guy seriously."

"I don't see that I have a choice. There's something to this."

Wendy took another glance at the note. "If this is real, Beck, you'll need help. Maybe Aaron can pull some strings with the SBI."

"He said he'd try, but I've got a feeling it'll take more than a note to make anyone take this seriously. At least until there really is a body."

"Do you think the girl is real or made-up?"

"I wish I knew. The rescue squad helped us search all over. They even drug that section of the lake. There was nothing. But the women's glasses I found are definitely from a real person."

Wendy took a closer look. "Something I can tell you for sure, you're dealing with a southpaw here."

"How do you know?"

"I've graded enough essays to pick up a few things about handwriting. Only a lefthander makes those crossover strokes from right to left. The O's are made clockwise too, another tipoff. I know that doesn't help much."

"It's more than I had," Becky said.

Wendy broke the gloom with a smile. "So, you've made progress this morning. Let's go grab an early lunch."

"Can't today. I have a meeting in Deaton with the district attorney. He wants to talk about Tolly's hearing."

Wendy lifted her bags. "Well, since it seems I have the day all alone, let me cook dinner for us tonight. You've never had my chicken piccata. It's out of this world if I say so myself." She started toward the door. "And, you will not let that silly note mess up our week. I want you happy. But be careful while you're at it. Happy and careful. That's what you're going to be or I'll kick your ass."

Becky smiled again. "Need some money?"

"No. This meal is on me. See ya later."

"Enjoy your day," Becky said.

"Say that again." Becky's words came after a half-minute of silence, long enough for anger to replace her disbelief. She barely stopped herself from going around District Attorney Martin Sawyer's desk.

"Calm down and listen, Chief. I know this isn't what you wanted to hear, but Tolly is ninety-five-damned-years-old. The people at Central Prison say he hardly knows where he is anymore. I can't try someone like that. He has to understand what's going on. But look at it this way—he's spent two years locked up. You put him there. You broke up his organization. You beat him."

"That bastard killed my husband. It's not some contest I won."

"Becky, the man is not competent to stand trial. I've talked to the doctors who've examined him."

"So, you're telling me you're not even having the hearing. Are you serious? This is the same act he put on before he shot Ed."

"Keep your voice down in my office. You may not think so, but I know what I'm doing, and I know when I have a winning case and when I don't. Going to trial costs money, tax payers' money. Consider what a jury is going to think when we wheel him in front of them, a man older than their grandparents. Even if he is found competent, it'll be impossible to convict him."

"And how do you know that?" Becky stood and leaned across the desk.

Sawyer rolled his chair back. "I know," he said. "I've prosecuted more than enough cases to know."

Becky glared at him, weighing if it would be worth her career and an assault on a court official charge if she grabbed his red bow tie and found out how many times she could twist it tight around his scrawny neck. She turned when a knock came and the office door opened.

"Hello, folks. Sorry I'm late. It's a bit of a drive for me." Drake County's Sheriff Donaldson, commanding respect in his summer khaki uniform with stars on the collar, removed his hat and studied the scene. "Did I interrupt something?"

"Sit down, David," said Sawyer. "Maybe you can help me explain some things to her."

Sheriff Donaldson took his seat and listened to Sawyer's spiel. His face remained matter-of-fact the entire time. "Well, Martin," he said, "I only became involved with this case because it ran over into my jurisdiction, but I know enough to tell you that Harrison Tolly is one of the most ruthless and conniving men you'll encounter."

"I understand that, but—"

"Wait. Tolly confessed straight-faced to Chief Hawk that he conned and coldly executed her husband from behind. He also admitted to participating in murders involving men, women, and children going back over sixty years. He even talked about how much he enjoyed it. There's no way of knowing how many he's killed in his life, but he fits the definition of a mass murderer in every way. And you're making the decision to cut this man loose before even a hearing? Am I understanding you correctly?"

"I know his history well, but he's lost his mind now. He's been evaluated by experts at the prison. If we have a hearing, they'll be there to testify. No evidence we present can get past that. And, by the way, that so-called confession he made to her has holes all in it. She was a civilian at the time and tricked him into it. His lawyer is good and will blow it to pieces. And our only other witness, Bud Sweeney, is dead. So why waste taxpayer dollars? Tolly will be dead soon anyway."

Becky shot forward. Donaldson put his hand on her arm. "Ok, Martin, if you want to forgo the hearing and proceed straight to a dismissal in a police chief's murder case, so be it. But I think you'd better understand that every law officer around will see this as a huge slap in the face. Through teaching criminal justice at the college and my job, I know about every one of them in your district. And each one has relatives and friends who vote. This could be a tough issue to get past next election year."

Sawyer sat back and smirked. "Is that a threat?"

"No. Just telling you the reality of it. You're the DA. You make your own choice. Let's go, Becky."

Becky calmed some while they walked back to their cars. "Do you think he'll change his mind?" she asked.

"What do you think?"

"Seems like the political slant got his attention. Thanks."

"He's just trying to avoid a messy trial of an old man. I agree with him, though, that Tolly very well could be found incompetent to stand trial. You need to be ready for that."

"Why can't they see he's acting?"

"I wouldn't doubt at all that you're right. Psychiatrists get played in the prisons all the time. But a ninety-five-year-old man would have an advantage when he's trying to convince a judge his mind has faded."

"Yes, I know. And I've prepared myself for the worst. At least we still have a shot now, thanks to you."

"Glad I could help. How about some lunch?"

"Sorry, I need to get back, but there's something else I'm dealing with. Mind if I get a little advice?"

Ten minutes later, Donaldson leaned against his car with a cigarette while Becky finished her story "What do you think, Chief?" he asked. "What does your gut tell you?"

"That there's something to it. It's kind of like that feeling I got when I knew there was more to Ed's murder. Now, I'm worried there's a girl dead somewhere, or in danger."

Donaldson tossed his cigarette. "First off, worrying never helps. If you're the worrying type, you'll get ulcers fast in this job. I can't tell you if there's anything to it or not, but I'll say that you're doing right by taking it seriously. When you don't take things seriously, they bite you in the ass more often than not. In the meantime, I'll make some calls to other sheriffs around the state, maybe see if they have any missing girls with a connection to here. Have you talked to Leroy Newton about it yet?"

Becky shook her head. "Can I have a cigarette?"

"I didn't know you smoked."

"I don't. Just want to now."

Donaldson lit it. "What's wrong? Something about Newton?"

"Not only him. The deputies, the highway patrol, and officers from other towns. You saw it back there in the DA's office. It's always the same. You can pick up a phone and call another agency and they'll listen. They stop taking me seriously as soon as they hear my voice."

"It's because you're something they're not used to. They see police work as a man's job only. It's a club, and in their minds, there's membership rules."

"It wouldn't also have anything to do with Sheriff Scotland, would it?"

Donaldson clenched his jaw and nodded. "In Bolton County, maybe. A few of the deputies there worked for him, including Newton. Some of them still may not believe he did all those things. Some of them may still hold a grudge over what happened. I'm just trying to be honest with you."

"Is that the talk?"

"I've heard it mentioned some."

"He fired a shot at me for Heaven's sake."

"I know."

"I shot him in self-defense!"

"Calm down, dammit. You don't have to explain anything to me." Donaldson watched her for a moment. "You Ok?"

Becky took a last draw on the cigarette. "Yeah, I guess. It's just that I bust my ass doing this job and still get treated this way. It's frustrating as hell."

"It's a tough job, Becky. Even when you do the right thing, sometimes you catch grief. Nobody's going to really give a damn about your feelings. All you can do is keep doing your best and be professional. You can't control what people think. Respect comes fastest when you understand it's nothing owed to you."

Becky looked at her shoes. "I understand that. I never thought it would come with the badge. I just didn't know it would be this way."

"Some things will never change, but enough will if you keep giving a damn. In the meantime, send me a copy of that note you were talking about. And keep on your toes. Because, whether this is a hoax or not, I have a feeling you'll be hearing from this guy again soon."

CHAPTER 14

As any other weekday, all except the older hobos left camp early that morning for their itinerant farm jobs. Breakfast was served before daybreak. Shiloh ate her serving of grits, eggs, and biscuits around the fire with them before going back to Andi's hut. Her blurred vision had begun giving her headaches. Rest seemed the only cure.

She felt tired from lack of sleep and lay down on a cot. Visions came to her when she closed her eyes, like in her nightmares—the man again. She didn't like being alone. Chris and Andi had sat up with her the previous nights. The three of them talked until late. Chris told jokes that bordered on dirty but made her and Andi laugh. She didn't know what it was she felt for him. It was something new to her. She only knew how good she felt when he was around, and she wanted him there all the time to keep away the darkness and nightmares. "Have you seen him?" she asked when Andi entered.

"He's gone to the other side of the lake to pick me a bucket of blackberries. I'm baking pies for the festival in town. He left early, so he should be back soon. Let me take a look at this before I head to work." She pulled back the wrap on Shiloh's neck. "Healing nicely," she said. "The bruise is fading." She patted the wrap back down. "So, I'm figurin' you've taken a shine to that boy."

Shiloh didn't want to deny it. "Yes." She felt her face warm.

"Is it first love? Or is that what you believe it to be at least?"

She pushed through her discomfort. "I think about him all the time. That's all I know. Yeah, it's the first time."

Andi chuckled and placed a hand on Shiloh's shoulder. "Sweet girl, don't think for a moment I'm laughing at you. I'm laughing only because I've been there and understand what you're feeling in your heart. It's a wonderful feeling, ain't it?"

"Yes. Have you got time to tell me about yours?"

Andi's eyes shined while she tied a bonnet to her head. "Well, I'll make it quick. I was fifteen. He was sixteen. Wavy, blonde hair. Eyes like Tony Curtis. A smile that would melt ya. We met one day at a church picnic. I fell head-over-heels. I couldn't have shook it if I'd wanted to. I imagine it's hard for you to believe an old bag like me was once in such a way."

"I can believe it. You're not an old bag."

"Bless you."

"What happened? How did it turn out?"

"He moved to Vermont with his family the fall after we met. He told me he'd come back for me sometime. I got one letter. I wrote back many times but never heard from him again. You could say it broke my heart some."

"I'm sorry."

Andi shrugged and put work gloves in her apron. "Long time ago," she said, with a half smile. "So, I worked for a bit in a sock factory in the town I was from. I'd go to work every day, holding out this fantasy that he'd come back for me and sweep me away. He didn't, of course. Let it hurt me far more than it deserved. A few years later, I decided that little town held nothing for me. That's when I began riding the rails." She smiled. "Don't get me wrong. I've met some wonderful people and been to many interesting places, but I often wonder now what life would've held for me if I'd waited a little longer, given myself a chance to grow up. I'm happy Chris makes you happy. But you don't really know him yet. So don't pin too many hopes on him just now. And don't underestimate the people that truly love you, Shiloh."

"I never would."

"Will you talk to me tonight and tell me about yourself? Where you're from? Why you really left?"

Shiloh's smile dropped, and she turned away. "Maybe."

"I'll be looking forward to it. I'll change your wrap also."

"Thank you. Would you mind if I read some of your books today?"

"You can see to do that?"

"I'm nearsighted. I can see up close."

"Well then, help yourself. Don't know what ya like, but there's a variety. Flynt and the others will be around if ya need anything. I'll have them look in from time to time. Call for them if needed."

"Thank you, Andi."

"They're coming, and they mean business, boys. Best get ready for a fight." The call rose over the camp soon after the working hobos left.

Flynt looked up from his repair work on a hut wall. "Plague take it. What now?"

Cotton carried his lead pipe and made fast strides while leading the tramps over the tracks. Flynt gripped his hammer tight by his side while the hobos gathered around him.

Cotton marched up. "Where's the punk?"

"He's not here. Let this go, Cotton. I told you I'd keep that boy away from your camp."

Cotton moved inches from Flynt's face. "Then you lied. I had ten dollars missing from my tent this morning. We're taking him back with us one way or the other. Turn him over to us so we won't have to tear down your camp finding him."

Flynt glanced at the tramps holding clubs behind Cotton. "I told you, he's not here. I'll walk you around and show you. How do you know he took your money anyway? Maybe it was one of your own men."

"Nobody in my camp is dumb enough to steal from me. So, move aside, old man. I don't wanna knock your block off."

"Let them see for themselves," Flynt said. "No sense in anyone getting hurt."

"Search every tent and hut," Cotton ordered. "Simon, come with me." He pushed past Flynt.

Shiloh laid her book down and stood when she heard the voices. Through a space between the plywood, she saw the movement around camp. She moved to the back of the hut and crumbled to her knees against the wall. Blankets draped over the entrance spread. Even as a blur, there was no mistaking Cotton's large frame. He walked in followed by Simon. The hut filled with the smell of stale sweat. "Where is he?" Cotton asked. The two men neared her. "Tell us unless you want trouble."

The moment brought back a memory to Shiloh. She imagined icy blue eyes. The wound around her neck burned. "He's not here," she piped, covering her face with her hands.

Cotton stood over her. "You're his Angelina, ain't you?"

She kept her hands over her face and felt the breath of his voice. "My name is Shiloh."

"He took money from me. Now, we're going to find him one way or the other. You can tell us where he is, or you can stay with us until he comes for you, if the punk has the guts." He turned to Simon. "Hold onto her."

Shiloh screamed when a lanky hand grabbed her wrist. It jerked her to her feet. Simon cackled while tugging her around. "Don't," she said. "I'll get the money for you somehow."

"Yeah, you'll pay for sure, Missy," said Simon. "Only no money needed." He showed his snaggleteeth while giggling.

Cotton scowled. "Tell us where to find him."

"I don't know. I promise I don't."

"Then, let's take a walk." Cotton held the blankets aside.

She cried while Simon tugged her outside.

The hobos blocked their way. "Why are you roughing the girl?" Flynt asked. "She had nothing to do with it."

Cotton shoved him. "Get out of the way, you antique."

The other tramps moved in with their clubs ready. They eyed Cotton, waiting for their cue.

Shiloh's heart pounded. It came hard for her to breathe. "Don't let them take me. Stop them." She jerked against the grip.

Cotton held his big hand out to Simon "Give her to me." Shiloh squealed when he jerked her powerfully.

Flynt's eyes flashed. "For the love of God, Cotton, there's no need for this. If it's only ten, I can get it for you now." He reached for Shiloh.

She cried out again when her arm was twisted.

Cotton raised the pipe with his free hand. "One more step, and I unleash my boys. I'll spill your brains myself, Flynt. I'm not a man to be tested. It's not about the money now. He came into my tent and stole from me. That won't stand no matter what you pay. You tell him that I'm holding her until he comes. Maybe I'll decide to go short of killing him if shows up on his own." He motioned with his head, and the tramps moved forward.

"She had nothing to do with it."

"Send the road kid over and I'll let her go." Cotton tugged Shiloh along.

"Don't let them, Flynt!"

Flynt stepped toward her but received a blow to his stomach from the end of Simon's club. He wheezed and fell to his knees. Simon cackled, his stringy hair waving over his face as he cocked his club back toward the other hobos. "Who's next?" he asked.

"Give the same to any others that get in the way," Cotton told his men. "Make a circle around us." Shiloh fell when he pulled her. Cotton jerked her back to her feet. "Move your ass."

She was forced to take steps while looking at the hobos and begging for help. They watched with sorrowful expressions. A few turned away.

With each resistance, Cotton twisted her arm more. The pain grew enough to force her to keep pace. She tripped on the tracks and was again roughly jerked up. "I never did anything to you," she said. "Let me go."

"She never did anything to you, Cotton," one of the tramps mocked. "Are you planning on changing that?" The others laughed.

"Walk faster or I'll break your arm."

She felt burning pain when he wrung her wrist. It took her to her knees in the middle of the tracks. She trembled and felt weak. Tears rolled from her eyes and further blurred her vision. She never saw him sprint from a clump of trees beside the tracks. The tramps did only when one had been knocked over. By then Cotton's head was held back by his hair with the point of a butterfly knife pressed against the base of his skull.

Chris eyed the other tramps moving in. "Move just a little and this knife goes straight in. Tell your boys to back off. Tell 'em right now."

Cotton jerked on Shiloh's arm as if trying to break it. "Fuck you," he said. "Jump his ass. Kill the punk bastard." But his eyes widened, and he bellowed when he felt the knife push in. "No! Stop! Back off. Back off."

Chris watched a red ribbon roll down the back of Cotton's neck. He leaned to his ear. "Just a little more and this blade slides right in before I scramble your brains. Then we'll just see who's fucked. Let her go. I won't say it again."

Cotton released Shiloh. "There. I did it. I let her go."

"Maybe I should kill you just for putting your greasy hands on her." He twisted the knife and listened to Cotton's tight groan. "What do you think, Shiloh?"

Cotton winced. It was he who trembled now. "I'll leave you both alone," he spluttered. "I promise." He sniveled when the front of his pants wetted.

Chris looked at the tramps' confused faces. "You're damned right you will, Cotton. But if any of your guys moves an inch toward us, your ass is dead. Tell them to turn and walk down the tracks. Tell them to keep walking until you call them back."

"Do what he says," Cotton said, then yelled it when the tramps hesitated.

Chris watched them. They walked slowly, each looking back every few steps.

"Get on your knees." Chris kept the knife pressed while Cotton complied.

"What are you going to do?" Cotton asked.

"Here's what you're going to do, fat boy. You're going to kneel right there and watch your boys walk. When we're gone, you can call them back. And, if you ever do bother us again, I'll come to your tent while you're sleeping. Only this time I'll slice your throat from ear to ear." He pushed the blade just enough to make Cotton yell out once more. "Understand?"

"Yeah. I understand." Cotton felt the blade removed. He heard feet running away behind him. He shook all over as he looked at the front of his pants, and then at his men walking away. He never called them back.

They sat close together on the lake shore. "Thank you," Shiloh said and leaned into Chris' arm. She felt safe again.

"No problem. Cotton and those guys are a walk in the park. I used to have to deal with some real badasses in Camden. Sorry they roughed you up, though. It's my fault that all happened. Maybe I'm not the best guy for you to be hanging around with."

She smiled. "Seems like you're always there when I need help. Maybe you are the guy I need to be around."

He blew a laugh and looked into her face. "Can you see me Ok?"

"Yes."

"Mind if I ask a question?"

"No."

"What are you doing here?"

"I told you. I ran away."

"Well, I've seen a lot of people on the run from one thing or another. But you don't look like any of them."

She rolled her eyes and grinned. "What am I supposed to look like?"

"You don't have that hard look most people on the run have. Those eyes may not see too well, but they say a lot. They say that you're unsure about what you're doing."

"I'm not sure about anything anymore, other than I don't ever want to go back to that camp. I don't know if I want to go home either. I've ever been so confused."

"Yeah, I get it. It's a big deal when you leave your folks. Once you really do it, things never go the way you planned. So, if you really are serious about it, you'd better always have a second plan. I can't tell you what that plan should be. You'll have to decide that, but I know another place we can go to if you need to think about it for a while. It will only be us. I mean, if you want to. I understand if you don't trust me enough yet."

"I trust you."

"Really? You're one of the few."

"You've saved me twice now. How can I not trust you?"

He looked down into her face. "Your eyes are pretty too."

"Would you say that even if they were behind thick glasses?"

"Yeah. No doubt about it." It came in a soft breath.

They kissed.

CHAPTER 15

With all the kitchen gadgets she'd received for her wedding, Wendy felt she had to try her hand at a few simple recipes and had discovered a hidden passion. She'd taken cooking classes and toyed with the idea of opening her own catering service as a side job to teaching. Normally, she sipped a glass of merlot while cooking. Milk in a wine glass was her substitute that day as she finished butterflying the chicken breasts and adjusted the gas flame under her pan. She was flouring the first cutlet when the phone rang. Irritation showed on her face as she wiped her hands on a towel and walked to the den.

"Hello. Hawk residence."

"Becky?" The voice was hesitant, some stressed.

"No. Wendy Powers. Becky should be home in an hour or so. May I take a message?"

"Yeah. Tell her, uh…Tell her…Never mind. I'll call back." The words were slurred.

Wendy heard a dial tone and stared at the receiver before hanging up. She took a look out the window, expecting Bobby and Aaron to return from their fishing trip within the hour. Flipping on the radio, she dialed it until she found The Four Tops.

She sang along to *Baby I Need Your Loving* while dancing back to the kitchen, where she finished flouring the chicken and set it to fry in a pan of hot butter. The stress from her nine months in the classroom was unwinding. She sipped her milk while she danced and sang, happy to have alone time.

Ten minutes later, the browned chicken bubbled in a buttery, lemony sauce. Wendy tasted a spoonful. "Exquisite. Don't you agree, darling?" she said, rubbing the bump on her belly. She tossed in a handful of capers before placing the lid on the pan. The phone in the den rang again.

Wendy huffed on her way back to the den and turned the radio down. "Hawk residence."

"Becky?"

"No. Wendy Powers again. I'm a friend of Becky's. She's still not home. I'd be happy to take a message."

"Ah, Wendy Powers. Formerly Wendy Martin?"

The corners of her mouth dropped. The voice wasn't the same as before. "Yes. How do you know that?"

"I've heard a lot about you. This is Pete Underwood, your friendly neighbor from across the lake. I hate to bother you, Wendy, but I noticed the door over your boathouse is open. You folks may want to check it. There's a problem of stealing around the lake in the summertime. Crooks in boats, you know."

"Thank you. Repeat your name please."

"Pete Underwood. An old friend of Becky's."

Except when she put it on and took it off, Wendy rarely thought of her prosthetic anymore. She did then, however, when she heard the names of the two men who'd intentionally caused the automobile wreck that placed her in a coma for two months. Her recovery had gone well, though not yet complete. The occasional phantom pains from where her right leg had once been still bothered and amazed her. "Thank you for telling me," she said.

"No problem. Be sure to tell Becky and Bobby I said hello. Hope to see them soon."

The caller's name stayed on her mind while she crossed the backyard. Coincidence only, she thought, but with lingering uncertainty. She walked onto the pier, looked up at the closed guesthouse door, and then carefully climbed the steps to it. The knob turned when she tried it. Aaron would need to remember to lock up before he went fishing. She opened the door and stepped into the room. Drawn window blinds blocked the sunlight. She felt certain she'd opened them that morning. Aaron must've closed them back for some reason. Wendy traced her hand over the wall until she found the light switch and flipped it. A check of her and Aaron's belongings found everything in order. She remembered the chicken on the stove, locked the door, and hurried back to the house.

The stove was off. She saw that before she made it to the kitchen.

"Becky, are you home already?" she asked, walking to the front bedroom. "Becky?" She knocked and eased the door open. The red, police emergency line telephone Becky kept on her nightstand lay on the bed with the receiver off. Instinctively, Wendy placed her hand over her belly. She heard a boat engine outside and hoped it was Bobby and Aaron returning.

Her eyes darted over the living room on her way back to the kitchen. There were innocent reasons for it all, she thought. She'd turned the stove off without remembering. Becky had been in a hurry that morning and left the phone on the bed that way. Wendy took a sip of her milk and tried convincing herself of that. She lifted the lid to stir the sauce but paused with her spoon over the pan, knowing there would be no innocent reason for the chew marks around the edges of each chicken piece. She stepped back, and her trembling hand went over her mouth. The girl in the picture stuck to the refrigerator door wore a cap and gown. A small flower was taped to her hand. Wendy trotted toward the back door as fast as her prosthetic leg would allow and yelled to Bobby and Aaron unloading their fish on the pier.

"Maybe you should think about taking a vacation," Sheriff Newton said. "My guys can cover the town for as long as you need. If this person doesn't have you around to screw with anymore, he'll probably take his games elsewhere."

Becky watched Newton's crime scene technician flashed his camera at the sliced open screen of her bedroom window. "This doesn't seem like a game to me, Sheriff."

"Yeah, but to him it is. He's getting some kind of kick from it. We get these clowns sometimes who like toying with law enforcement. I once had a guy who'd call me every week, pretending he had information on the Lindbergh baby kidnapping. It stopped when I quit taking his calls. My guess is this is high school kids who are out for the summer and have a lot of time on their hands. Or it could be someone in for the Blackberry Festival. Something like that brings in all kinds. Regardless, you kill their fun if you get away for a while."

"That doesn't sound quite the way a police chief should handle a problem," Becky said. Newton's dismissive tone had her steaming. "Seems to me our concern would be finding out who the girl in the picture is."

"Ok, Chief. I'm just suggesting what I think's best."

Becky wondered, as she often did, if the smirk she saw on Newton's face was normal or reserved only for her. "I'll be inside," she said. "I'd appreciate your man dusting the window glass and the phone in my room for prints." She walked back inside to the den, where Aaron paced with the phone to his ear. Evidence bags containing the picture and the flower lay on a table. Becky took a seat on the sofa beside Wendy and Bobby.

"What do you make of it?" Wendy asked. Her voice still carried a tremble. "Are we dealing with a jokester or a real psycho?"

"A jokester, I hope."

"But you think it's more, don't you?" said Bobby.

Becky shook her head. "There's no way of knowing for sure. But we all need to be a little more careful from now on. I should know better than to leave my window open like that."

"Why would somebody do this?" Bobby asked. "It makes no sense."

"I don't know," said Becky. "But he knew we live here. He knew the house phone number." She looked at Wendy. "He knew your name and what Pete Scotland and Max Underwood did to you, and he was smart enough to figure out he could call the home phone from the police line. He's studied us, maybe watched us, and I don't believe this will be the end of it. I have no idea who we're dealing with, but the first step is learning who the girl in the picture is."

"Any theories about her?" Wendy asked.

"Only that the glasses she's wearing are the same glasses I found in the phone booth. That's the girl whose scream I heard. I'll guarantee it. That flower he taped to her picture may be something symbolic."

"Symbolic of what?" asked Wendy.

"Th-the girl is dead, isn't she?"

"Maybe he just thinks she is, Bobby. She's the girl he mentioned in his note and his phone call to Curt. She could be in the lake. The currents could've moved her. But I don't believe he would've put her there. I think he wanted us to find her body and his note together.

Since we didn't, I think there's a possibility she's still alive and he doesn't know it yet."

Wendy bit a nail. Her hand stayed on her belly. "So, this could be a sure enough killer who was here."

Becky saw fear in their faces. She felt it too.

Aaron hung up the phone. He sat close to Wendy and entwined his arm with hers. His worried look hadn't changed over the last hour and a half.

"What did they say?" Wendy asked.

"I gave them the girl's description. They're passing it on to my district supervisor and sending an agent down from Raleigh tomorrow. I'll need copies of the girl's picture. They're going to send them to all the field offices in the state and compare it with current missing person reports. Maybe we can get a name and find out where she's from."

"But, that could take a bit, right?" Wendy asked.

"Yeah, but it's about all they can do for now. There's no body. The only real crime we have is a break-in, so they're going to let the locals handle that. But I agree with Becky. We need to be careful of this guy." He looked at Bobby. "Looks like our fishing may be on hold, buddy."

The conversation continued, but Becky's attention was elsewhere when she looked toward the living room at her and Ed's anniversary picture on the fireplace mantle. She tried keeping her voice calm when she spoke. "I'll be right back."

"Where are you going?" Wendy asked. She followed and met Becky at the mantle. "What's up? What's with the funny look? Oh, dear God."

"Before she died," Becky said, "Pearl Wilson told me she wanted only certain flowers at her funeral. Under no circumstances were there to be chrysanthemums, because they symbolize death and mourning. Pearl didn't want that."

To preserve fingerprints, Becky lifted the picture frame by the edges. On it were two chrysanthemums, one taped to Ed, the other to her.

CHAPTER 16

"You're way too far out to be in a rowboat, kids." The fisherman stopped his boat near them. They bounced in the wake. "The water is deep here, and the currents are strong."

"I've rowed here before," Chris said. "I've got the currents figured out."

The fisherman's boat puttered closer. "Here." He tossed two life preservers. "Put these on. I'll give you a tow back."

"Thanks, but no thanks," said Chris. "We'll be fine."

The fisherman cocked his head toward Shiloh. "You Ok, young lady?"

She nodded, keeping her chin low and a hand on her cheek, partially concealing her face.

"You're not headed to Boar Island, are you? If you are, don't. There's sinkholes everywhere there. Fall in one and you'll never be found."

"No," said Chris. "I'm just showing her around the lake. She's a little shy, doesn't get out much. I'm going to rest for a minute before we head back."

"Keep the preservers. You may can paddle it, but you'll never swim it if you tip over."

Chris fished the preservers out of the water. "We really appreciate it, man." He handed a preserver to Shiloh and slid into his while watching the fisherman drive away.

Shiloh uncovered her face. "Boar Island? That's where we're going?"

Chris paddled again. "Yeah. Right over your shoulder. So close, *you* can probably even see it. He's right. There's sinkholes, but I know where they are. I've spent more time there than I have in the hobo jungle."

Shiloh tightened her preserver and turned. She made out a tree line. Behind it, on a hill, protruded the roof of a large structure that she knew once had been a hunting lodge. "I've read bad stories about this place," she said.

"Yeah? What have you read?"

Shiloh watched as they neared the island and its ancient cypresses draped in Spanish moss. "Bodies were found here, buried in hollow trees to hide them. They were all murdered. One of them was a girl named Shannon Monet."

"Yeah. I heard Flynt and the others talking about it. The club that used to own the island and lodge killed them for some reason."

"The Manticores," said Shiloh.

"You must've read a lot about it. They say the sinkholes started opening up not long after the bodies were found. It's like the lake is swallowing the island because of the bad stuff that happened here. Some of the hobos say the place is cursed. You're not superstitious, are you?"

Shiloh watched over the bow as they glided toward a cove under leaning trees and waving moss. "No. But how long will we be here?"

"Not long. I'll be leaving Black Lake soon. You'll have time to think about things without being bothered. I can probably arrange it for you to get home if you like. It's up to you."

"Where are you going?"

Chris rowed and smiled. "A place I've dreamed about for a long, long time."

Something didn't seem right. There'd been nothing in the papers about the young girl. Even a little police department with a female chief would've found her by now. The crowds gathering in Black Lake made him comfortable enough to go there, pull his fedora low, and walk around. He listened for talk of a murder. There was none.

He thought about it all again. She'd been lifeless. There'd been no breath when he left her against the tree. Or could he have been mistaken? Maybe he'd become too confident. Her scream and fight, after all, had rushed him. She would've seen his face.

Runaway or not, she'd come to Black Lake for a reason. If she were alive, she probably would still be there. It could be a problem. Finding her in a small town shouldn't be difficult. However, she would've told others. His hunt was becoming risky. That was fine with him, though. Risks energized him. They were addictive and, like any other addictive thing, he felt the need growing stronger.

He wouldn't leave Black Lake. Too many good things had fallen into place there. He would push his plans as far as possible. And, by chance he failed, he simply would render his own destiny. There would be no prison cell for him, only a darkness that didn't frighten him.

He drove around the town, familiarizing himself with its settings while he looked for her. He found the police station, and then cruised the waterfront. He stopped often to let pedestrians cross and gave them smiles and waves. A lumber barge on the lake blew its horn. People turned and snapped pictures. A Ferris wheel and carousel were going up in a vacant lot. The town was alive.

Knowing that each person he saw could be his next stirred his desires. He made another pass through town, this time finding a road that traveled along the lake. Boaters and swimmers filled the recreation areas. There was a campground too. A small boy on a bicycle came from it and rode down a backroad. He thought about it while following from a distance. He hadn't planned on a kill that day. But maybe it was time to show Black Lake and Becky Hawk exactly whom they were dealing with.

Even the giant bald cypresses bowed toward the cove. Smaller trees had surrendered to the sinking ground and formed a watery maze, which Chris rowed through. Shiloh rode with her hands braced on the sides of the boat. Even if she didn't know its history, she would've found the place unpleasant. It smelled murky with clouds of gnats dancing in the humid air. Spanish moss brushed her face when they passed beneath dead branches. The chance of a snake dropping into the boat seemed high. She swatted her arm.

"Yeah, mosquitos are bad in the cove," Chris said. "But there's always a good lake breeze at the lodge that keeps them away. That's where we're going. You won't believe that place, Shiloh. It's more like a mansion than a lodge. I found some canned stuff there too. Soup, vegetables, lots of good stuff. I'll fix dinner for us tonight. You sure you're still Ok with this?"

The sun was low over the lake. The cove was darkening.

"I guess," Shiloh said. "Are there lights up there?"

"There's no electricity, but I found some candles. There's a fireplace too. We'll have to be careful, though. The lake patrol came and almost caught me one night when I had the place lit up. On that hill, it shines over the lake like a freaking lighthouse."

"Are there still wild boar here?"

"Nah, they killed them off after they shut the hunting club down." Chris rowed into a small opening between a grove of trees and landed the boat. "So, you've never been to Black Lake before?"

"No."

"But you sure seem to know a lot about it."

"I know its past. That's why this island scares me."

He followed the boy to a sparsely populated area with derelict buildings and eroded streets. A condemned sign was nailed to the front entrance of the large, two-story building the boy went behind. He drove slowly and found him riding his bike up and down a weedy and cracked concrete ramp that descended under the building. The layout of the place told him it had once been a hospital. The ramp would lead to a morgue.

He pondered the boy's fate for a full minute, watching him appear at the top of the ramp and roll downward over and again. The boy had yet to detect his presence. He crept the van toward him. The boy appeared once more at the top of the ramp and, seeing the van this time, sat on his bike and stared. No one else was around. It would be an easy kill. He gave the boy a friendly smile, opened the glove box, and took his parachute cord out. His hand was on the door handle when he had second thoughts. As tempting as it was, the old hospital offered something more practical for his stay in town—concealment. He placed the cord back then cranked the window down an inch.

"Security. No trespassing." He watched the boy shoot away and laughed. "Lucky, lucky boy," he said, backing the van down the ramp and disappearing under the building.

Dusk had settled when Chris helped Shiloh slide through a back window of the lodge. The inside smelled musty when she dropped onto a polished stone floor. Chris landed beside her.

"Take a look at this place," he said. His flashlight beam fell on a large animal. Shiloh flinched. "Relax. It's only a stuffed bear." Chris swept the light over more eternally posed animals. Though the details were unfocused and dark, the size of the main hall they stood in surpassed Shiloh's expectations. She stayed by Chris' side, and he held her hand as they walked to a giant hearth in the center of a lounging area.

"Look at the size of that pig in the middle," Chris said, pointing his light upward.

Shiloh barely made out mounted deer and wild boar heads on the wall. She squinted at an enormous boar's head with pointed tusks when the beam settled on it. "Is that from a real animal?" she asked.

"Yeah, it's real. I heard there were more that big here once. I've been told there were lots of animals the club stocked this island with. But, in all the times I've been here, I've never seen the first one, other than a few birds and snakes. They must've all been killed off." Chris shined the light over the heads again before taking her arm. "Want to go upstairs?"

She stiffened and pulled away.

"No," he said. "That's not what I meant. I just want to show you the rest of the place, if you want to see it."

"Sorry," said Shiloh. "I'm just feeling a little nervous. Yeah, I want to see the rest."

They toured the second floor and its rooms before entering the once secret meeting room of the Manticores. An opening to it in the oak paneling of the hall wouldn't have been noticed had it not been left propped open two years earlier. Chris' light shone over hardwood bookshelves and a meeting roundtable with plush, leather chairs around it. There was an open floor safe.

"I hear this is where the cops found the records that the club kept. There were lists of big shots on the take and the payoffs these guys were giving them. I hear they even found the badge of a police chief they'd shot and killed. They must've been some really bad guys. But I guess you already know all that."

"Are those pictures on the wall?" Shiloh asked.

"Yeah." Chris led her there. "I'm guessing by the nails in the wall, there used to be more pictures up there. The cops must've taken them to identify the guys in them. I'm guessing they left those old ones behind because all of those guys are dead."

"What's the big one at the top?"

"It's their group picture from eighty years ago. Look at them, posing like a damned football team."

"Take it down for me," Shiloh said. "I can't see it from here."

"Sure." Chris stood on his toes, removed it, and then laid it on the table while holding his light over it.

Shiloh sat down and brought her eyes close to an old, wide-angle photograph of about thirty men. They wore an array of slouchy hats with badges on their coats and stood with arms laced in front of a horse and wagon. Two men and a boy knelt in front, holding a banner that read "MANTICORES 1884." Shiloh studied the men and noticed the one in the center didn't lace his arms with the others. His hands were on the boy's shoulders in front of him. There were similarities on both faces. Neither was pleasant. Shiloh's heartbeat increased. A cold and wicked look in the man's and boy's eyes reminded her of those she'd watched when the rope tightened around her neck. She sensed evil in the picture. She pushed it away and wrapped her arms around Chris. "Get me out of this room," she said. "Get me out of this house."

"But there's something else I want to show you."

"Please, Chris!"

CHAPTER 17

It was still dark when Becky showered and put on her uniform. She carried the girl's picture with her to the kitchen and found coffee already made on the stove. Aaron and Wendy sat on the back porch, watching the sunrise over the lake. Aaron wore his pistol holstered.

"Have you guys been up all night?"

"Aaron has," said Wendy. "I joined him around four. You're headed in kind of early, aren't you?"

"I'm meeting Sheriff Donaldson in Drake County first thing. He's been making phone calls for me. How are you both?"

"Scared some," Wendy said. "Didn't sleep much. I don't think Bobby did either. I heard him watching TV until late."

Becky sat and took a sip of strong coffee. "I hate you can't stay in the guesthouse now, but I think it's safest if we all keep close at night until we find out something about this guy. I'm sorry your vacation is ruined by all this."

"Pfft," Wendy blew. "Dolly, I'm sitting here with my man, watching a beautiful sunrise, and feeling my child squirm in my belly. No chicken piccata loving creep is going to ruin that."

"He's squirming?" Aaron asked and placed his hand on Wendy's stomach.

She, Wendy mouthed to Becky.

"Listen," said Becky. "You know I love you both being here, but I have a request. Go home and take Bobby with you. I'll feel much better if you do. Once this is settled, you can come back for as long as you like."

Wendy made a face. "And leave you behind? Forget it."

"I'll keep an eye on things while you're not here," Aaron said. "I won't let anything happen again."

"John Wayne there is right," Wendy said. "So, let's concentrate on finding that girl in the picture. I say we make copies of her picture and post them all over town. If she's been around, somebody will recognize her."

Becky frowned. "I don't know. If this guy thinks she's dead, maybe we shouldn't tip him off."

"I agree," Aaron said. "I think it would be better to find out who she is and why she came here first."

"May I see her picture again?" Wendy asked. She studied it after Becky handed it to her. "Well, it looks like a new picture. But there's nothing there to identify what school she was graduating from. One thing I can tell you, Becky, is that you have a young doppelganger in this world. Take away the glasses and tie her hair in a ponytail, and we have a teenage you."

Becky took the picture back and stood. "I'm going to work. You guys be careful today. Call me right away if you need anything." Her eyes repeatedly fell on the girl's face while she walked to her car and gave her ponytail a tug.

"Good morning, Sheriff." Becky took a seat at Donaldson's desk.

"Morning, Chief. I hope you're not as tired as you look. Long night?"

"A visitor dropped by my house yesterday. You said I would hear from him soon."

"He came to your house?"

"He came into my house."

The abridged version of the events Becky told him made Donaldson lean forward in his chair. He sat back and lit a cigarette when the story was done. "Want one?" he asked. "Sounds as if you might."

"No. I just want some answers." She handed him the photograph. "This is what he left on my refrigerator door. I've checked with the bus company. None of the drivers that stop in town remember her."

He put on reading glasses before taking it. "Well, this could help. I'll make some copies before you leave."

"Please say you have some useful information for me."

"Only a theory," Donaldson said. "And it's a bit of a wild one. I called every sheriff within a fifty mile radius. Most I spoke with have missing girls in their counties, but none knew of a connection with any of them to Black Lake. I also passed around the note with my senior guys. Our major over detectives noticed something about it. And this is the wild theory part. Have you ever heard of The Axeman of New Orleans?"

"No."

"He hacked up six people between 1918 and 1919 and sent letters taunting the police to the New Orleans newspaper. In one, he wrote that he'd spare anyone who was listening to jazz music on a certain night. It's said he had the whole city listening to jazz on their phonographs. It must've worked, because nobody got axed that night." Donaldson made an amused smile, but it quickly dissolved. "He was never caught."

"I'm really not following you," said Becky. "Surely you're not saying this might be the same person nearly fifty years later."

"Of course not. But the note your guy left for you is worded similarly to the ones The Axeman sent to the paper. He wrote about being a spirit and a demon from the depths of the earth, crap like that. It looks like the author of your note may have done some reading on The Axeman. I'm hoping the writing style is his only inspiration from him. The Axeman liked toying with the police, just like Jack the Ripper and others like them have. They get a kick from it and love following the news about their killings. It's a game for them that makes them feel powerful and in charge. Maybe your guy is the same. As I said, it's sort of a wild theory but not totally baseless, because it seems we have a person like that here in our own state. Has Aaron said anything about the bodies found along the new section of interstate in the mountains?"

Becky felt cold tingles. "No."

"Well, he's new in the bureau and may not even know. There have been three women found between the Pisgah Forest and foothills and two more near the Tennessee line. All were within less than a two year period, and all were along or near I-40. They all died of manual ligature strangulation and were left where they could easily be discovered. There were no obvious signs of sexual assault in any of the cases. This person apparently enjoys killing just for the thrill of it."

"So, we may be looking at someone who moved his killing ground here for some reason."

"We don't know near enough yet to draw any conclusions, but it's a possibility we should consider."

"Were flowers or notes left near the murder scenes?"

"I didn't know that detail when I was asking. It wasn't mentioned. The women were drifters and prostitutes that frequented the truck stops along the highway, so the SBI believes it's a trucker. They don't have much more than that. Their investigation has been mainly concentrated in that area. Keep in mind, though, that the interstate has cut down traveling times across the state significantly. Someone could make the drive from the mountains to Black Lake in less than five hours now. Plus, your town's only highway connects directly with Interstate 40."

"It's consistent," Becky said. "He told Curt that he left the girl against a tree, where she could be found easily."

"Except no body was found."

"He made it clear to Curt that he'd killed the girl. He must've been trying to taunt me by placing her picture in my own home. But maybe he made a mistake this time. Maybe we have a victim somewhere who survived him."

Donaldson nodded. "It's possible. You're sure the glasses you found in the phone booth are the same ones the girl in this picture is wearing?"

"Yes. They're identical anyway."

"Well, given everything, it seems the interstate killer's motive is simply the thrill of killing and the notoriety he gets from it. If this *is* the same guy, something or somebody brought him to your town. Whoever came into your house got his hands on that girl's picture, and we need to find out how. If this girl came to the little town of Black Lake and was trying to make a call, I'd say there's a good chance she knows someone there. It would be valuable if we could find out who that person is." Donaldson stared across his desk. "Are you with me, Becky?"

She came out of thought. "Yes, Sheriff, I really want to know that."

CHAPTER 18

They'd slept on a hill that overlooked the lake. It had been a pleasant night with a light breeze and a meteor shower. Chris told Shiloh when shooting stars traced over the sky. She tried seeing them. Only one had been bright enough for her eyes. It was late when the lake breeze lulled them to sleep. Nightmares tried entering Shiloh's dreams, but the feel of Chris' arms around her kept them away.

He smiled at her when she woke up. "Are you better this morning?"

"Yes, much better," she said.

"Bet you're hungry too. I am. Would it bother you if we went back to the lodge so I can cook our breakfast?"

"In a minute. I want to stay here a little longer." She sat up and rested against him while looking toward the lake. "That must be a wonderful view."

"Yeah. It sure is."

"Tell me about it."

He sat up a little more and held her from behind. "Well, the sun is still behind the tall pine trees on the far bank. It's shining yellow light through them. You can see the rays in a mist under them. There's birds flying around in it. No boats are out yet, so the lake is like a big, smooth piece of dark glass. Ducks are swimming and catching minnows on our side. I wish you could see it. This is my favorite part of the island. Sometimes I come here just to sit and think."

She smiled with her head resting against his chest. "What do you think about?"

"Oh, I guess the same stuff most people think about. The future. Being happy. Not having to look over my shoulder."

"I like dreaming about the future too," said Shiloh. "My guidance counselor at school told me that these are the best years of my life because of all the opportunities ahead of me. I think he was trying to say that anything is possible."

"Before I left Camden, I wouldn't have believed that. But I do now."

Did you hear the whippoorwill last night?"

"Did I hear the what?"

She smirked. "Whippoorwill. It's a night bird. My daddy would always say that you're getting your wish granted when you hear one."

Chris squeezed her shoulders. "Oh, really? Huh. I guess that's the sound I've been hearing in the woods the nights I've slept up here. I was thinking it might be a ghost."

Shiloh laughed.

"Anyways, it's great to wish and hope. But you have to have the guts to go after the things you want. I knew guys who had all these big dreams, but all they did was sit back and wait for it all to come to them. Then they'd talk about all the breaks they didn't get." He squeezed her shoulders and pulled a broken breath. "You know something, Shiloh?"

"What?"

"I mean…man, it's awkward. But, you know, you watch the movies and read the stories and listen to the songs about love and stuff, and you wonder what's such the big deal. Then you meet someone that shows you just what it's all about, and it, uh...." He chuckled. "Oh, wow, I feel stupid. You must think—"

Shiloh turned and looked him in the eye. "Tell me. Don't be embarrassed."

He grinned while looking away and then turned back to her with a blush. "I'm feeling something for you, Shiloh. I'm feeling something that I've never felt before for anybody. I can't describe it in words, other than it's flat out blowing me away."

She let it settle for a moment. "I cannot believe it."

"It's true. I'm not lying."

"No. I mean, I can't believe something like that is being said to me."

"Really? Why?"

"Because no boy has ever even given me a second look. I mean, never. Sometimes I believe I'm invisible when I'm around them. Why are you so different?"

He blushed more and struggled. "Well, I don't know. When you like somebody, you just like them. Before we met, I didn't know it was possible to feel this way. It just seems like all the bad stuff inside me has washed away now. I don't pray a lot, but last night I did, and I prayed you'd never go away."

Her eyes shined. "I won't."

"Are you sure? You're not just saying it?"

"I mean it more than I have anything before."

"If you're serious, I want to ask you a question, and I want you to be honest. Would you like to go to Florida with me?"

Shiloh made a confused smile.

"There's a train with lumber leaving town Monday morning. I'm in good with the conductor, so no worries about getting caught. It'll make a stop in Atlanta, and then it's on to Miami. I'll catch a bus there to Cudjoe Key. That's been my destination since I read about it in a magazine back in Camden. I really want you to go with me."

Shiloh's smile faded. "For good? We won't come back?"

"No. We'll live there. I'll take care of you, and you'll take care of me. We'll get us a place near the beach. It'll be sunny all the time, never cold. Soft sand and crystal water according to the magazine. We'll live like other people dream of living."

The idea overwhelmed her. It would've sounded impossible from anyone other than Chris. "But how will we get us a place? How will we make money? I'll need glasses."

He stood and took her arm. "Let's go to the lodge. There's something there that'll answer your question. You'll have to see it to believe it."

Becky gave her ponytail a long tug after she sat down at the steel table. For years she'd dreaded the coming conversation. She'd rehearsed the words she'd say but couldn't remember them while she waited. She heard a heavy door slam down the hall. Chains rattled until they were outside the room. A female guard took a peek through a small window before the door opened.

Cynthia Billings' bunned hair had turned white. She wore prescription glasses now and looked more wrinkled and thinner in her baggy, orange jumpsuit. She smiled, shuffled across the floor in her shackles, and extended one of her cuffed hands. "Becky."

"Will you be alright alone with her?" The guard asked.

Becky stood and briefly took Cynthia's hand before sitting again. "Yes."

Cynthia took a seat across from her. "I wondered if you'd ever come. How's Bobby?"

"He's better, but it still bothers him that his Uncle James thought he killed a little girl and her mother."

Cynthia looked down. There was an extended silence. "I don't think Jimmy ever believed that. Tell Bobby I said that. Let him know I love him. I hear he got his inheritance back. I'm happy about that."

Becky remained straightfaced. "We had to get a good lawyer and spend a lot of time in court. But, yes, he finally got back what was rightfully his."

"Why haven't you accepted my calls?"

"I didn't feel like talking to you."

Cynthia nodded. "I can't say I blame you. I wish I could apologize to you and Bobby more. I just never knew the whole thing would turn out like it did."

"Don't lie, Cynthia. You knew from the beginning what you were doing when you married James. You knew their plan included setting Bobby up. You knew a young girl would be killed. You even helped plan it." Becky felt anger renewed while she watched Cynthia wipe tears from under her glasses.

"Papa would've killed me if I didn't go along with his plans. I've told you that before. He controlled me. It was something I couldn't break. I'm so sorry, Becky."

Becky refrained from saying all the things she wanted to. "Does he still control you?"

"No. It took prison to do that. I may die before I get out. My baby brother has a date with the gas chamber next year. And it's all because of him. That man is dead to me now."

Becky's brown eyes were unblinking. They examined Cynthia's every motion for signs of deception. "I really hope you've changed."

"I have. I teach needlepoint classes in here. I help in the yard with the gardening. I counsel young inmates." Her eyes begged Becky for approval.

"You know that your grandfather is trying to play the courts and be declared incompetent. Have you talked to him?"

"No. I mean, yes. Just once. He called me here, right after my trial."

"What did he want?"

"What he wanted doesn't matter."

Becky's voice rose. "I want to know."

Cynthia's fingers trembled. She interlaced them and looked at the wall. "Do we have to go into this?"

"Yes, we do."

"I told him I wouldn't, of course. And I told him that I never wanted to speak to him again. But he said that, if I ever get out, I must kill you." She turned back to Becky. "He's consumed with anger. All he thinks about is revenge. I hear he's already gotten it from Bud."

"Yes. His throat was sliced while the guards weren't looking. He bled out in seconds. Central Prison stayed on lockdown for a week while they searched for the weapon. The rumor is Papa did it himself."

"He couldn't have. He's too old and fragile. But it had to have been through his orders."

"He's conniving, isn't he, Cynthia?"

"Yes, and he's terrible. You saw that yourself when he described how he killed Ed and what he and the other Manticores did to that poor family on Boar Island. Be careful of him. For all I know he may have contacts on the outside."

"It's no surprise to me that he wants me dead," said Becky. "But, perhaps you can help me with something else I'm dealing with. I won't go into the details, but it could involve another terrible guy."

"Not as bad as Papa, I hope."

"Every bit as."

"I'm sorry," Cynthia said. "Has anyone been hurt?"

"I don't know that yet. But I think someone will be unless he's stopped. So, tell me, how does someone become like that? Tell me what I don't know about Papa."

Cynthia gloomed. "In Papa's case, it was sewn early in his life. His father, my great-grandfather, was one of the founders of the Manticores. Papa admired all of them. They were his family as he saw it. He saw the things they did, and it molded him. There's a horrible story Papa told me once that I wish I could forget. Have you heard of The Burning?"

Becky shook her head.

"It was during the final stages of the war, just before Sherman's March. The Yankees began a scorched earth campaign in the Shenandoah Valley. Sheridan's cavalry pillaged and burned homes and farms. One of those places was my great-grandfather's. Years after the war, when Papa was a young boy, the Manticores learned that one of Sheridan's officers was living on a farm near Richmond. They went there in the middle of the night. Papa was with them and saw them kill that man and every member of his family. He watched them cut up each person with swords and burn the body parts. Papa told me that he later bragged about it to some of his school friends. As punishment for talking, he was tied up, placed into a box, and buried alive. His own father was the one who put him in that box. Papa thought that's where he would die, in the ground. They never told him otherwise. They kept him buried until he could hardly breathe. Then they dug him up. It was their way of teaching him loyalty and secrecy."

Becky scowled.

"I'm sure there are some simply born evil," said Cynthia. "Maybe Papa was. But his childhood ensured it. If there ever was a conscience in him, it died at an early age. I'm very glad he's near the end of his life now."

"Me too," Becky said. "However, he's still a very dangerous man. What happened to Bud and the phone call to you prove that. His competency hearing is next Monday in Bolton County. I want you to testify about everything you know about him. I want you to tell them what a deceitful man he is. Give them examples. Tell them about what you've seen with your own eyes. I don't know if it will help, but it can't hurt."

"Becky, I don't want anything else to do with that man. I don't want..."

Becky burned a stare at her.

"If I do it, he'll want me dead."

"Welcome to the club. You say you've changed. I won't believe that until I see you do something besides saying you're sorry. This is his last grasp to avoid a trial. You know him better than anybody. The judge may listen to you."

Cynthia blew a sigh and nodded.

"I'll let the district attorney know. I'll be here myself to transport you if I have to." Becky waved to the guard watching through the small window.

Cynthia stood and looked Becky in the eye when the guard stepped in. "The last time I saw you," she said, "you told me you'd visit me one day and decide if you'd forgive me. Do you?"

Becky leaned forward. "Every night in bed, I think about all the times you lied to me and wonder how many more lies there were I don't know about. Bobby will wonder for the rest of his life if his uncle died thinking he was a murderer. And every night I wonder if you were with Papa the night he fired two bullets into the back of my husband's head."

"No! I wasn't!"

Becky held up her hand. "There's nothing you can say to change any of that. So, forgiving isn't easy, Cynthia, but testify at that hearing and we'll see."

They entered the lodge from the back again. Chris guided Shiloh through the main hall to the kitchen. He opened the pantry closet door and shined his flashlight on the canned goods and spices inside. A mouse shot away.

"I was looking for food in here once," Chris said. "That's when I found this." He held Shiloh's hand, walked into the pantry, and pushed on the back wall. It swung open to darkness and damp air. "Keep hold of my hand. Go slow. The steps down are steep."

Shiloh squeezed both his hand and arm. "I don't know. What is this?"

"It's Ok. I won't let you fall."

They walked carefully down stone steps. Shiloh heard flowing water below. "What is this place?" she asked.

"I'm guessing the Manticores dug it after the lodge was built. Stay right with me. That water you hear is at the bottom of a sinkhole. It's in the middle of the room and deep. But don't worry. I won't let you get close to it."

Shiloh hesitated. "Chris, wait."

"It's Ok. We don't have far to go." His beam led them to the bottom of the stairs and a dirt floor. Chris then guided her along a wall to the corner of the room. "Look," he said. "Right there."

Shiloh barely made out what he shined his light on. Her first thought was coffins. Once closer to them, she saw they were rotten and collapsing. She counted ten. "What are those?"

"I found them the first time I came here. They dug this room to hide them in. Half of those crates were still full when I found them." He turned the light to stuffed and tied burlap sacks. "There it is, all they left behind, all packed and ready to go with us when we leave." He walked her forward and knelt her down. "Take a look," he said, untying and opening the first sack.

The contents glittered under his flashlight. Shiloh placed a hand over her mouth.

"It was all just left here," Chris said. "I separated everything. This sack is nothing but gold and silver coins. The others are full of things like silver plates and candlestick holders—jewelry too, with diamonds and gems like you see movie stars wear. Who knows how old some of these things are." He lifted a silver coin and handed it to her. "It's true. I found a real treasure."

Shiloh took the coin and held it closely to her eyes while Chris gave her more light. "1861" was struck beneath a seated Lady Liberty, both still in sharp relief. The edges were reeded with no wear. She turned it over to a shield and wreath of cotton and wheat. "Confederate States of America" bordered the top. "How did all this get here?"

"They stole it," Chris said. "I'm sure they did. You can bet the people who rightfully owned it are long dead now."

"I don't know about this, Chris."

"Listen to me," he said. "I've already made phone calls and have it all planned out. There's a rich collector in Miami. He wants to meet me at the freight station there and look it all over before he offers me a price. Whatever that may be, you can bet it'll be a fortune. This isn't a scheme, Shiloh. For once, things are going to work out for me." He squeezed her arm tight. "It's funny how things work, isn't it? I've spent years thinking up crazy ideas about how I could live a good life. Just when I thought it wouldn't happen, I stumble over this, and then I find you."

Shiloh looked once more at the coin before dropping it back. "Things like this don't happen. People don't become rich just by stumbling over something. It's impossible."

"When we watched the shooting stars last night, did you make a wish?"

She nodded. "Yeah, on the bright one, the only one I could see."

"Think of the odds of that one star being the only one bright enough in the sky for a girl named Shiloh to wish upon. How impossible does that seem? Plus, you heard a whisper wheel."

She giggled. "Whippoorwill."

"It doesn't matter. You saw that one shooting star." He placed another coin in her palm and closed her hand over it. "Keep it," he said. "So you can always remember that impossible things *do* happen."

CHAPTER 19

The Black Lake town council concluded their Monday night meeting in closed chambers, with Becky updating them on the events since the previous Friday. When she was done, only Councilman Phillips' face was readable, with the red hue and jaw twitch that even his slightest stress caused him. He was the first to speak:

"Someone is screwing with you, Chief. If this was real, something would've happened by now."

"Something *has* happened", Becky said. "My house was broken into."

"I mean something serious, someone hurt. Look, what happened here two years ago was broadcast all over the country. A lot of people heard your name and read about you. It shouldn't surprise us that things like that can attract crackpots. We don't need some wild-assed story flying around town right before our festival."

"I hope that's all it is," Becky said. "But I think it's best that we consider this in the worst case scenario."

"What's that?" Mayor Clayton asked in his usual calm voice.

Becky pulled the evidence bag containing the girl's graduation picture and flower from her file. "This is what was stuck to my refrigerator door. He also taped two of the same flowers to my and

Ed's anniversary photograph. Maybe some of you have seen mums on funeral wreaths before. It's a flower sometimes symbolic of death. Some sophisticated criminals leave calling cards for recognition. Mums appear to be his calling card. The worst case scenario is we have a killer here in search of notoriety. But killer or not, the guy who broke into my house while my friend was there enjoys taking great risks and playing games. That in itself makes him dangerous. And I'm betting he'll be at our festival. We'll need to be prepared for that possibility. In the meantime, Curt has taken time off from the lumber plant. He'll be covering the town at night. I'm asking that you contract with the sheriff's office to provide extra security both days of the festival." She saw discomforted expressions. Councilman Johnson rarely asked questions in meetings but seemed to have one. Becky locked eyes with him until he spoke.

"Why would he leave his calling card on your picture?"

A silent, uneasy air settled in the room. "Think about it, Councilman," Becky said. "You all saw what happened when the last chief of police was marked for death in this town. Maybe that will help you understand why I'm taking this so seriously."

After several moments, Mayor Clayton spoke somberly. "Thank you for the update, Becky. Considering everything we've heard, I think we should motion Chief Hawk's suggestion."

"Well, I suppose some extra security wouldn't hurt under any circumstances," said Phillips, his jaw twitching even more. "I motion it. But let's not go blabbing this all over the place and starting a needless scare."

"Second," came in unison from the others.

"Also," Clayton said, "I would like having the volunteer fire department boys spread out at the festival so we can have some extra eyes. And I want you to be particularly careful, Chief."

"Thank you for hearing me out," Becky said. It had been a long day. She walked out, ready for food and bed.

"What did the agent say today?" Becky asked Aaron while they walked the property boundaries of the lake house after supper. Each wore their gun by their side.

Aaron roamed his flashlight beam over the woods. "Not much, other than he'd send the copies of the picture to all the offices in the state. I tried convincing him that there's something to this, but he acted kinda put out that he had to drive all the way here just for pictures of a girl in a graduation gown." He glanced back at the house. Through the bay windows, Wendy and Bobby could be seen playing Monopoly. He jerked his light back to the woods and placed his hand on his gun when a twig cracked.

"Probably a deer," Becky said after a few moments of silence. They walked toward the pier. "I think this is worrying you about as much as it is me."

"Probably more. I can't tell you how much it scares me knowing that guy was in the house with Wendy alone. She's putting on a good face, but it's got her terrified. She couldn't sleep last night. That's probably not so great for the baby."

"I want you to do like I said. Go home and take Bobby with you. Do it for your baby's sake if nothing else. I'll be Ok."

"Only if you come with us."

Becky stepped onto the pier and checked the boathouse locks. "You know I can't do that now. Keep an eye on the house while I check up here." She climbed the steps to the guest quarters.

"Yell if you need me," Aaron said. He looked again toward where the sound in the woods had come from.

Satisfied that the property was safe, they walked back up the yard. "What do you know about the bodies found along Interstate 40?" Becky asked.

Aaron stopped dead in his tracks and looked at her. "You don't really think this is…" His voice trailed as he shifted his eyes to the window. "Oh, hell."

"I don't know for sure. Just tell me what you know."

They walked slowly.

"There's been five of them. All were strangled with some kind of a rope or cord and left near the highway. The women were all streetwise, not the kind to be conned easily, and the murders appear clean and quick. He's very adept at what he does and organized. They think it may be a trucker who drives that area. The guys investigating it aren't saying much more than that. I hear they've been staking out the truck stops." He looked through the window at Wendy rolling dice. "Dear Lord, don't let this be the same guy."

Becky stopped at the back door of the house. "I don't know if he is or not, but I would like for you to do something for me. Try to get the exact locations where all five bodies were found. And find out if any bodies were being found in that area before the interstate came through. Check on missing person reports from there too."

"Sounds like you may have a theory."

"Maybe. Get that information, and we'll talk more about it. Let's go inside. I need to call and check on Sharon."

Wendy made a playful frown when they walked in. "Guys, we have a tycoon on our hands. I'm down to my last fourteen dollars and Bobby has the board covered with his freaking hotels."

Becky listened to them all chuckle while she lifted the phone. "He's ruthless when it comes to Monopoly," she said.

"I'll loan you five hundred if you want," Bobby told Wendy.

"Oh, so you can draw out my misery?"

Becky had smiled while dialing Sharon McDowell's number but it faded, and her stomach began a slow sinking on the fifth ring. After the tenth, she trotted to the living room window and looked down the path in the woods. A lighted window with a wide-open blind allowed her to see clearly into Sharon's living room. The television set flickered. Across from it, beneath the light of a floor lamp, a cat stood on the arm of the recliner. He pawed at Sharon while she lay there in her pink bathrobe.

Wendy groaned when she landed at Park Place. She made a face at Bobby, throwing her last bills at him, but the following laughter stopped when Becky ran out the door with her revolver in hand. "Don't leave this house, Aaron," she said.

CHAPTER 20

Curt was still on duty when Becky walked into the police station at eight AM. He gave her the desk, watching her sit and stare away. He waited through silence before she looked at him with reddened eyes. "I'm sorry," he said.

"Thank you." Her voice was just above a whisper. "Thank you for working over also."

"Don't mind at all. Do you want to talk about it?"

Becky made a face of disbelief while shaking her head. "No. I don't *want* to talk about it, but you need to know. She was attacked from behind while she watched television in her recliner. It was ligature strangulation. When I found her, her hair was damp. There was still steam in her shower stall. It had to have happened not long before I found her. We don't know yet how he got in. All the doors and windows were locked. I presume he'd been inside hiding, waiting for his chance, and locked a door behind him when he left. The sheriff's detectives are still out there processing the scene."

"So, what do we do?"

"Mainly, be very careful. There's no doubt in my mind now that this is the same person who's been killing women in the mountains. He'll be around town. He'll probably be looking for another victim. Keep a razor eye on everything. I can't tell you what to look for. You'll have to use your instincts. Stop and talk to anybody who doesn't look quite right. Find out all you can about them. Fill out a field contact card. Don't hesitate to call for help. I'll have my radio on even when I'm home. There'll be plenty of deputies around town too. This guy is toying with us. He'll be right under our noses."

Curt's hands fidgeted. "I never knew I'd be dealing with something like this when I took the job."

"Feel free to step down," Becky said. "I'll completely understand."

It took him a moment before he shook his head. "No, Chief. That ain't happening. Only a coward would leave you in this situation."

Becky smiled at him. It would be her only one of the day. "Go home and get some rest, Curt. I'll be working over if you want another hour or so before you come back in."

"Thanks. Chief. I might take you up on it. There's a girl I met that I'd like to take out for dinner. She wants to ride in my Mustang."

"Sure. Have fun."

Curt snapped his fingers. "Oh, damn, I almost forgot. There's a drunk locked up in the holding cell who needs to be let out when he sobers up. Public intoxication."

"One of the regulars?"

"Nope. Out-of-towner. I left the arrest report in the basket."

They'd washed the dust out of the sheets and pillow cases with soap and spring water and then hung them out to air beside the mattress and pillows the day before. It made the canopy bed they chose in the lodge smell clean and fresh. The sleep it provided was the most comfortable Shiloh had in days. The sun was up when she woke and rolled over. It didn't bother her much that Chris was gone. He'd promised to get up early and cook breakfast that morning. She called for him while taking slow steps down the stairs. The lodge was quiet. She tried to suppress the apprehension growing in her as she found her way to the front door and out to the barbecue pit that Chris cooked on. The coals from their dinner still smoldered in it.

"Chris?" She squinted and turned in different directions. "Chris?"

"Right here," he said from behind her. He held his burlap bag.

She turned and slapped his back after hugging him. "Where were you? Don't ever leave me like that."

"I'm sorry. I thought I'd be back before you woke. I brought eggs. I was hoping to have omelets ready when you got up. And there's a gift in here for you." He brought a glasses case from the bag and handed it to her.

Shiloh pulled the glasses out. The frame and lens were like hers. She slid them on and saw the bleared images of the island focus enough to remind her how much she missed seeing clearly.

"Better?"

"Yeah. Some. Where did you get them?"

"That doesn't matter. I know they won't give you twenty-twenty, but at least you can make things out enough to get around. We'll buy you your own when we get to Florida."

Shiloh took another look around before taking them off. "No, Chris. They're stolen. I can't take these."

He shrugged. "Well, you need them. You're almost blind without them. The person they were for will just get another pair. Then, both of you can see."

"I don't like your stealing," she said. "I especially don't like you stealing in Black Lake."

He made a puzzled face. "Ok. But you have them now. Might as well wear them until I can take them back."

"Why don't you make the omelets? Then I believe it's time we talked about our pasts—and our future."

Worry showed on his face. "Yeah," he said. "It's past time we did that."

CHAPTER 21

After Curt left, Becky walked with key in hand to the small, white brick building behind the police department. Under the circumstances, she wished Curt had spent his on-duty time with things other than locking up drunks. She put the key into the steel door and turned it while taking a glance at the arrest report she held. The key stopped in the lock and was left hanging. Becky paced to the police department, reading the full report while she walked before turning and coming back. She took deep breaths to calm herself. Please, no, she prayed before pushing open the door.

From the cot he sat on, Dan Bowman's eyes glanced up then cut to the floor again. His head fell between his hands.

Becky came to the bars and watched him silently. The thick, dark hair she remembered was now thinned and white. She waited for him to look up, and then saw in his face only a vestige of the features she remembered.

"Hello, Becky."

It seemed like another of the unpleasant dreams she'd had last as a child. "I was sure you'd be dead by now," she said.

He wiped his nose with a finger. "I was too."

"Why are you here?"

He stood and turned his back to her, looking at the lake through the barred window. "I came here to find someone. She ran away from me this past Friday. You don't know her. She's my other daughter."

Becky was too stunned for it to click. Memories she didn't want invaded her mind. She could hear her mother's cries and the thuds of fists striking. She remembered how scared she'd felt when she'd run to stop it, and how warm the blood in her hair had been after he'd shoved her down and her head had banged against the floor. She could see his younger face looking down at her with drunken fear on it before he ran from the house, never to return. "You bastard." It broke from Becky with all the resentment she'd stored for nearly thirty years.

He sighed. His eyes were down again when he turned. "I don't blame you for saying it."

Then it clicked for her and felt like a punch to her gut. "Who's your other daughter?"

"Her name is Shiloh. She's seventeen." He looked up into Becky's blank stare. "Years after I left your mother, there was a woman in Asheville I met. Shiloh is hers and mine. But I raised her myself."

Becky shook her head in disbelief. "And here you sit in jail after pulling a drunk while she's out there somewhere. Why am I not surprised? Have you even filed a missing person's report?"

He shrugged. "I talked to the sheriff back home. Don't know if he put anything on paper. My neighbor's boy was the last to see her. She was walking toward the highway from our house with a bag late Friday afternoon."

"Have you got her picture with you?"

"Yes," he said, reaching for his billfold.

Becky took the photo he passed through the bars. She had many questions but chose the most pressing ones first. "Where did she come from, and why did she come here?"

Dan's eyes flashed. "She *is* here?"

"She's been here. Where did she leave from?"

"Millpark in Linville County. It's where I lived before I married your mother. I moved back there just after Shiloh was born. How do you know she was here? Have you seen her?"

"Answer my questions first. Why did she come here?"

"You," Dan said. "If she came here, she came here because of you. I guess her big sister was the only person she felt she could go to."

"But I don't even know her."

"Yeah. But she knows about you. The older she got the more questions she had—who her mama was, my past, things like that. I told her everything, including that she had a half sister who got married and moved away. She wanted to know your name, so I told her. Then she saw the stories about you in the paper back home. She cut them all out and saved them. I think it made her kind of proud. She wanted to meet you. I'd always tell her that you and I weren't on good terms and meeting you probably wouldn't be a good idea. When I didn't find her, I thought she may have found a way here."

Becky reached through the bars and grabbed his shirt. "Why the hell didn't you call me first thing?"

"I drove here yesterday and planned to. When I got here, I was nervous about meeting you. I felt like I needed something to settle my nerves. I called your house, but you weren't home. So, I went out looking for you. That's how I ended up here."

She pulled loose his shirt and looked at him in disgust. "You haven't changed at all. You're still the same drunk who beat my mother."

"No. I've changed. I tried raising Shiloh right. I go to church with her. Every day I feel terrible about how I treated you and your mother. There's been many times I've wanted to call you and apologize, but I just didn't have the guts to. I was scared to talk to you. Yeah, I'm still a drunk. I'm every bit the drunk you remember. I'd move Heaven and Hell to change that. But I am not the man you remember."

Becky shook her head. "I'm not really concerned if you are or not. But I am concerned about Shiloh. Do you know of anyone who would want to hurt her?"

His hands grabbed the bars. "No. Why?"

"I found her glasses in a phone booth Friday night. I think she may have been trying to call me when someone attacked her. My neighbor was strangled to death last night. The person who did that probably attacked Shiloh too."

His face paled, and he dropped sitting on the cot. "Oh, great day! Please don't tell me she's dead."

"I don't know, but I think it's possible she's alive. If she is, she's still in danger. You need to go home in case she calls."

"She couldn't. My phone has been cut off for months."

Becky unlocked the cell door and pulled it open. "Come to the police department with me. We're going to make sure there's a missing person's report filed. And you're going to give me every detail there is about her."

For the first time, he hadn't watched the eyes. He'd been too fixated on the cat in her lap and its comedic entertainment. It had cocked its head and struck different poses while the woman croaked. He'd watched it over her shoulder, trying to keep the cord tight despite his laughter. With the final gasp, the cat hesitantly pawed at the woman's bathrobe. The cat continued looking on quizzically while he'd posed the lady nicely, with her hands crossed and a flower slipped under her wedding ring. She'd looked very natural lying there on the recliner. He'd spotlighted her with the reading light and opened the window blinds. It would only be a matter of time before Becky Hawk and her friends across the way noticed her.

He'd returned to the morgue sally port and was resting and reading a book in the back of the van when distant sirens told him the discovery had been made. He'd felt happy about it and slept soundly that night.

His excitement renewed when he woke late the following morning. Things were going well, very well. He wanted to hear the talk about it around town before he went about his other preparations. He drove to the waterfront and wasn't disappointed when he ate breakfast at Perkins' Restaurant. Sharon McDowell was the woman's name, a retired store clerk and widow. She was the main topic at a long table where older men ate and talked.

After he'd eaten, he walked to the lot where the big festival was to be held. More vendors and food trucks were setting up there. A crowd gathered around a juggler flipping clubs of bright colors, and an idea made him smile.

It impressed him that the small town would throw a festival the size this one would seem to be. That was good. The more people the better. He surreptitiously listened to the talk going around. Was it fear in the voices? He thought so, and it delighted him. He wanted to stay and hear more. He yearned to meet Chief Hawk and talk to her, but there would be time for that. There was much to do before the festival and his grand finale. The groundwork would need to be laid thoroughly.

There was also a decision to make: How to get that one advantage over the Chief he needed? Which of her friends would it be? From the woods, he'd watched them through the big windows of the house.

Aaron was much too formidable. Bobby was a possibility. Wendy, however, would be the most valuable because of the baby in her belly. He'd noticed that when he'd watched her cook and come a breath from taking her in the kitchen. But that would've ruined his grand plan. It had been too early. Now, the time was drawing near.

He walked and thought about his plans. They were even riskier now. He hated second guessing himself but wondered if he should've been more secretive. The other players were on guard. He'd seen that through the shadows of the woods when he'd slipped away from Sharon McDowell's back door. This game couldn't go on forever anyway. The Luger under his shirttail was a reminder of that. He would win regardless of when and how it all ended, simply because the dread of his name and the stories of him would be left behind in the world he hated.

An elderly man and woman walking ahead of him stopped at a light post and read from a scrap of cardboard taped to it. He joined them and felt his spirits soar when he saw the picture of a familiar face attached.

"Poor child. I hope they find her," the woman said.

"So sad," added the man.

"Yes," he said. "I'm sure someone is heartsick with worry." He watched the couple walk away before removing the cardboard and folding it into his pocket.

CHAPTER 22

"You could be a chef," Shiloh said when she tasted her omelet. They sat on the wide porch of the lodge and ate from china plates.

"Well, where I came from, I had to learn to cook if I was going to eat right," said Chris. "A guy gets tired of Cheerios and peanut butter sandwiches after a while. Can you cook?"

"Yeah. I did some back home. My father taught me." She enjoyed one more distorted view of the lake before removing the glasses. "These are going to give me a headache worse than when I'm not wearing them."

"Sorry. They were the thickest I found."

"Thank you for the thought," Shiloh said.

"I wish I'd known my stealing bothered you. But it's not like I clean people out. I only take the things I need. You needed glasses."

She nodded with a half smile. "Yeah, I need them bad. I've been nearsighted for as long as I remember."

"Which reminds me, we were going to talk about our pasts. Mine's simple. My mom was a drug addict who slept around with every guy on the block and never gave a hoot in hell about me. I decided to get away from her after I caught her in bed with the same guy that killed my dad."

"Oh, Chris. I'm sorry."

"Yeah, it was a tough deal. He'd shot my dad eight years earlier in a fight over her. The son of a bitch got out on parole and smiled at me when I walked in from school. She was either passed out or dead asleep. I seriously thought about killing the guy but walked out instead, and I haven't looked back."

"I wish you'd have told me before. That must've been hard for you."

"Nah, don't worry about it. If it hadn't happened, I never would've met you."

"Do you miss your father?"

Chris pulled a broken breath before speaking. "Yeah. He wasn't a bad guy. He kept the bills paid and food on the table, made sure I had what I needed, and took me to ball games. He deserved a hell of a lot better than he got." He looked away for a moment to wipe his face. "So, you're on. What's your story? Start with why you know so much about this place and why you don't want me stealing, especially in town."

"Because my sister is the chief of police there."

Chris snorted a laugh. "You're kidding. I know you're not serious."

"Her name is Becky. I've never met her, but I've read about her and this place in the newspapers. She's really my half sister. My father left her and her mother when she was really small. I came to meet her, but she doesn't know I exist. I'm not even sure she'd want to see me." She could tell Chris was staring and wished she could make out his expression.

"Why haven't you told me that?"

"Because I was afraid to. I thought having a sister who's a police officer might make you not want to be around me, since you're a runaway and you... you know."

"Have sticky fingers?"

She nodded and suffered through silent moments.

"Wow," he said. "A big sister who's the head cop in town. That's cool. I've seen her out shaking doors at night. Never got a good look at her, though. I was always hiding."

Shiloh let out a laugh of relief.

"Of course I want you around. Do you really think I'm a big enough jerk to not like you over that?"

"No. But I worry so much that you'll find something wrong with me. It seems everyone else does some time or another. I worry because I'm the happiest I've ever been and I don't want it messed up."

He chuckled. "You know, that's funny because I've been worried about the same thing in reverse. God knows there's enough flaws here to keep someone from wanting to stay around me."

"I'm happy when I'm around you," she said.

"So, tell me why your face hasn't been showing it today."

Shiloh slid the glasses back on and looked at him. "It's nothing to do with you. I've been thinking about my dad. I'm wondering how he's getting along. I think he might be taking my leaving him hard."

"Yeah, I get it. He's your dad. I'm sure you love him, but you're almost eighteen. He couldn't have expected you to stay with him forever."

"I know, but there's more to it."

"How?"

"He never liked talking about it," she said. "I'd ask him questions sometimes after he'd been drinking. That's when he'd open up about himself and tell me things he wouldn't sober. I never knew my mother. He never married her. He said she wanted to abort me. So, he offered to raise me on his own if she gave birth. I think he always felt like he'd failed Becky. He wanted to do better with me. He named me Shiloh because it means peace. I guess that's what he thought I would give him. He did the best he could. There were just some things he couldn't beat. He lost his job last week, and then he lost me. I'm worried about what he must be feeling now."

"Be honest," said Chris. "Are you thinking about going back?"

She felt torn. "No. I want to go with you. I've never wanted anything more. But I know if I do, I'll always wonder what became of him."

He took her hand. "If you go back, it's fine. I'll come for you one day and we can be together again."

"That scares me. There's too much that could happen. You might meet someone else."

"No. I'll come for you. You have my word on it. Listen, I only want you to come with me now if it's without regrets. I won't feel right if it's any different. Think about it a little more. We've got until next Monday."

CHAPTER 23

A North Carolina map mounted on poster board stood propped against a chair in the den. Aaron stood at it with his notepad and pressed the final of five, orange-headed straight pins into the mountain section. Becky watched beside him. Wendy and Bobby glanced up between the rolls of their Monopoly rematch.

"That's close," Aaron said. "Three east of Pisgah Forest and two within fifteen miles of the Tennessee Border. Roughly one hundred and sixty miles between the farthest east and west. The three bodies in the foothills were near the interstate. The two near Tennessee were along Highway 19, which connects to the interstate around Asheville. But there was no flower left behind in any of the cases. No calling card of any kind."

"Still, he left them all where they could be found easily," Becky said. "This guy wants attention and is becoming more confident in himself. That should make him easier to catch but more dangerous. What's the time period between the first body being found and the last?"

"About a year and a half. The two near the state line were the first. The three others were more recent. He seems to like operating in the warmer months. All five were between April and September. His last was May second of this year."

Becky leaned close to the map. She found Linville County easily but had to look harder to find the dot that represented Millpark. She placed her finger on it. "Stand back and look at the pins," she said. "Does that look about the midpoint between them?"

"Yeah. Almost exactly."

"Eighty miles at the most each way from Millpark, less than an hour and a half drive on highway."

Wendy and Bobby left their game and walked over. "Looks like a little town." Wendy said. "You would think there would be someone there who could give you a rundown of the local psychopaths."

Becky stepped away from the map. "We know for sure Millpark is where Shiloh ran away from. If this guy picked her up along the way, she wouldn't have gotten this far. He must have followed her here. We need to find out how she got here, Aaron."

"I'll have some agents check with the bus stops in that area and show her picture around," he said. "And there's something else. I called around to some tire shops today about the tread marks you found. It sounds like they could be from rain and snow tires on a truck or van."

"That makes sense," Becky said. "That area gets a lot of snow and ice in the winter. A vehicle almost has to have snow tires to get around on the back roads and up the hills."

Aaron added to his notes. "Just another tidbit: This guy probably doesn't know much about car care if he's driving around on those tires now. They tend to wear down fast in the summer."

"First thing tomorrow," said Becky, "we need to start calling all the tire shops in Linville County and find out what we can about anyone who's purchased snow tires for a truck or a van."

"Better than television, right, Bobby?" Wendy said. "All we need is our popcorn."

"It's nothing to joke about, Wendy. Don't you know people are dying?" Bobby's words silenced everyone as they watched him walk to the living room with his head down."

"Honey, I didn't mean it that way. Becky, I'm sorry. I was only trying to lighten the mood."

"It's my fault," Becky said. "I should've realized what a strain this is putting on him. We shouldn't have been discussing it in front of him."

Bobby sat on the sofa when Becky entered the living room. He looked at her with concern. "I didn't mean to hurt Wendy's feelings."

Becky sat down beside him. "You didn't. She understands. Bobby, I'm sorry if we scared you."

"I was that way already. How could you not be?"

"I am. But we have to catch this man."

"Even more scared than you were with the Manticores?"

"Yes. Then I was so desperate to find out what happened to Ed that there was no room inside me for fear. But knowing a killer was here inside our house has me terrified. Bobby, I want you to—"

"Let me tell you what I want first. Quit your job. Let's leave this town. Only b-bad things happen here."

"I can't just leave. Not now. I swore an oath." The tight chuckle she heard from him hurt her.

"Ed s-swore an oath too, and that's what got him ki-killed. When they gave you your oath, was it to check doors and write reports, or was it to catch cra-crazy killers? When did they teach you how to do that?"

Becky wished her cheeks didn't burn. In their time together, Bobby and she had never argued. She felt they were close now, and she took a deep breath. "I can't run away from it."

"It's not about running away from it. I know you've got guts. But you-you saw what it did to me when Ed and Uncle Jimmy died. I never want to go through that again. You don't have anything to pr-prove. Don't pl-play this man's game. Think about me if you don't for yourself. We can pack and move tomorrow. You know we have the money to do it."

A mixed feeling of sadness and relief surprised Becky. "I'll make a deal with you," she said. "If you go home with Wendy and Aaron, and give me time to find my sister, I'll think about it."

After searching all day, Dan needed solid sleep but his gut gnawing dread had grown. There were no leads other than Becky's terrifying one. Horrible thoughts swirled in his head during his walk back to the motel. In his room, he prayed. He prayed for a lot, mainly that Shiloh was alive.

He dialed the lobby and asked if there had been any calls for him. There were none. He hung up and realized he should be hungry. There was another urge, however, and it was strong. "No," he said to the closet his bottle was in. "Not tonight."

He turned off the lamp, dropped onto the bed, and hoped sleep would come fast. The temptation and his worries grew stronger by the minute. His exhausted body, however, showed him mercy, and he drifted off. It seemed late to him when he woke and felt his way around to find the ringing phone.

"Hello."

"Dan?" It was a cheery voice. "Dan Bowman?"

"Yes. Who's this?"

"Someone who may can help you. I noticed the poster concerning your missing daughter today. Shiloh is her name?"

"Yes! Yes! Have you seen her?" He was fully awake now and flipped on the lamp.

"Indeed, I have, sir. I recognized her picture on your poster immediately."

"Where is she? Is she Ok?"

"Oh, she's fine. Never better, I'm sure. I want to help you reunite with her, Mr. Bowman."

Dan's eyes moistened. "Thank you. Thank you so much. Where is she?"

"Well, of course I need to be sure that I'm not placing the girl in any danger by telling you that. Could you please tell me just why she ran away from you and came here?"

"I'm her father, for Christ's sake. Who is this?"

"Answer my question first, Mr. Bowman."

Dan ran his hand through his hair and paced. "She ran away last Friday and came here because her sister lives here. But her sister hasn't seen her. She's been reported missing."

"And whom may Shiloh's sister be?"

"Why are you asking me all this? I want to know where my daughter is, and I want to know now."

"I understand your haste, Mr. Bowman. We both hold the girl's safety as our top priority. I only want a few facts before we proceed. Now, tell me who Shiloh's sister is, and why she felt it necessary to come here."

"Why she ran away is none of your damned business. But her sister is Becky Hawk, the chief of police in town. So, I think you'd better tell me where she is, because I'm pretty sure it's a crime if you don't." He heard soft chuckling while he waited. "Who is this?"

"A crime do tell?" The chuckling became louder. "The name is Kage, sir. K.A.G.E. Be sure to write it down and have it handy when you report my crime to your hero daughter."

CHAPTER 24

"Please, Father! Please, don't!" The boy tossed on the ground with his hands and feet bound. He looked up into steely, harsh eyes. The brim of a slouch hat adorned with a golden badge hung over them.

"You were warned," his father said. The men looking on held shovels and hammers. "You were told clearly."

"But it was only Peter and Zack. They can be trusted. I swear to you they can be." He cried louder when his father lifted him and placed him into the wooden box. "No! I'm your son!"

His father's face still showed no mercy when it looked down into the box. "When you tell our secrets, you remove yourself from us. All our love for you dissolves. You're only a traitor now. I no longer claim you."

The lid closed over him. Through the slats, the boy caught glances of the men hammering. He screamed when nail points broke through the boards over him. The box moved and tilted while he was lowered. He felt it settle, and then he heard dirt falling from above. It leaked in between the slats. His cries became labored breaths. The dirt gradually blocked the sunlight. Darkness came while he twisted and kicked. The sweet smell of clay entered the box. "Father!" he cried repeatedly after everything quietened. He thrashed while bawling.

Later, his body exhausted. As his mind faded, he talked to himself to break the silence in a voice raspy from his screams. He felt himself drifting while he breathed in his remaining air. There was comfort in knowing that death was near. His thoughts and fears reduced to a haze while he closed his eyes and waited.

Imaginary sounds entered his head. He thought the distant scratching was one of them. It became clearer, though. Shovels were digging. Light showed between the slats again. Fresh air brought him back. He heard voices and felt the box moving up. The tip of a crowbar came between the boards before the lid was ripped off. His father looked down, this time with kindness in his eyes. Sun blinded the boy when he was pulled from the box and the ropes binding him were cut away. He lay on the ground, sucking in air while his head cleared more.

His father knelt and hugged him. "Do you understand now, son? Our rules must never be broken. Loyalty and secrecy are sacred to us."

"I understand, Father," he said and received another hug. The other men joined around and helped him up. Light no longer burned his eyes. Only yards away, Peter and Zack were bound to pine trees. Two men with rifles across their shoulders stood in front of them.

Peter's voice was shrill. "Harrison, let them know we will not tell anyone."

"We always keep secrets," yelled Zack. "You know we do." He was crying.

"What are you going to do with them, Father?"

"They know things now. There's only one thing that will change that. That's the problem created when you break our rules, Harrison. But, I'll let you decide. They're your friends."

He looked again at the two boys, and then at the men with rifles. "Shoot them dead," he said.

His father and the other men smiled. A cheer went up. "Congratulations, my son," his father said. "We can feel comfortable giving you this now."

Harrison's eyes lit at the gold badge handed to him. A winged lion with a curled scorpion's tail stood in relief on it. "It's mine? I'm one of you?"

"Yes. Forever you're one of us. Go home now and rest."

He walked down a dirt trail. Even when he heard the gunshots, his eyes never left the badge he carried, nor did his smile fade.

The clang of a door from the far end of the cell block brought Harrison Tolly out of his thoughts. He closed his eyes while he lay on his cot and listened to the guard's footsteps approach. He waited until a flashlight beam waved over his cell and the door clanged at the other end of the block before he opened his jumpsuit and reached under the left sleeve.

It was a wicked weapon he drew, fashioned from the bottom of a large soup can by an inmate who worked in the kitchen. Half-moon shaped, the curved edge had been sharp when Harrison received it, but it was razor-like now from the hours he'd spent grinding it over the concrete floor of his cell at night. Two small holes had been cut just above the flat end for fingers to grip it. Another inmate in the tailor shop had sewn a pocket inside the jumpsuit so the weapon could be carried under Harrison's armpit.

Harrison brought the weapon out, studying the edges by dim light for imperfections. There were none. He'd taught himself a method of slipping his little finger and forefinger into the holes and flicking the blade from concealment at the intended. Hours of practice at night had trained him to perform the maneuver fast.

He sat and practiced more, taking pride in his still sharp reflexes. Time and again, his hand and blade flicked like a snake's strike. He imagined sitting in the courtroom. Becky Hawk would be there. If the opportunity came, he wouldn't wait for the judge's decision. Maybe she would pass close enough before court or during a recess. If his hands were locked to a belly chain, it would have to wait. But if they were only handcuffed, the Manticores' revenge would be carried out spectacularly for all in the courtroom to see.

He held his hands together as if cuffed and flicked the blade again. Bud Sweeney was proof of how easily it sliced through flesh and arteries. He pictured Becky Hawk's throat with his next flick.

CHAPTER 25

Becky shoved open the door of the police station after taking her first report of the day. She grabbed the phone and dialed fast. "Aaron, what have you found out?"

"What?"

"What have you found out? You've made the calls, right?"

"Yeah, but you can't expect me to know anything yet. The guys are going to do some checking at the Linville County tire shops, but you know any list of snow tire sales in the mountains will be a long one."

"What about the town—Millpark? Are they sending someone there?"

"Why are you talking so loud?"

"Answer the question, Aaron."

"They're going to check arrest records and see if anyone from there stands out. The agent over that area says it's just a tiny place. There used to be some textile factories there that closed down. The place then stayed afloat from the tourist traffic that passed through. The interstate killed that. Hardly anyone lives there now."

"Then, it shouldn't take long to find the locals there with violent criminal records. Have them get on it now."

"I'll do the best I can. Are you forgetting I'm only a rookie agent? I can't order people around like you are me."

Becky took her seat behind the desk and caught her breath. "I'm sorry. Are Bobby and Wendy all right?"

"Yeah. They're eating breakfast. I've got my eyes on them. So, tell me why you're acting like your hair's on fire."

"I just took a break-in report at Black Lake Optometry. There--"

She looked up when the door opened and Dan walked in. "There were a pair of strong prescription glasses stolen within the past few days."

"Well, that sure sounds like a lead, but it could be a coincidence."

Dan sat down in front of the desk.

"Nobody steals glasses from an optometrist, Aaron. It's too much of a coincidence."

"Ok. I'll get on the phone now and try speeding things up."

"Thanks. Sorry if I sounded pushy, but she's around town somewhere and so is he. We need to get some things figured out now."

"She's alive?" Dan asked, leaning forward when Becky hung up.

"I think so. Tell me Dan, how nearsighted is Shiloh?"

"She can hardly see without glasses."

"Have you ever known her to steal?"

"Sakes, no. She'd never think of it."

"Someone jimmied the backdoor of our eye clinic and took a pair of glasses being held for an elderly lady in the nursing home. I think someone took the glasses for Shiloh. Even if she did steal, I doubt she could've seen well enough to have done it herself."

"It doesn't sound like her to be with someone like that."

Becky stood. "Maybe not, but the glasses taken were for someone very nearsighted. I need to get to work on it before he finds out she's around. If he attacked her, he'll know she can identify him. You need to go home in case she comes back. I'll let you know when I find out something." She started toward the door with her keys.

"Becky, I came here to tell you something."

She rolled her eyes. "What is it, Dan?"

"I got a phone call at the motel last night. He was asking questions about her."

"Who? Who called you?"

"He said his name is Kage."

She flinched and turned. "You talked to him? How did he even know where to call you?"

"Well... I put up a poster with her picture and my room number on it. I thought it might help."

Becky placed her hand over her eyes and brought it down her face. "Why did you do that without telling me first? There's a reason I haven't put posters up. What were you thinking?"

"I wish I'd have known."

"Tell me exactly what he said."

"I don't remember it all. He was asking questions about her. I thought he was trying to help me. I told him she's my daughter. He was asking about you too."

"Please, please tell me that you didn't let him know I'm her sister."

His face tensed. "Yeah, I told him that. I didn't know. Who is he?"

Becky stepped closer to him. "You couldn't have messed things up worse if you'd tried. Tell me why you didn't call and tell me right away. No, never mind. I know why. I smell it on you."

He hung his head and turned away from her.

Becky reached for him but closed her hands. "Look at me." Her voice seethed. She waited for him to turn back. "I don't know who he is. I think he could be from Millpark and he followed her here. Is there anybody from there you would suspect?"

"No. I know everyone there. We have our share of roughnecks, but nobody who'd do the things you've talked about. How sure are you that this person is from there?"

"I'm not sure about a lot right now, but I am sure the person who called you wants to find Shiloh before we do. And I'm pretty sure he thought she was dead. Only now he knows differently, thanks to you. And you decided to go have a drink or two before you even told me about it ."

"I'm sorry, Becky."

"You're still the same," she said. "Don't tell me you're not. You still put booze over everything, even your family." She walked to the door and put her hand on the knob. "I don't know where Shiloh is or who she's with, but I do know she came here to get away from you." Becky didn't care that she shouted. "There's nothing you can do to help find her. I want you out of town. Leave now. I don't want to see you anymore." She shoved open the door. Mayor Clayton and Councilman Phillips stood outside it.

"I know this must be stressful," Clayton said, "but I've never heard you speak to anyone that way. Are you sure you're alright?"

Becky placed her elbows on her desk and her chin on her fists. She looked at the two of them and didn't feel like lying. "It's a lot, Mayor. First Sharon is murdered and now my estranged father shows up, telling me it's my half sister in the picture. It's a hell of a lot to take in."

The redness in Phillip's face was brighter than normal. His jaw twitched a steady rhythm. "This is a small town's worst kind of nightmare," he said. "In a few days, we're going to have more people in Black Lake than any other day in our history, and there's a killer running around. This town was doing a pretty good job of changing its image. If something bad happens during the festival, there may be a stigma we can't shed this time."

"I'm worried over a lot more than a stigma, Councilman," said Becky.

"I didn't mean it that way."

"Of course," Clayton said. "Everyone's safety is our main concern. We want to be sure we're doing all we can. We followed through on your suggestion and contracted with the sheriff's department. They're sending as many deputies for the festival as they can spare. The fire department's guys will be out too. So, we should have plenty of coverage in town. Which leads me to my next question." He and Phillips exchanged glances.

"Shoot," said Becky.

"You admitted yourself in our meeting," Clayton said, "that this person is getting his kicks by playing games with you. That didn't seem like such a big issue until we saw how high the stakes are in his games. So, we were wondering, is it wise for you to even be at the festival? Why give this guy more motivation? You haven't had a real vacation since you took this job anyway."

Becky's ire rose and showed on her face. "This man is a cold-blooded killer," she said. "That's his only motivation. He won't stop whether I'm here or not. And my sister is around here somewhere. He knows that now. He also knows she's the one person who can identify him. You can place me on leave if you want, but I'm going to look for her until I find her."

"Ok, Becky," Clayton said. "I trust your judgment. How can we help?"

"I'll make up a missing and endangered juvenile poster. I'll pay for the printing costs myself, but I'd appreciate any help I could get distributing them around town and getting them in the papers and on the local news broadcasts too."

"Charge the printing to the town," Clayton said. "I'll call the newspaper and the television stations. Anything else?"

"Yeah, make sure the chamber of commerce folks and the fire department guys report anybody they see who looks even a little out of place at the festival. Because, with the crowd we're going to have, I believe he'll try something. And I have a feeling he just may overplay his hand."

CHAPTER 26

The batteries in Chris' much-used flashlight had finally died. Candlelight, however, glowed in the dining room of the lodge. It waved over an assortment of canned fruit and vegetables on silver platters. Chicken noodle soup steamed in a porcelain serving bowl. Salmon patties surrounded a remoulade-like sauce on an oyster serving dish.

The candles reflected in Shiloh's glasses when she walked down and smiled at Chris. He met her at the bottom of the stairs, wearing the blue dinner jacket he'd found in a bedroom closet. "So, this is why you told me to wait in the room," she said. "What's the occasion?"

"You don't know? We met one week ago today."

"Are you serious? It doesn't seem that long."

He took her hand and led her to the table. "Yeah, it's been a week. I decided maybe we should celebrate and enjoy what this place has to offer."

Shiloh looked over the spread while she took the seat he offered her.

"I'd planned on steaks until you told me you didn't want me lifting. We'll have to settle for junk from the pantry. At least it's fancied up junk from the pantry." He poured wine into her class.

She beamed him another smile while he took a seat across from her. They toasted their glasses, and she coughed and spit when she tasted hers. "Holy…" She wiped her hand over her mouth, grabbed her water glass, and gulped. "Kind of ruined the mood there, huh?"

"Sorry. Wish I'd known you don't like riesling."

"I thought it was wine." She reached across and thumped him on his head when he leaned over and laughed into his napkin. "Ok, wise guy. I don't know about stuff like that. I've never even drunk it before."

He wiped his eyes and sat back with a wide smile. "I picked that wine because I heard it pairs well with salmon. I don't know if that applies to salmon patties too. There's plenty of other kinds if you want me to get another bottle."

"No thanks. I'll stick with my water."

He sipped his wine while he watched her face in the candlelight. "You look beautiful tonight, Miss. Bowman." The engaging look she returned excited him.

"Thank you, Mr. Heath. And thank you for this wonderful meal." She tasted her salmon patty and looked at him wide-eyed.

"Oh no. Terrible also?"

"Delicious," she said while chewing. "It's really delicious." She dug another portion onto her fork. "Chris, where did you learn to cook this way? How do you know about wine and things?"

He tasted a bite and nodded approval. "Had an uncle in Philly who cooked at some fancy place. I used to visit him in the summer."

"He was a chef?"

"Maybe. I don't remember him calling himself that. Whatever he was, he cooked like nobody's business. I used to go to the restaurant and watch him. I thought it was the hippest thing in the world, the way he'd slice up food with his big knife, throw it in a pan, and toss in spices without even thinking about it. He never looked at a recipe or a measuring spoon no matter what the dish. The waiters would hustle in, grab a fresh plate, and yell things like 'Table ten sends their compliments.' He'd just grin and give a thumbs up while he went from pan to pan. I always thought he was really something. He taught me a few dishes. I'm not as good as he was, of course."

"Is that what you'd like to be?"

"Well, yeah. It's a thought anyway."

"I think that's wonderful. Why haven't you told me?"

He shrugged and chopped his food with a fork. "I don't know. Maybe I don't see myself doing it. I might can throw together an omelet or a salmon patty. But doing things like lighting a match to booze in a pan and flipping the food around while it flames, people all snazzed up and being seated by a maître d' so they can eat it. Nah, it seems far-fetched."

"I thought you were more of a dreamer than that," Shiloh said. "Anybody who can take canned food and do with it what you've done here could surely do that."

"It's so freaking nice," he said.

"What's so nice?"

"Having somebody around for once who tells me that I can do something instead of laughing about it." He ladled soup into his bowl and hers. "I'll be honest with you. If I looked into my heart of hearts, I don't think I ever really believed I'd pull off this deal about going to Cudjoe Key with a haul of treasure. It was just something to shoot for. But with you, it really seems possible."

She felt a nervous tug, looked down, and took a spoonful of soup.

"I know the time is pretty close for you to make a decision," he said. "So, I've been thinking. There's envelopes and stamps upstairs.

Why don't you write to your dad and tell him everything? Tell him about me, where we're going, all of it. Ask him to give us a little time to get settled down, only a month or so. Then we'll come for him. He can live with us. It'll be like in the stories—happily ever after."

A sob broke from her.

Chris' smile faded. He spooned over his soup. "Yeah, I know. You can't pin your life's hopes on a crazy Jersey guy and a shooting star." He looked at her tear trails glistening. "No, I understand. I'm not going to hold it against you. Would you at least spend the weekend with me?"

"I'm not crying because I'm sad," she said. "It's because I believe what you just said. When I left home, I was terrified that I was making a mistake. I never imagined that a week later I'd be eating a wonderful meal in a place like this with the man I want to spend the rest of my life with. I never dreamed I would ever feel this alive. So, I can believe anything now. Yes. I'll write to my dad tonight, and I'll go to Florida with you, and he'll come live with us. I believe it all."

His hand reached across and grabbed hers. "Thank you. I'll make sure you'll never regret it. I swear to it."

"I believe you. Chris?"

"Yeah?"

"I won't be afraid this time if you invite me upstairs."

He came around the table and lifted her.

CHAPTER 27

It was early morning when he'd left the morgue and late at night when he returned. The items he'd bought in Wilmington lay on one of the porcelain slabs. By dimmed lantern light, he ate a cold meal, knowing his time in Black Lake, maybe on earth, was drawing to an end. Only one thing remained to ensure the addition of the crown jewel to his shrine. And that would happen. He was confident of it. There was an energy that favored him in Black Lake.

He replaced the old ammunition in both clips with the new he'd bought and then cleaned and oiled the Luger before pulling the lantern closer. He wrote notes beside his maps and diagrams, making sure it was all large enough for old eyes to read. It took him over an hour, and he grinned when he was done.

He buzzed with excitement and knew it would be hours before he could sleep. So, instead of trying to rest, he carried his lantern and some jars to an adjoining bathroom. He heard thunder rumble outside while he wiped dust off a mirror and pulled his hair from his face. Lightning flashed from the upper window when he dug his fingers into one of the jars and smeared a white streak over his face. He rubbed more on and vowed to find the girl named Shiloh at any cost.

Dan watched headlight beams wave over his house while the car he rode in bounced up his rocky driveway. He felt relieved that his truck had made it up the steep grade of the mountain and surrendered only when he could coast it into a Piggly Wiggly parking lot, ten miles from home.

"Thank you. I'm sorry I had to call you out this late at night," he said, avoiding eye contact with the driver. The ride had been long enough for him to tell some of his story.

"I'm happy to do it," Pastor Henry Owens said. "We were all worried about you. You should've let someone know before you left."

"Sorry, Pastor. I'll pay you for the gas as soon as I can." Dan reached for the door handle.

"Dan, you can always rely on your church family when you're having problems. We draw on one another for comfort and strength."

"I know. And I'm thankful for that, but comfort ain't coming easy now. I prayed that Becky would have forgiven me and that I'd find Shiloh. I was scared to death that neither would happen. Here lately, it seems the things I fear are the only real things."

"You took your daughter by surprise when you went there. You can't expect forgiveness to come instantly. Give the grace of God time to work within her. Would you like for me to call her?"

"No. I doubt she would listen. I don't know if I'll ever see either of them again, and I don't know that I want to unless I can beat this once and for all."

"You're never alone in your fight, Dan. Paul tells us to take the sword of the Spirit, which is the Word of God."

Dan opened the door and placed a foot out. "Pastor, didn't Jesus face his final temptation from the devil on a high place?"

"Yes, he did. Where he could see all the kingdoms of the world. Why do you ask?"

"No particular reason. Thanks again."

"Would you like to pray with me?"

"No. Right now I want to pray in private. But, if I happen to not be in church Sunday, I'd appreciate you and the congregation offering me a special prayer. Because I think it's time I had my own final showdown with the devil."

CHAPTER 28

We've created a monster. That was the thought that entered Becky's head more than once on the first day of the festival. Traffic and parking problems began that morning and climaxed with a backup that extended all the way to the highway. In the humid heat, irritated drivers honked their horns. Several times, Becky heard curses directed her way while she directed traffic. Minutes of panic ensued when it seemed every possible parking space in Black Lake was taken. But the day was saved with the idea for overflow traffic to be directed to the neighboring community of Cypress Cove, where local church buses were used as shuttles.

In between the traffic snarls and bump-ups, Becky's radio sent her a steady stream of "investigate a report of the missing juvenile" transmissions. The posters that covered the town had created another monster. It seemed every good-intentioned festival-goer would eventually, somewhere, see a dark-haired young girl whom they thought resembled Shiloh Bowman. With the help of the sheriff's and fire departments, all such reports were checked out, but the initial hope each provided faded over and again.

The evening provided relief from the traffic and heat of the day. Becky, feeling the cool from her sweat-soaked uniform, took time for a hotdog and lemonade at a stand. She watched the passing people while she ate. "Does anyone have anything new to report?" she asked into her radio, not for the first time that day.

"All's good around the lakefront area, Chief."

"Thanks, Curt," she said, irritated that he'd been the only one who'd replied. She moved among the food smells, music, and chatter while watching the crowd. One lone man with a rough beard caught her eye.

"Show us what you can do, Officer," the man at the shooting gallery yelled. Another man seated in a dunking booth called her a rag-arm and dared her to prove him wrong.

She gave them smiles and dismissive waves while keeping a distance and following the man toward a gathering where the blackberry pie eating contest was to be. Her suspicions dissolved when she saw him kiss a woman and lift a toddler. A tap on her back made her jerk. It was Aaron. "Where's Wendy and Bobby?" she asked.

"At the pizza stand. Don't worry, I'm not letting them out of my sight. Anything unusual so far?"

"Nothing."

Aaron took a glance around. "Who knows what to look for in this crowd anyway."

Becky watched the crowd also and shook her head in disgust. "I should have my fanny kicked over that poster idea. We've been tied up all day over false calls. I think everybody's tired of chasing their tails. If Shiloh *was* here, I'm sure she'd have been scared away by now."

"Well, maybe that's not a bad thing if he's around. If he is, this could be our only chance. The weather report isn't looking too good for tomorrow. Heavy rain all day is the forecast."

Becky twisted her face. "I was hoping he'd overplay his hand tonight, but now I have a feeling we overplayed our hand with all the uniforms here and kept him away. This is getting frustrating as hell, Aaron."

"Then I guess you're in the mood for information that might be meaningful."

"Absolutely."

Aaron lowered his voice. "The western district office put together a list of currently missing persons in the Linville County area. In the past ten years, there have been eight women and one man, who've vanished from camping sites and hiking trails, all in a small, rugged area north of Millpark."

Becky gave him a look of disbelief. "Good grief, nobody's picked up on that until now?"

"As I said, it's rugged country. There's waterfalls, cliffs, and caves, lots of places people can get lost in or fall off of. People going missing there has never been unusual. Still, it seems like a high number for that time period."

Becky watched Wendy and Bobby paying for their food. "No remains found at all?"

"No, not even bones or clothing."

"Nine people don't just disappear, even in the mountains. When was the most recent one?"

"Over two years ago, roughly the time bodies began showing up on the interstate."

Becky turned to him. "There's a connection. He lives in the Millpark area. I guarantee it."

"But thrill killers normally keep the same M.O. The interstate killer left bodies where they could be found. The ones in Linville County just vanished."

Becky rubbed her face. "Criminals evolve for different reasons," she said. "If he went ten years without being caught, maybe he became confident enough to change his M.O. The new interstate would've provided him mobility and a bigger area to find and dispose of victims. I've got a strong feeling about this, Aaron. Your guys need to do some serious checking in Millpark."

"I agree," Aaron said. "But what are they supposed to look for?"

"There's a reason this person is the way he is. Since he most likely followed Shiloh here, I'm betting he still lives in that area. Maybe he suffered a brain injury or some type of childhood trauma. There should be something to make him stick out in a small town like that. And the remains of those people have got to be there somewhere. I bet if you find one you'll find them all. You'll need to convince your higher-ups to look there, Aaron. I'm sure they won't listen to me."

Aaron huffed. "Convincing them to look into the medical and childhood histories of an entire town will be a tall order."

"I understand, but…We'll talk more about it later." Becky gave Wendy and Bobby a smile and wave. "Are you guys having fun?"

Bobby nodded. "Except the guy in the dunking booth pissed Wendy off."

Wendy took a bite of pizza. "He called me Fatso. I'm going to dunk that sucker if I have to spend my last dollar doing it."

"Want to try the shooting gallery, Bob?" Aaron asked.

"Sure."

"Out shoot him, Bobby," Wendy said, turning to Becky. "Nice festival. Great food vendors too, a pregnant woman's dream."

"Yes. It's went over even better than I thought it would."

"Except no Shiloh, I suppose."

Becky shook her head.

"She'll show up, Beck. Don't worry. If she's anything like you, she can take care of herself." Wendy smiled and waved at someone. "I have just one suggestion for future festivals. If you're going to have a mime, don't go so low-budget."

Becky looked and saw the man with a beret and white-painted face. He drew laughs near the eating contest while he stuffed pretend pies into his face. He smiled at her and waved with his fingertips.

CHAPTER 29

Chris' heart skipped a beat when Shiloh walked down the stairs in a white sundress and wide-brim straw hat. She'd applied a touch of makeup. A red, silk scarf covered the fading scar on her neck. He whistled. "Wow. Where did you find all that?"

"In one of the bedrooms. It looks like the Manticores may have entertained a few women here from time to time."

"You're knockout gorgeous."

She smiled and let him embrace and kiss her. "Maybe we should stay here tonight," she said, feeling for the first time every bit like a woman.

"First things first. I want to take you on our first real date. We can mail your letter to your dad while we're in town."

"And return these glasses."

"You'll need them for the trip. Why don't you keep them for now? When we get to the Keys, the first thing I'll do is get you the best ones money can buy and mail those back."

She grinned. "Well, it *would* be nice to see on my first ever train ride. I'm really getting excited about it."

"Me too," he said. "Especially now that I know you're going with me."

"So, where are you taking me on our first real date?"

"How do fireworks and cotton candy by the lake sound?"

She giggled. "Very romantic."

"Then let's head to the boat."

The mime gave Becky another smile and then pulled his way toward her and Wendy on an invisible rope. A crowd of kids laughed and followed. He stopped and made a frustrated expression while tugging hard and placing his foot on air for leverage. He stumbled backward. Looking at the broken, imaginary rope in his hand, he wept silently while the kids cackled. Next, he was stuck in a box, making puzzled facial expressions while feeling for a way out.

"He's really not bad," said Wendy. "Though he certainly could use some advice on applying makeup."

Becky watched him find the door to the box, open it, and step out. "I never cared for mimes," she said, taking a glance at Bobby and Aaron at the shooting gallery. "I think they're creepy. Let's go join the guys and see who's out shooting who."

But the mime held up a white-gloved hand toward her and made his way over with the kids in tow. He pulled a red bandana from the back pocket of a passing man, whose wife laughed and stopped her husband to watch with the gathering crowd. The mime displayed a black ball in front of Becky. He covered it with the bandana, swiped his other hand over it, and revealed a white ball. The crowd clapped.

"Very good," Becky said. She couldn't help but notice the icy blue eyes watching her from behind the makeup. They stayed emotionless despite his jesting.

"He's palming the black ball," Wendy whispered. "Easy trick to do."

The mime held up the white ball and repeated the motions, only this time he dropped the black ball while attempting the transition.

"Easy trick if you don't drop it, that is." Wendy said.

The crowd laughed while the mime hung his head in pretend shame and rubbed tears from his eyes. He turned and held his hands behind his back, waving them at Becky, ready to be arrested for his flub.

"Play along," Wendy said. "I want to see what he does."

Everyone watched and chuckled while Becky drew her cuffs and clicked them on the mime's wrists. He waved the bandana behind him. Becky took it and covered the cuffs. The mime turned to face her and the crowd. He made a series of twists and turns with exaggerated facial expressions. The crowd laughed more with every second. After a minute, he made a sad expression and looked around at everyone sheepishly. Then he brought his hand up with the cuffs dangling from his fingers. The crowd applauded.

Becky took the cuffs and smiled. "Have you got a key, or did you shimmy the teeth?"

The mime brought his finger to his lips before tossing the man back his bandana and shuffled away with the kids still following.

"How'd he do it?" Wendy asked.

Becky kept her eyes on him. He drew another crowd near the carousel. "I don't know. Come with me." She hustled to the nearby information desk and excused herself through the line. Cindy Brewer represented the chamber of commerce inside the booth. "Cindy, who's the mime?"

"Who?"

"The pantomime guy. Check your list."

"You mean the white-faced people who don't talk? I don't remember one registering. We've got clowns and jugglers and magicians, but none of them."

Becky looked back at the carousel then around everywhere else before transmitting a BOLO.

Chris docked the rowboat amongst reeds near the waterfront and walked Shiloh down a winding trail in the woods. They heard the music of the festival before they reached the back side of a grassy, car-filled parking lot.

"Looks like the perfect place to me," Chris said. "Nice and dark and private. The fireworks show should start in half an hour or so. Think you'll be able to see well enough?"

She sat down on the grass with a sly grin. "Yeah, well enough. I guess we have a half hour to kill."

They were well into a kiss when they heard walking in front of them. Shiloh clung to Chris when a flashlight beam waved around before falling on them.

"Chris? Shiloh?" The voice was Andi's. She turned off her light and came to them. "Well, if you two aren't a happy sight. We've all been sick with worry over ya at the camp." She sat down beside them.

"We decided it was best if we left," said Shiloh.

"Cotton would've caused you all problems as long as I was around," Chris said. "I don't think Flynt ever cared for me much anyway."

Andi waved her hand. "Oh, Flynt didn't mind ya being there. He only wanted ya behaving." She looked Shiloh over and made a hum of approval. "Well, look at this young lady all decked out. Looks like she might be seeing better too."

"She got the clothes honest," Chris said. "I snatched the glasses, but we're returning them soon. She's reformed me."

"Well, the dickens." Andi gave Shiloh a grin. "Ya must've really hit his heart in the right spot to have pulled that off. That's worth celebrating." She reached into her jeans pocket and removed two dollars. "My pies were a hit at the festival. Chris, being it was you who picked the berries for them, why not run down there and buy you and Shiloh some treats before the fireworks begin. I'll stay here and keep her company. Hurry back though."

He took the money. "Thanks Andi. I'll mail the letter while I'm at it."

Andi waited until Chris was a distance from them before she spoke. "Who's the letter to?"

"My dad. I wanted to explain some things to him."

"Wrote that ya love him I suppose."

"Yes. And other stuff." Shiloh listened to the festival sounds and became uncomfortable when she saw Andi studying her. "I don't want to get into it all."

"I'm very glad ya wrote to him. Whatever your reasons for leaving, he deserved that much."

"I'll see him again. Chris and I have a plan."

"Oh, do ya now? He'll be delighted to know that. He must be worried to death over what could've happened. Is it your plan to stay around town?"

Shiloh sensed Andi was wheedling her for information. "Probably," she said, and instantly felt guilty for lying to the woman. "What about you? Are you staying here for long?"

"No, dear. Come fall the farm work will be done, and I'll be leaving." She made an ambivalent smile. "This will be the last of my riding the rails. It's time for this old lady to rest."

"Where will you go?"

"I'll be headed to live with my sister in Virginia. Her husband passed away last year. She has two sons and a daughter living near her. Should be a good life for me."

Shiloh didn't understand why she felt so sad. "I hope you'll be happy," she said. "Thank you for helping me when I first came to the camp."

"Oh, think nothing of it."

"You've been kind to me. I won't forget you. I wish I could've had a mother like you."

Andi chuckled but looked away. "How sweet." Her hand wiped her eye. She cocked her head at the coin Shiloh held out. "Now, what might that be?"

"Just a gift for you. I hope you'll carry it with you, so you won't forget me."

"Oh, I won't forget you, sweet child." Andi took the coin and held it close to her eyes. "Well, I'll declare. A Confederate coin. Where did this come from?"

"It doesn't matter. And it doesn't matter what it is. It's what it represents between you and me."

Andi slipped it into her pocket. "Thank you." She swallowed, and then noticeably struggled with her thoughts. "They're looking for ya, Shiloh," she said. "Your posters and pictures are all over town."

A crashing feeling came.

"They say you're endangered. I was headed back to camp to talk it over with Flynt and the rest. They don't like reporting matters to the police, but this one seems an exception."

"Please don't, Andi. It'll ruin things. Chris takes care of me. Let us handle it. We love each other."

"I so do hope you're right, but there's more you'll have to tell me than that. We'll need to start with the first night ya came to the camp. What happened then? Who made that mark on your neck?"

Shiloh dreaded recounting the story but knew no way around it. She was about to speak when there came a high whistle, followed by an explosion in the sky. She and Andi looked up. The crackling starburst illuminated the surroundings. The silhouette of a person making strange movements caught Shiloh's eye. He walked toward them from the parking lot, stopping for a moment in front of a couple returning to their car. He did some sort of hand display before leaving them and walking closer. Another starburst crackled and lit a white face and black lips. The mime noticed Shiloh and Andi, pursed his lips, and waved his fingertips under his chin. He did a penguin-like walk toward them.

"Well, hello," Andi said. "Come to give us a show?"

The mime bowed and flipped his beret. He looked down at them and pointed to the black ball he held. His other hand reached and tugged away Shiloh's scarf. More fireworks exploded while the mime's eyes settled on Shiloh's scar. She reached to take back her scarf, but the mime held it tightly. She squinted when he gazed into her face. Their eyes locked and it sent an electric chill through her that stole her breath. She pulled hard for air, making whooping sounds before her scream broke through. Then, she was running down the trail, her hat sailing off with Andi following and calling her name.

Chris heard the scream halfway across the parking lot and knew it was Shiloh. He dropped the orange sodas and corndogs he carried and sprinted with his hand digging for his knife. He met the mime where he'd left Shiloh and Andi. "Where's the girl and the woman who were here?" His hand gripped his knife in his pocket. The mime pursed his lips and shrugged his shoulders. Chris took a step towards him. "Cut your bullshit, man. They were right here. Where did they go?"

The mime propped a hand over his eyebrows while gazing toward the trail and pointing.

Chris glared at him. "Did you hurt her? You're dead if you did."

With that, the mime turned and made a high-stepping run in the opposite direction.

Chris debated going after him but, instead, sprinted down the path. He heard Andi yell his name. Shiloh wept frantically at the boat with Andi holding her when he arrived. "What's wrong?" he asked.

"I don't know," said Andi. "She's completely panicked. I can't get her to talk to me. There was something about the man back there, the painted mime."

Chris looked back. "Stay with her, Andi. I'm going to find that asshole."

"No!" Shiloh cried. "Don't leave me. Take me back. Take me back now!" She lunged and latched her arms around him.

Her trembling and clammy touch scared Chris. Her unyielding grip reminded him of when he'd fought to save her from drowning. He pulled her face to his. "What is it? Did he hurt you?"

"He...he's the man," she stammered. "He's the man who choked me!"

Chris glanced at the trail, Shiloh, and then Andi. "What should I do?"

"Take her away. The poor child is petrified. I'll fetch the police. Tell me where you'll be so I can send them."

Chris hesitated and listened to Shiloh's weeping. "It'll ruin our plans if you do," he said.

"Chris, this ain't a blasted game." Andi's voice was sharp. "The time's come to do the right thing. Now, tell me where you'll be."

Chris thought of Cudjoe Key one more time. Soft sand and crystal water. Only a dream. Nothing more. "Boar Island. The old hunting lodge."

"Take her there then, and do not leave. I'm trusting ya, Chris." She kissed Shiloh's head. "Easy, child. Things are going to be fine." Andi watched while Chris led Shiloh to the boat. She then turned and sprinted toward the festival. "Be careful, Andi," she heard Chris call.

The fireworks show was drawing to its grand finale. Andi ran up the trail as fast as her aged legs would allow her. Not wishing to go through the parking lot again, she cut into the woods and followed the sounds of the festival while she ran. She stopped for a moment to gather her bearings and catch her breath. Leaning over, she huffed while clutching a twitch in her side and watching the woods around her.

Andi wasn't a woman who scared easily, but a feeling of dread fell on her with the sudden sound of rustling from somewhere in the woods. She turned a circle, looking through the trees as explosions overhead strobed colored light through them. The rustling came again, and she crouched down. Two deer ran past, their white tails high and waving. Andi had heard once it was their way of signaling danger. She waited longer, giving her legs some more rest while she watched and listened. She stood but kept low, walking softly over dry leaves and pine needles. Despite the humid summer night, she felt coldness slipping over her.

He appeared as a dark outline between the trees directly in front of her. Andi froze in hopes he hadn't seen her, but quickly realized his stare was on her.

"Who are ya?" she asked.

He walked toward her and stopped close enough for Andi to see the smudged remnants of wiped away makeup. The beret was gone too. Black strands of hair hung over his glaring eyes. "Kage." The voice reminded Andi of a snake's hiss. "Call me Kage."

"Well, Mr. Kage, I'll be leaving now, and I'll ask ya to kindly let me be." She turned and made three running steps before she felt his hands shove her down. She fought with him on the ground. The festival crowd's cheers and the rocket explosions drowned her yells. She felt herself jerked onto her back. Hands closed around her throat while she gouged at his face and arms with her fingers. She kicked with all she had and rolled away, trying to gain her footing. But he was on her again, wrestling for the upper-hand. His hands found their grip. She felt her throat constrict until her head became light. Still, she struggled against it, but her strength was fading. She kicked feebly twice more and then lay still.

"Where are they?" he asked. "Tell me if you want to live."

The pressure eased. Andi coughed and looked up at his soulless eyes. End of the line, she thought. "Kiss my Irish ass," she said. She felt the grip again and looked beyond his face. Silence fell on her. The grand finale of fireworks lit the sky with bright colors.

CHAPTER 30

Becky heard rumblings of the approaching storm soon after she showered and went to bed. She felt tired but worry prevented the sleep she craved. Her thoughts stayed on the mime. Nothing, she thought. Only somebody who'd come to the festival to join in on the fun. Nobody had taken him seriously, even Aaron. Forget him and rest, she thought. Still, she wondered how a man with a painted face was not found in an area so well patrolled. He'd simply disappeared. No, it had been him. She felt it. He'd found her and played his game. He had overplayed his hand, exactly as she'd thought he would, and she'd failed. He wouldn't give her another easy opportunity. The thought of her sister reminded her of how horrible her failure had been. She was losing the game.

"I will enter your mind and be the worst spirit in your reality or fantasy." She'd scoffed when she'd read those words in his letter. Not now. It wouldn't end. He would watch her. He would pick his times. He would kill again and torment her until she found a way to stop him. Kage. There was a reason he'd picked that name. Shadow.

Headlights from the road flashed across her room. She took her revolver from under her pillow and looked out the window. Thunder sounded closer while she walked into the hall and checked on Bobby sleeping. She looked out each window before returning to her room and closing the door.

She thought she may be able to sleep when she lay back down. Lightning flashed. Thunder clapped. But it was the ring on the police department emergency line that startled her. She flicked on the lamp and grabbed the receiver.

"Chief Hawk here," she said with her stomach tightening.

"Surprise inspection, Chief." The voice was overly cheery, almost cartoonish. "Are all your fine Black Lake citizens accounted for tonight?"

"Who is this?"

"Nice to speak to you finally. I didn't mean to be rude earlier, but I dared not break character, you know."

Becky tried keeping her breath controlled and her voice steady. "What exactly do you want from me?"

The voice lowered and turned menacing. "We will discuss that later. You'll hear from me again very soon. I promise you that. And I would suggest that you stay a little more on the ball in the coming days. It will be vital to the people you've sworn to protect. You've already lost one feisty, old lady tonight."

"Oh, my God," tore from Becky.

There was a terrible chuckle. "No, I'm not God, but I feel close to it now. Maybe you should beg me for mercy on your fair citizens, since it seems I hold the fate of each one in my hand. The one tonight wasn't planned but quite a fortuitous find. I'll tell you more about her later when we meet. There are preparations to make first."

Becky felt anger overtaking her dread. "No need for all that," she said. "If you want to meet, we can do it right now."

"You don't know how happy that makes me. But I make the rules in our game. Get some rest. You'll surely need it." The cartoonish voice returned. "Second surprise inspection, Chief. Is all your crime-fighting, keeping-the-world-safe-from-bad-doers, equipment accounted for?" Then came a dial tone.

She hurried to her closet and, from her duty belt, removed a pair of cheap, five and dime store cuffs. Becky studied them and caught herself reaching for the ponytail she'd undone before bed. "Made in Taiwan," the stamp on the cuffs read. And there was something else there, jammed between the metal strands of the cuffs. She pushed out a tightly folded piece of paper, opened it, and read the bold, red letters.

"You had me! You let me go! Shame On You!"

She sat down on the bed while still looking at it. The paper was old and moldy with a hole punched in the top part. A toe tag, she realized. She turned it over. The stenciled words were faded. The handwritten ones were in fresh, red ink:

Name of Deceased: *Chief Becky Hawk.*

Cause of Death: *Yet to be determined.*

Date and Time of Death: *??*

Physician(s): *Dr. Kage.*

A portion of the bottom of the tag had been torn away, but halves of letters remained, enough for her to deduce: "Black Lake Community Hospital."

Becky took another look at the tag before tossing it and going for her raincoat and boots.

CHAPTER 31

He loved storms. This one was particularly pleasant. While the rain pounded outside, he rested and thought about the old, Irish lady again. She'd surprised him with her fight. The fingernail gouge marks she'd left on his arms and face wouldn't heal quickly. Fire had remained in her eyes even as her life ebbed. She'd been his toughest. He admired her and was happy their souls were now bonded. He'd done his best to give her a defiant look and balled fists when he'd posed her against a tree near the grass lot.

He held up the coin he'd taken from her pocket. Lightning flashes lit it. He thought again of the story he'd once read about a Civil War swindle played by the Manticores. His luck was beginning to astound him. Maybe there was an unknown spirit guiding him now, compensating him for everything before. Whatever the case, his game was hitting full stride and playing out past his expectations. He thought of the possibilities of the coming days—and even that night.

Becky nearly told Aaron the truth when he answered her knock on his bedroom door. After second thoughts, she lied that she was only leaving to assist Curt with an alarm call. She knew that what she was doing violated every tactical rule of police work, but *he* was an exception to the rule. With backups, he would slide away again, like the shadow he claimed to be. Finding the hospital name on the toe tag had been too easy. He was smarter than that. He wanted her alone, so that's the way it would be. No one else would die. She was ready for it to end, and it would end that night.

As she drove through the rain and down empty streets, she ran in her head scenarios of what may play out. Black Lake Community Hospital had closed in the early fifties after Bolton Memorial was built, long before Ed and she moved to town. She'd been inside it twice while running out vagrants. She tried remembering the inside layout while she took side streets on her way there and turned off the car lights well before she neared the old building, hoping surprise would be to her advantage. She parked on a street without lights and watched the hospital from a distance for several minutes before stepping out.

Selecting the darkest areas on her approach, she walked through blowing sheets of rain. She knew the morgue was in back and elected to not go directly there. Instead, she checked the perimeter doors first. Thick chains and padlocks secured them now with "No Trespassing" signs attached. The windows had been patterned with grooved designs that prevented transparency. Some of them had been cracked or broken over the years. Becky tried sneaking peeks when she came to them but only saw an occasional bed or chair in the dark rooms. It soon became apparent to her that there would be no easy entry except for possibly the one room she knew he'd been in. She kept her revolver in front of her while she walked to the back.

The ramp down to the morgue was slick with moss and rain. She wanted to inspect the surroundings but didn't dare shine her flashlight. Farther down, however, she was left with no choice. The ramp led into complete darkness. She felt her way along with careful steps and then crouched and placed her fingers over the flashlight before turning it on. She controlled the beam by spreading her fingers slightly and shining slivers of light around the sally port. A concrete walkway with an awning led to a wide, metal door. "MORGUE" in faded black paint was stenciled above it. A chain and broken padlock lay on the concrete.

Becky crept over, crouched to the side of the door, and listened. Rain and thunder drowned away any possible sounds from inside. Her easy turn and tug on the latch proved the door would open. She turned off her flashlight, placed it under her arm, and held her revolver out. A lightning flash showed her the latch again. She took and pulled it, keeping low while she moved into cool, stale air and recoiled when the heavy door slammed behind her. She knelt lower.

Muffled thunder rolled. The absence of lightning flashes told her the room was without windows. She kept still and listened. More thunder filtered into the room. Then came a soft shuffling. Becky eased her breaths. She pulled her flashlight from under her arm and held it against her revolver. A barely audible whisper came from where she'd heard the shuffling. She listened longer, trying to be certain of the direction of the sounds. More movement made her confident enough to act. She stood and flicked the flashlight switch.

Two porcelain slabs with neck rests showed in her beam beyond a steel table in front of her. The shout of "Police" was coming from Becky's mouth when a man rose from behind the far slab, squinting his eyes in her light with a shotgun pointed. In a second, she had her light beam on his chest. The stress of the moment made time slow, and her revolver's report came as only a popping sound. She heard the man's grunt and the clatter of his shotgun on the floor clearly while she watched him slump and fall.

Ringing stayed in her ears as she kept her light and revolver in front of her and made a circle to the far side of the room and the man lying there with blood spreading over his shirt. His breathing came in labored gasps while he winced on the floor. He looked at her with his hand fumbling his pocket.

"Don't move." Becky's voice trembled. "Don't move. I'll get you help." A dreadful feeling crept over her while she shined her light and looked at his brown eyes. She holstered her revolver and reached for her walkie. Then a shout came from behind her. The man on the floor brought a gold star from his pocket.

The shout came again, and this time Becky understood the words. "Sheriff's Department! Put your hands behind your head and drop to your knees!"

She did and prayed it was all a bad dream.

He'd cleaned up and dressed in his suit before he watched from down the street. Becky Hawk's stealthy tactics had amused him when she'd checked the building before going to the morgue. But the patrol cars and an ambulance speeding to the rear of the hospital a few minutes later worried him. He drove away, hoping he hadn't overplayed the game and rendered her destiny too soon.

CHAPTER 32

Torrents of rain rattled the upstairs windows while they watched the storm from their bed. Lightning showed Chris a swelling lake and whitecaps. The black water had already pushed onto the lower parts of the island. Shiloh saw enough to be worried. She set aside the meal of oatmeal Chris had brought her.

"Are you sure we're safe?" she asked.

"Sure. We're on high ground. Nothing to be afraid of. This is probably the leftovers of a tropical storm. It'll move on soon."

She held tight to his hand. It had been a long, sleepless night so far for her. "I'm sorry I've ruined your plans," she said. "I'm sure you're mad."

"I told you already, I'm not. You haven't ruined anything. You've only made things a thousand times better for me."

"But we'll be separated when they come for us. They'll send us both back. We might not see each other again."

"Listen, I should've been smart enough to have gone to the police first thing after that guy attacked you. We're doing the right thing now. Like I told you before, you always have to have a second plan. Whatever happens now, I'll find you again. That's a promise."

A clap of thunder made them both flinch. Shiloh pressed tightly against him. "When do you think they'll come?"

"Not until this storm lets up. The lake is dangerous when it's this way."

"You do think Andi is all right, don't you?"

Her question riled a worry he'd tried to avoid. "Sure," he said. "She can take care of herself."

"I wish we didn't leave her there. But, when I saw him, the only thing I could think of was to get away."

"And you're sure it was him? I mean, he had makeup on and was wearing a hat."

"Yes. It was him. I can't forget his eyes. They were the lightest blue I've never seen on a person before. But the color isn't why I'm sure it was him. I saw them close while he was choking me, and it was like staring into evil. The mime's were the same." She put her head on Chris' chest while her heart drummed. "I'll never get it out of my mind."

They both bolted upright with a rumbling that shook the lodge. Booming crashes outside caused Chris to hurry to the bedroom window and look out. Another lightning flash gave him a glimpse of a bare section of woodline near the cove.

"What was it?" Shiloh asked.

"Another sinkhole opening near the cove and swallowing everything around it. That was the biggest yet." He walked back, lay down, and held her tightly. "Everything is fine."

"I'm beginning to think this place really is cursed."

"Don't be silly," he said, trying to sound confident. "Just rest. You're safe. You're safe, Shiloh."

The clock in the Bolton Memorial Hospital waiting room showed a quarter after two. Becky sat alone there. She watched deputies arrive in groups and go straight to the elevator. Some gave her silent glances. Despite her requests, no one had given her an update on Detective Sergeant Mitch Evans. She tried holding her emotions in check when Wendy entered through the main door and hurried to her. Aaron and Bobby followed.

"What in the world happened?" Wendy asked, taking the adjoining seat with rain dripping from her hair. "Are you hurt?"

"No. I'm not hurt."

"What happened?" Aaron asked.

"Bobby," Becky said, "would you go get me a cola? The vending machine is down the hall."

"Not now." He took the other seat beside her. "I want to hear about it first."

Becky took a breath and avoided their eyes. She tried telling the story calmly but stopped several times when her voice broke. Only when she was done did she look at them.

Wendy placed an arm over her shoulder. "Dear Lord, honey, why didn't you tell anyone what you were doing?"

"Why didn't you tell me?" Aaron asked. "You can't just go out and approach a violent suspect on your own. You should know better than that for goodness' sake."

"Don't lecture her, Aaron," Wendy scolded. "Now's not the time for it."

"I'm glad you weren't hurt," Bobby said. He leaned in with a hug that reminded her how much she loved him. "Quit this job. Please," he whispered into her ear.

The idea had never sounded so good. And what she had to do next, Becky thought, might determine her decision. "We'll talk about that later," she said, standing. "Wendy, would you and Bobby wait at the security office while Aaron goes upstairs with me? I want to check on the sergeant."

"So, he's killed again." Aaron said on the elevator ride up.

Becky watched the lighting numbers. "He claims he has. Curt's out looking for the body now. All he told me was that it was an old lady. This guy is having too much fun now to stop. He's toying with me and trying to make my life hell. If he can't find Shiloh, it's only a matter of time before he comes after Wendy or Bobby. You've got to get them out of town immediately."

"You know Wendy won't allow that unless you—"

"I can't leave, dammit." Becky felt her frustration boiling. "Tolly's hearing begins the day after tomorrow. I have to be there. And I don't care how hard-headed Wendy is. You're going to have to put your foot down. Her and your baby's lives could depend on it. Be the man of the family, Aaron."

The elevator jerked to a stop on the fourth floor, and her anxiety peaked when the doors slid open to a gathering of deputies in the hall, locking stares on her. Their eyes cut away when she and Aaron approached.

"How is he?" Becky asked. Sweat rolled down her back while she waited for their answer.

The one with Lieutenant bars on his collar spoke. "Oh, I guess about the same as every other man who's been shot in the chest, seen his better days. At least he's alive—for now."

"Can we see him?"

"No. He's in surgery. They're trying to dig your bullet out without killing him."

"Listen, guys," said Becky, "I'm sorry. Your sergeant and I surprised each other. There was a lot of confusion."

The lieutenant gave the others a head motion, and they all walked toward the waiting room at the end of the hall.

Aaron took Becky's hand. "Let's go. They're all shook up over this. There's no use trying to talk to them now."

Sheriff Newton stepped from the elevator in civies when they turned. His hair was uncombed, and his jaw was set tight while he walked toward them. Becky realized she was tugging her ponytail only when she felt it.

"What the hell are you doing here?" he asked.

Aaron stepped in. "What do you think, Leroy? We're concerned about your man."

"Stay out of it, Powers." His eyes cut to Becky. "Tell me Chief, why is it that in my twenty-four year career and thousands of high-risk calls, I've never once heard of an officer shooting another until tonight?"

Becky detected a hint of whiskey on his breath. "I'll talk to you about it later, Sheriff. You should go check on your man. I know saying I'm sorry doesn't help now."

Newton blocked their way. "Oh, you'll be sorry if he dies. I intend to be on the phone with the D.A. first thing Monday morning to talk about charges. Manslaughter seems appropriate."

One long stride brought Aaron's face to Newton's. "Then maybe you'd better be ready to do some explaining too, like why your deputies were in that building without informing Becky. Are you not aware that it's inside her jurisdiction, or did you just decide not to tell her?"

Newton's jaw twitched.

"Why were they there, Leroy?" Aaron demanded.

"Because we had a tip that someone had been driving in and out of the morgue sally port for a few days. The caller thought it might be our murder suspect. We were staking the damned place out. Nobody expected her to show up and start blazing away."

"Who gave you the tip?" Becky asked. "Did they give a description? What kind of vehicle did they say was coming and going?"

"It was anonymous, and he didn't give any details."

"Your person taking the call didn't ask?"

"The call was short and sweet. He hung up before we could ask questions. Now, I'm done with both of you. I have a deputy fighting for his life because some small-town cop decided to go out and play Lone Ranger without even picking up the damned phone and giving me a call."

"So, none of it's your fault," said Aaron. "All Becky's, huh? No regrets for not picking up the damned phone and giving *her* a call."

"Don't tell me how to do my job, Powers. I don't care if you *are* an SBI agent now. I was a deputy when you were still crapping yellow. Now, get the hell out of my way so I can check on my man."

Aaron didn't move. "Then it seems as if you'd have learned a little something about communicating with other law enforcement agencies."

Becky wondered if the situation was about to come to blows. She tried using a calming voice. "Listen guys, we're all on the same side here. There's still a killer out there. There's another body somewhere too. I understand you're angry with me, Sheriff. But our arguing isn't solving anything. We have to catch this man."

Newton pushed by. "We'll catch him if you stay out of our damned way."

"Your tip came from him," said Becky. "It was his plan to lead your guys and me there at the same time. He was toying with us just for kicks. He'll keep playing these games until we stop him."

"So, when did you learn to analyze the criminal mind? Did a couple of years of doing petty larceny reports and writing parking tickets teach you that? Maybe learning how to not shoot other cops should be your first step."

Becky saw Aaron's eyes flash and grabbed his arm before he went for Newton. "Let's go." She tugged until Aaron walked with her.

"But I guess you enjoy pulling the trigger a little too much for that, don't you, Hawk." It came loud and clear as they neared the elevators. "As long as you do it ambush style."

"You want to clarify that?" Aaron shouted while Becky struggled to hold him back. Nurses and deputies spilled into the hall.

"You know what I'm talking about, Powers. You were there. What really happened the night she shot Sheriff Scotland?"

With her arms around Aaron's waist, Becky was dragged away from the elevators. The deputies formed a barrier between Newton and Aaron.

"So, that's what this is all about," Aaron said. "You still haven't accepted the truth about Scotland. Is that true with you other guys?"

"Hard to say what the truth was since he died before he could get a trial," the lieutenant said.

Becky felt Aaron pulling from her grip. "This isn't worth your career," she said into his ear. "Let it go. Let's get out of here."

An intense staring match between Aaron and Newton ensued before they departed.

Aaron calmed some during the elevator ride down. "Sorry I lost my cool," he said. "Sorry you heard all that garbage from Newton too. He was just drunk and full of it tonight."

Becky closed her eyes and tried rubbing away a gnawing headache. "Booze only brings out what a man thinks when he's sober. I can only wonder how many of the deputies up there feel the same way he does."

"Don't worry about it," Aaron said. "Let's just get home so you can get some rest."

The elevator stopped, and the doors opened to the lobby. Becky felt she was close to a decision. "Aaron, would you know of any homes on the market near you and Wendy?"

CHAPTER 33

The second day of the Blackberry Festival would've been canceled even if another band of storms hadn't moved in overnight. Word that a killer was stalking the town spread after the body of an elderly female had been found displayed under a willow tree near the lake, her hands duct taped to a low branch in a pugilistic pose. She wore her mum in a soaked, silver strand of hair. A steady stream of campers and cars began moving toward the highway shortly after breakfast. News trucks passed them on the way in.

Under a blue tarp tent, SBI agents photographed and processed the scene. This time, Aaron hadn't been required to pull strings. The bureau had sent its best men, along with some from the interstate murders task force team. They were meticulous in their search for evidence while news cameras and reporters waited just past the crime scene tape at the parking lot.

Becky watched, praying that he'd made a mistake this time and left behind that one small but crucial bit of evidence that so often turns the tide in an investigation. She also remembered words from his letter: "It will be futile to look for clues because clues will not connect you to me. I do not exist as a human being." They were words stolen from The Axeman of New Orleans—the Axeman who certainly had been human but had managed to kill time and again unseen, never to be caught.

"Becky?" Curt stood beside her with his rain hat dripping when she turned. "The mayor would like to see you at town hall as soon as you're done here."

She'd expected it. "Thank you, Curt. Would you mind staying here until they're done?" She ignored the reporters' questions as she walked past them.

Mark Clayton made a quick half-smile and pointed to a chair when Becky entered his office. "How's it going out there?" he asked. "Any leads at all?"

She sat and removed her hat. "Other than that, it's another case of strangulation, no. It appears he attacked from the front this time and used his hands only. She put up a hell of a struggle. We haven't identified her yet."

"Nothing on her that might give a clue to who she is?"

"Nothing but a roll of soggy bills in her pocket."

Clayton fiddled with a pen. "What about your missing sister? Did the posters and newscasts shake up any information?"

"No. I'm afraid she may not even be in town now."

Clayton nodded while still studying his pen. "Becky, we had an emergency council meeting this morning. It was about what happened last night."

"Yes. I'm working on a detailed report about that for you. To put it in a nutshell, I used some very poor judgment. As I'm sure you've heard, the deputy is still in serious condition." She bit her lip while waiting for a reply. "You don't have to be afraid to tell me I'm fired, Mark."

"No. No. Nothing like that. It's just that we're all concerned that… well that this guy has gotten into your head. Has he?"

"With the crowds leaving, I think things will be less confusing. He won't be able to blend in as well."

"That's not what I asked. I asked if—"

"Yes, Mayor. I think it's safe to say this guy is in my head some."

Clayton nodded. "I understand. Hell, you wouldn't be human if he wasn't. He's in all our heads." He looked at his pen once more before tossing it onto his desk and sitting back. "This town will forever be grateful to you for uncovering the criminal operation that was going on under our very noses. You did a great job there. Two of those men were town councilmen, and I never once expected anything. We also appreciate the job you've done as police chief. But what we have now is something no small-town police department should be expected to handle. It's why we have county and state agencies. They have resources and training. So, since this killer seems to be motivated by taunting you personally, we believe it best that you take a leave of absence. That's our unanimous decision. Why allow him to play his games with you? Let the sheriff's department and SBI handle this. Take a vacation, Becky, and enjoy it. You've earned it."

He appeared surprised when Becky nodded without argument. "Ok, Mayor. It sounds like a good idea. Except for the Tolly hearing tomorrow, I'll consider my duties on hold. As soon as it's over, Bobby and I will be gone for a while."

Clayton made an uncomfortable smile. "Thank you. We're only wanting what's best for us all, you foremost."

She stood and walked but stopped at the door. "One other thing, Mayor. Maybe you should start looking for your next chief, just in case I enjoy my vacation too much."

The Harrison Tolly file Becky kept had grown thick in the two years since she'd become chief. She felt a mixture of emotions while she drove to the police station to retrieve it for the hearing. Relief, strangely, seemed the strongest. But the envelope she found slid under the office door instantly changed that. She recognized the handwriting that spelled her name on the outside while tearing it open, unfolding, and reading:

> I'm happy to hear you're alive and well. Be home alone late tonight. No assistance. No tricks. Follow my simple rule if you wish to spare others.
>
> Respectfully,
>
> Kage

CHAPTER 34

The guard behind the desk at Central Prison visitor registration jotted information down from the identification card presented to him. "Does he know you're visiting him today, Reverend?"

The man in a black suit with Band-Aids on his face and a Bible tucked under his arm took the card back. "I assume, sir. I scheduled my visit a week ago."

"And what is your relationship with him?"

"Not much, other than having offered spiritual guidance on a few occasions. I understand he chose the wrong path. So, since I was visiting Raleigh today, I thought I might drop in and offer him a prayer and a few words."

"You understand that he's been in the geriatrics section for over a year. His capabilities are limited."

"Yes. I'll keep my visit brief. Also, I wonder if you might let him have this Bible."

The guard took it and thumbed through it. "We have Bibles for the inmates here."

"Yes, but I underlined some Scripture in it and jotted a few notes that I thought might enlighten him, if he's still capable of reading and understanding, of course."

"I doubt he can, but we'll see that he gets it. If you would, empty your pockets on the table before we take you back."

"Yes, sir."

Behind a thick glass window, he sat and lifted the phone when another guard rolled Harrison Tolly in his wheelchair into the visitation room. "Sorry Reverend," the guard said into the phone on the other side, "but you're wasting your time here. He doesn't even know where he is anymore."

He studied the vacant look on the old man's sunken face. "I understand. Please try getting him to hold the phone to his ear for a few minutes. I only want to share some Scripture. The Word seems to find a way for those who listen."

Tolly cast the guard a confused gaze when the phone was pressed to his ear. He fumbled with it before taking it.

"Ten minutes, Reverend."

"Thank you, brother."

He waited for the guard to step back to watch the line of other inmates conversing with visitors. His eyes watched Tolly's for a moment, and then he smiled. "Just listen, old man. Continue your act. I know you understand. You don't know me, but I'm like you in many ways. You and I are two of the rare souls on this earth, void of the cumbersome emotions that plague others. We don't care that the world hates and condemns us. If I didn't know your past, I would still know that by what your act can't hide in your eyes."

Tolly continued to stare at nothing.

"Neither of us are long for this world. I suspect that doesn't bother you, just as it doesn't me. But I also believe we both have the same last wish. The wish I'm sure you've craved since you've been here. The elimination of one, Becky Hawk."

Tolly's bony hand squeezed the phone. His eyes focused.

"I can't make you trust me. You'll just have to believe I am who I say. I understand your desire to avenge what that woman did to you and the fraternity that was your life. I'm not a plant. My motivation is something I believe you understand. You know the thrill. The power over life or death, that one thing that fuels the spirits of aberrations like us."

Tolly's lips moved hesitantly before he spoke low. "They can monitor these conversations."

"Continue your act and don't speak then. They care nothing about talk between a pastor and a confused old man." He looked at the guard and closed his eyes. "Pretend to pray with me."

They bowed their heads.

"I've sent you a Bible. Check the book of Titus. I've detailed my plans on the page borders. There's a map and a diagram too. Don't worry, the guard who checked me in has already done his compulsory search."

"I don't trust you."

"That's entirely up to you. All I ask is that you read my plans. Who knows how your competency hearing will go. This is your best chance, maybe only chance, to get your revenge. If you follow my directions precisely, I can deliver that woman to your mercies. Amen?"

Harrison's appearance had changed when he looked back up. His eyes were sharp and unblinking. "What's your interest in this?"

"Only for this shitty world to know and remember me well. I've been merely a shadow all my life. Now, I want my name to be mentioned forever in the same breath and in the same tones as those of people like you."

Tolly looked at the gazing eyes behind the glass for a moment. He smirked while taking a glance at the guard. "I still don't trust you."

"Listen to me, old man. You have your reason for wanting Becky Hawk dead and I have mine. There's only one thing I will need from you. I know of someone who's dear to her. I only need to find this person to make the rest work." He watched the guard and reached into his shoe. "The lesser documented, side stories of history have always been some of my favorite reading. That's why I know that during the last months of the Civil War, an outlaw gang by the name of the Manticores kept just ahead of Sheridan's cavalry. They offered to take and secure precious items from rich southern families so that it wouldn't fall into Yankee hands. It was all promised to be returned after the war. The Manticores, being what they were, of course, never returned it. The stolen treasure of the Confederacy is considered a myth by many. I believe differently."

"So that's what this is about," Tolly said. "You go to hell."

"I don't give a damn about treasures, old man." He glanced again at the guard and then pressed the Confederate coin he'd taken from the old Irish lady against the glass for a moment. "I need the person who will bring Becky Hawk to us. She's most likely wherever this came from. You can tell me or not. I can find another way, but you will never get this chance again." He palmed the coin and waited for an answer.

CHAPTER 35

The rain had slowed but still clicked on the windows while they lay in bed and looked out at the water still rising over the banks. Silence added to the gloom. Neither of them felt like conversation.

Shiloh finally spoke. "Something happened to her. Someone would've come by now if it hadn't."

"The water is still moving fast," Chris said. "I think they're only being careful."

"I don't think so. I think he found her before she could get help. I think she's dead. And it's my fault because I panicked. We never should've left her there alone." She scowled and put her head on his shoulder. "Oh, Chris."

"We don't know what happened," he said. "So, don't let your head start making up stuff. If the worst did happen, it's not your fault." He sat up. "Tell you what, I'll cook a nice dinner over the fireplace tonight. We'll eat by the fire, and then get a good night's sleep. The rain is slowing down. If they haven't come by morning, I say we cross the lake ourselves tomorrow. How's that sound to you?"

Shiloh nodded. "I think we should."

"Fine. Now, let's both cheer up and try to enjoy our last night here."

"I'm a police officer, for Pete's sake. I can take care of myself." Becky's argument with Wendy continued in the lobby of the Courthouse Square Inn. The bespectacled man behind the front desk was doing a good job of pretending to concentrate on the registry book.

"Yeah, I know you're a big girl and you can take care of yourself and all that jazz," Wendy said. "But don't you understand how much we'll all worry if we leave you here alone?"

"I have to stay. You all don't. I'll be safe here. All I have to do is drive to Raleigh and pick up Cynthia for the hearing tomorrow. If this wraps up quickly, I'll be at your house tomorrow evening."

"I don't like it," Wendy said. "I'll stay with you."

Becky looked annoyed. "Aaron."

"Come on, Wendy," he said. "She'll be safe. I'll have a few deputies I trust to come by and check on her from time to time."

"There's nothing to worry about," Becky said. "I'm looking forward to spending time with you guys without all the stress."

Wendy held out her arms. "Call me tonight."

"I will." Becky received Wendy's hug then Bobby's. She held him tight and didn't want to let go.

"Why are you shaking?" he asked.

"Am I? I don't know why."

"Yeah, you are. What's wrong?"

"I'm fine. I'll see you soon."

"Be careful," he said.

She made herself smile.

"Can't wait to have you as our guest," Aaron said. "Wendy should have the itinerary all ready by the time you get there."

Becky took his hand. "I'm sure she will. You watch after them."

After another round of goodbyes, she watched them leave the parking lot. Wendy's hand waved from the car window. Becky felt an emotional tug while waving back and watching them go down the street.

"I just need you to sign here, Mrs. Hawk," the man at the desk said, holding a key. "You'll be in room fourteen."

She picked up her suitcase. "Never mind. I won't be checking in."

The for sale sign on Earl Gammon's eighteen foot Lynman runabout had been in his yard since the previous fall. The ten-year-old boat still ran well. Despite the rain, Earl was happy to allow the interested man to see for himself when the two of them took it out for a test run. At full throttle, the hundred horsepower engine skimmed the boat over the lake as if on air. It was an exhilarating ride. Earl went over all the operating details in the half hour they spent on the water. Neither of them could wait to get back to the lake house and make the transaction.

Lucille Gammons even threw an extra chicken-fried steak into the skillet when they returned. It was delicious, the gravy perfect to his liking. Her fresh green beans, fried squash, and biscuits made perfect additions.

He sat with them in the living room, watching the local evening news while enjoying a bowl of peach cobbler. The unidentified woman whose body had been found tied below a tree in Black Lake was the lead story. He said little while he watched and enjoyed the somber expressions of the reporter and the people he interviewed. Yet, there was one disappointment.

"It seems they would've interviewed your chief of police too," he said. "Even though she's in over her head, I'm sure the people of this town would like to know what she has to say about these terrible happenings. What do you folks think about it all?"

The Gammons simply stared with unblinking eyes and bullet holes in their foreheads.

The sleep Becky got after she returned home was broken, no more than a half hour at a time. She got up and ate a small meal, not because she was hungry. She felt she'd need the energy for later. She'd hung up from talking to Wendy and Bobby when she sat on the sofa and wrote two letters. Things she felt but rarely said went in them. She let her heart pour out, holding nothing back. She wrote for over an hour before folding the letters and placing them in separate envelopes. "Aaron and Wendy," she wrote on the first, and "Bobby" on the second. She placed them on the kitchen bar. In the trash can, she found a piece of cardboard and took a Magic Marker from her desk drawer.

There was still over an hour of sunlight left when she drove her patrol car far enough up the driveway for it to be seen from the road. She removed her twelve gauge Winchester shotgun from the trunk and found an extra box of buckshot. Back at the house, she turned on the front porch light and then reclined on the sofa with the shotgun in her hands and her revolver in her holster.

On the patrol car windshield, there was a handwritten sign: "I'M ALONE."

CHAPTER 36

"What do you think will happen tomorrow?" Shiloh removed her glasses and watched Chris extinguish the candle.

He climbed into the bed with her. "I'm not sure. There will be a lot of questions. They'll check us out and find out we're both runaways for sure. I guess they'll contact my mom and your dad and send us both back home."

"I wish things were different. I wish it could've worked out the way we planned."

"Things will work out. The next time we're together, we'll be adults. We won't have to hide. We can live our life without looking over our shoulders. Who knows, maybe one day we'll even make it to Cudjoe Key."

"I'll be looking forward to that," she said. "Tell me again that it'll really happen."

"It will. I promise."

She snuggled against him. Their last meal in the lodge had filled her, and she felt a relaxing sleep coming.

"Two pints." Dan held out his money with a satchel over his shoulder and a sleeping bag under his arm. He'd interrupted Rylie and Brant Holbrook's evening of watching wrestling on TV.

"Two?" Rylie asked. "You must be planning on yourself a whale of a night." He and Brant shared grins.

"Yeah. You could say that."

Brant stood from the sofa and walked toward the back room of the house.

"Where are you going with all that?" Rylie asked. He took the bills from Dan. "You look like a man with something on his mind. Are you all right?"

"To tell you the truth, I don't remember when I was all right."

"Your girl running away has gone hard on you, hasn't it? Why don't you come in and watch some matches with us? Company would probably do you some good."

"No thanks. I've got plans."

"What kind of plans, Dan? At least tell me where you're going." Rylie took the jars from Brant and handed them to Dan.

"Never mind. I can't explain it, so you'd understand anyway." Dan put the jars in his satchel and tied the flap. "Just do me a favor. If Shiloh were to ever show back up and I don't, tell her I love her." He turned and walked.

"Dan? Wait a minute."

He paid Rylie no mind. In the distance, the light from a rising moon fell on Overlook Hang. Dan walked toward it.

The sound of the boat's engine first came to Chris in the form of a dream. He woke when the humming grew louder and went to the window. The rain had stopped. He spotted the boat by the light of a high moon. It glided across the water without running lights, making a straight line toward the old dock at the bottom of the hill. There was cause for alarm—Chris felt it. He walked back to the bed and began putting his pants and shoes on.

"Shiloh. Wake up. Someone's here."

She rolled over and put on her glasses. "Who's here? The police?"

He went back to the window. The boat was now tied to the dock. From the shadows of the trail that led to the lodge, a man appeared, stepping quickly.

"I don't think so. Get up and get your clothes on now."

His urgency brought her fully awake. She felt a tremor of fear. "Who do you think it is?" She saw him place his butterfly knife in his pocket. "Chris?"

"I don't know, but we're going down to the cellar until we find out. Hurry up." He lit the candle and held it for her while she threw on her clothes and tied her shoes. Chris grabbed her the moment she was ready and pulled her along.

"I'm scared," she said when they reached the bottom of the steps and hurried across the stone floor, passing the taxidermied animals on their way to the kitchen. A tight shriek broke from her when the knob of the front door rattled.

"Hurry," Chris whispered. His fast pace caused the candle he carried to blow out. He cursed under his breath while pulling her along to the pantry closet. They stepped inside. Chris closed the door and felt along the wall until he found the moveable panel and pushed it open. He pulled Shiloh close when he heard glass breaking in the main hall. "We're going to be Ok," he said. "Keep quiet. Hold on to me and follow me down."

"It's too dark." Her voice trembled. She prodded for the steps with her feet. "I'll fall."

"No. I've got you. Listen, reach behind you and find the panel door. I won't let you fall."

Shiloh extended her hand into the darkness. There were footsteps outside the pantry now. "He…He's in the kitchen," she squeaked. "He's right outside."

"Relax and quietly push the door to."

She found it and eased it shut.

"Good. Now, reach in front of you. Put your hands on my shoulders. We're going to take it one step at a time."

Shiloh held him tight. She huffed her breaths while he led her down to the hidden room. The air smelled different this time. It was a murky stench, like the cove but stronger. The sound of the water at the bottom of the sinkhole was different too. It gushed. She thought she heard another noise from behind her and looked back at the darkness.

"We're almost to the bottom," Chris said. "Stay right behind me. That moving water is from the storm. It may have opened the sinkhole more."

"Can you see at all, Chris?"

"No, but I know the way around and can feel ahead with my feet. We're going to take our time. One more step down, and we're turning to the left. We're going to walk along the wall. Just be ready to stop if I do."

She turned at the bottom of the steps and walked with him. The water sounded all around. Her hands squeezed his shoulders tighter. She walked until Chris turned and eased her down.

"We'll stay here until we're sure he's gone," he said.

She curled against him and felt his arm go around her. "Who do you think it is?"

"Probably just someone that heard about the lodge and wanted to check it out."

"At this time of night?"

Chris hadn't believed it either. He was trying his best to not let Shiloh know the danger he felt. There'd been something about the man's movements that had reminded him of the mime's. "Whoever it is," he said, "probably won't stay long. We'll be good here until he leaves. Lay your head against me and try to rest." He pulled her closer while he patted his pocket to be certain his knife was still there.

The panel at the top of the stairs rattled before slamming open. Chris felt Shiloh flinch and his stomach sunk. He threw his hand over her mouth, barely muffling her cry. "Be quiet," he breathed, and pulled her with him, past the crates and sacks of treasure to the far wall. He dug for his knife and saw a flashlight beam coming down the stairs. His wrist flicked and the blade clicked ready.

The man coming down the steps moved slowly. He reached the bottom and shined his flashlight around the room. His silhouette showed he wore a long coat. He stood still as a statue with his hand in a pocket. The flashlight flicked off. A low laugh began and carried on for several moments.

Chris' hand couldn't stop the sound of Shiloh's hard breaths.

"Hello, children," came a playful but malign voice. "Are you enjoying our game of hide and seek? You should come out now. It's past your bedtime. Time to sleep."

The knife rolled around in Chris' hand. His eyes stayed fixed in the direction of the voice. He listened for movement but heard only the rushing water. A humming, similar to a lullaby came for a moment before more silence. The humming came from another place, and then another. Laughter mixed with it. Playful singing followed: "Here we go 'round the mulberry bush. The mulberry bush…"

Chris rose to a crouch and removed his hand from Shiloh's mouth. Her breaths were loud, sure to give away their hiding place, but Chris didn't care now. This guy had pissed him. His muscles coiled for a fight.

The light flicked back on and shined a beam just to their right. It began sweeping toward them. Chris waited until it was nearly on him before he uncoiled and sprang forward. The light glared in his eyes. Blindly, he reached and felt an arm, sweeping his knife toward it. He felt it make contact with cloth. Fabric ripped. He grabbed for the light and felt the hand holding it. He jerked it. The flashlight fell to the floor. A sharp pop combined with a metallic racking sound reported near Chris' face. He saw a quick muzzle flash and dodged before he thrust the knife, feeling it sink into flesh and strike bone. There was a grunt and a jerk that pulled the knife from his hand. Another pop came with a second muzzle flash. It lit the man's face for a split second—scraggly black hair over a scarred, pale face and icy blue eyes. Chris reached for him, this time grabbing the arm holding the gun.

Chris had been in fights before. He knew early in them when he was losing and when he was winning. He was winning this one. He'd hurt the guy. He had momentum. All he had to do was wrench the gun away and this sleazeball would be sorry he'd ever crossed his path. He'd be sorry he'd ever messed with Chris Heath's girl. He jerked the arm he held and swung his fist toward where he judged the face would be. He felt it land solidly and ignored the pain in his knuckles. One more would do it. He spun the weakened man around and moved his back foot to plant for another punch.

Except there was no floor where his foot went. He felt himself tip backwards and pulled on the arm to catch his balance. He felt a shove and then his stomach rose. The sound of rushing water at the bottom of the sinkhole filled his ears. While he fell, Chris resisted screaming. He didn't want Shiloh to hear that.

CHAPTER 37

His body protested and told him how far he'd declined since he'd last climbed the mountain. It had been five years since he'd been to the top. Shiloh came with him then. They'd brought sleeping bags and spent the night there. They'd stayed up late and watched the sky while Dan pointed out constellations and planets for her. It was the darkest place he knew of, no lights within miles. On clear nights, even the Milky Way sparkled. Shiloh had liked it when he'd told her they were closer to Heaven there.

He dropped everything and caught his breath when he made it. The place was the same, but the view was different. More dots of light showed in the valley below. Beyond that, he saw the new interstate, tiny flows of red and white lights. He carried his satchel to the giant, pale rocks the place was named for. Shiloh had wanted to play on them when she was there. He hadn't let her. Anyone venturing too far out risked slipping down the slope and falling over a thousand feet.

He removed the jars from his satchel and placed them on the rocks. He then rolled his sleeping bag out and sat on it with his back against an oak. The moonlight shining on the rocks made the clear whiskey glow invitingly. He looked toward the heavens. "I'll need your help with this," he said.

A pendulum clock in the living room clicked seconds away through the otherwise silent lake house. A lamp near it spread soft light to the den, where Becky waited with her shotgun and an uneasy feeling growing. Was this another of his tricks? Could he be in town somewhere, killing again while delighting in the fact that he'd fooled the chief of police into staying home?

It was past midnight when she got up to make another round through the house. She checked outside through the front and back windows while feeling the effects of her stress and lack of sleep from the past days settling on her. Her eyes were heavy. She fought it for ten minutes before walking to the kitchen and using almost double the grounds she normally brewed her coffee with.

Just what the doctor ordered, she thought when she sat back down, blew steam away, and sampled the harsh taste. It felt good going down, and the effect was immediate. But it sloshed over her shirt when the phone beside her rang. Fully awake and alert now, she calmed herself before answering.

"Hello."

"Becky, I hate to wake you," David Donaldson said with some tension in his voice, "but a few things have happened here in Drake County tonight that I think I need to fill you in on."

"Go ahead, Sheriff."

"I may have a lead on your last victim—Andrea Fitzgerald, approximately sixty-five years old. She goes by Andi. She'd been staying in the hobo camp just our side of the county line. A couple of the men from over there came to the office late today and reported that she'd been missing since yesterday afternoon. She'd left out for your festival to sell some pies and didn't come back. Her description fits."

Becky carried the phone to her desk, flipped on the lamp, and found paper and pen. "Can I have those men's names and contact information?"

"William Flynt and Clay Graham. But, as I said, they're hobos so there isn't any contact information other than their summer camp. They couldn't give much in the way of her next of kin. If there are dental records, they're unknown. But they agreed to ride to the medical examiner's office with a couple of my detectives tomorrow morning and try to make a positive identification."

Becky peered out the windows again when she finished writing. "Thank you, Sheriff. It's a start."

"Wait. There's more. We interviewed these guys for a while tonight. It turned out they recognized your sister from her picture. Another runaway by the name of Christopher Heath brought her to their camp late a week ago Friday night. They stayed in the camp a few days before leaving. They said this Heath guy has a rowboat he gets around in. Me and my guys decided it might be worth checking out the old hunting lodge on Boar Island."

Becky paced and tugged her ponytail. "Did you find anything?"

"Yes, we did. Someone has been staying there for sure. One of the bedrooms had been slept in. The barbecue pit outside had been used to cook food from the kitchen. But the real kicker was a hidden panel door in the back of the kitchen closet. We missed it when we searched the place two years ago and would've again if it hadn't been left open."

"But did you find her?"

"No. The place was empty."

"Do you think it was Shiloh staying there with this Heath guy?"

"Maybe, but we don't know anything for sure yet. I want you to understand that before I tell you the rest. There are stairs behind this panel I told you about. They lead down to a cellar under the lodge. Someone apparently went down there recently and found something our old friends left behind. You wouldn't believe it, Becky. It looked like a damned pirates' treasure, Confederate coins, jewelry, silverware, all very old stuff. My guess is it was stolen and brought there when the Manticores built the place. Someone had transferred it from the crates it was in to burlap bags and must've been planning to move it all out."

"That's interesting, Sheriff, but my only concern now is finding my sister."

"Just listen. We found footprints in the dirt down there. One set appears to be from a girl. There's a wide sinkhole there too that's close to swallowing the whole damned lodge. And we found blood on the ground near it. There were two spent cartridges and a bloodied butterfly knife there also. People scuffled down there, Becky, and somebody got hurt. The blood was fresh. There was a trail leading up the stairs and out the front door. It was on the old dock too. Whoever got hurt left in a boat."

Becky paced faster. "You are looking for her, right, David?"

"Of course. I've got deputies searching the island now and a boat checking everything that moves on the water. We're getting another boat ready too. I know Tolly's hearing is tomorrow. I'll understand if you need to sleep, but I wanted to give you a chance to get in on it, since this may involve your murders. And your sister."

"Send the boat over," she said. "You can pick me up at the pier."

She swore under her breath while throwing on her uniform and duty belt. It *had* been a trick. "You're smarter than this," she hollered while walking out her bedroom door. She twirled around when the emergency line beside her bed rang.

CHAPTER 38

Fully expecting county dispatch to be calling with terrible news, she picked up the receiver. "Becky Hawk. Go ahead."

"Good evening, Chief. Sorry I'm so late calling. Nice speaking with you again. Your little incident in the morgue had me worried. I'm happy that you're proficient with your weapon."

She listened to his chuckle. "What have you done with my sister? If you hurt her, you son of—"

"Seems we're putting the cart before the horse. We'll get to that right after we chat and get acquainted. I want to say that I'm impressed with you. It took courage to show up at the old hospital alone. I'm beginning to believe you are all I've read about. That's important to me."

"I don't guess it matters to you that you almost caused me to kill a man."

"No, I can't say it does matter to me. Does it really bother you? I'm curious."

"Of course it does."

"What about Sheriff Scotland?"

"Tell me where Shiloh is. I'm not playing your game."

"I'm afraid you must. You're in no position to make demands. So, answer my question. I want to know what you felt when you killed Sheriff Scotland? Was it exhilarating? Come on, Chief. You can be honest with a fellow killer."

Becky squeezed her mouth for a moment. "I was protecting myself. I didn't enjoy killing a man, but if you've hurt my sister, I swear to you, I'll find you. And then I'll see if my opinion has changed about that."

"I don't like what I'm hearing in your voice. I understand emotion can creep up and turn volatile. You'll need to check yours. I want you with a level head and unflustered. I asked the question only because I'm curious about the makeup of your spirit. I want to know that because we're nearly done with the preliminaries. We're about to play the real game."

"Leave Shiloh out of it. Let her go."

"Be quiet and listen. You're the one I've chosen. You have the traits I was hoping to find: courage, resourcefulness, and a certain measure of fame. Though you may not like it, this is your fate now. Of course, you may choose not to participate this time but, if not, I will only return later and begin again. So, you should take careful note of all I'm about to say. There's more you need to know besides my name. I'm not human, not in the sense most are. I realized that early in my existence. But I'm more than just a shadow. I'm an expense to this world. Always have been, Chief Hawk. You'll do well to remember that."

Becky listened for sounds that might come over the line. His ramblings blocked out most, but she heard a car pass, confirming that the call was from a phone booth. "Listen," she said, "I've already told you that I'll meet you anywhere. All you have to do is tell me where. Are you in town now?"

"Sorry, Chief, I admire you, but I don't trust you that much yet. The cardinal rule of this game is that it's played between us only. I'll be watching. You'll forfeit the moment I see that you've broken that rule. I don't expect for my game to last forever. I'm more than ready to make my exit from this world whenever my own destiny calls for it. Therefore, the moment I am approached by any law enforcement officer other than you, your little sister and I will make that exit together. Time will be a factor also. You will need to act swiftly. But I'm fair, so take note:

"At the start of the hunt, the young jackals go before the experienced lion. Find the young jackals and they will lead you to where two sows lay. If you've listened to what I've said, from there, you will be led to a praying man. He will tell you where to find me and your sister. So, there you are."

"Wait! That's not fair. I don't know what you mean by any of that. I'll never find you."

"You're disappointing me already. But I don't want to make this more difficult than your capabilities. The afternoon I was at your house, I left something for you. I'm going to hang up now, but you should look under your bed mattress."

At the sound of a click and dial tone, Becky turned, jerked the sheets off her bed, and pulled the mattress away. The beige and green walkie talkie she found there was similar to one she'd seen in a photograph Ed brought back from the Pacific War Theater. She inspected the dials and buttons before extending the antenna and turning a dial to the "ON" position. Static crackled and grew louder when she turned the volume switch. She pressed the transmission button. "Are you listening?" she asked. The static continued. She tried again and heard a faint disruption. There came a voice, low and indiscernible. Static took over again before the voice returned, this time a touch clearer.

"Becky!" The cry pierced through the speaker and conveyed the young girl's desperate horror.

"Shiloh?"

"Help me! Help me, Becky!" Sobbing followed.

Tears streamed from Becky's eyes. "I will. I'm going to find you, honey. I promise." She listened to more static before the next transmission came.

"And now you know the stakes of the game, Chief. I've told you the rules. If you break them, I won't hesitate to dispose of her. I'll be watching and listening for you. Keep in mind that if you fail, we will begin our game again at a later time of my choosing with another person of importance to you. Your friend Wendy's child, one day, might be a lovely possibility. Don't you agree?" He snickered. "Gotta keep you motivated, right, Chief? I'll go now. There's still preparations I must take care of before our meeting."

"Listen to me," Becky said. "I still don't understand what I'm supposed to do."

"You'll have ample time to figure it out. And I would suggest you conserve the battery in your radio. The charge is only good for about two hours."

She stared at the walkie for a moment, flicked it off, ran to the den, and grabbed a notepad and pen. Her mind spun while she jotted notes of what she remembered from the conversation. Two sows and a praying man. Something about jackals going before the lion in the hunt. Her fast scribbling helped her to recall some of it. The young jackals were at the start of the hunt. She knew of only one possibility for that and grabbed her car keys.

CHAPTER 39

The first time came soon after he slid into his sleeping bag and closed his eyes. He fought the temptation by remembering when he'd camped there with Shiloh and their late-night conversations. He focused on the sounds of the cicadas and owls also. It helped him drift off and sleep for a few hours, though fitfully. At one point, strange dreams interrupted it. He didn't remember the details of them when he woke. He only knew they'd made him feel guilty and bad about himself. Moonlight still shined on the jars when he looked. Dan felt the beckoning.

"No," he said. "Not this time."

It had been more than a day since he'd had his last drink. His hands trembled. Cold sweat beaded on his forehead.

Sleep, he thought. Think about good things and sleep.

But the good things, his marriage, Becky's birth, his years with Shiloh, all had unhappy endings for him. He'd lost them all. Any peace he'd felt when he'd come there left him. He closed his eyes and prayed for calming. His hands shook harder, and the sweat beads spread to his face. He realized there would be no more sleep that night, not without help.

Too much, he thought. You're trying too much at once. Go slow. Be smart when you fight the devil. Just a sip or two to calm you, that's all.

He believed it until he unscrewed a jar lid and took a taste.

A Bolton County Sheriff's Department jail van left Central Prison just after seven o'clock that morning. Past the razor-wire-topped walls, a Black Lake patrol car fell in behind it. Curt Nickles had wanted to be a part of the excitement buzzing around the county. He'd volunteered to be the escort weeks before.

Tuned to the chosen frequency, the radios crackled in the two vehicles.

"Curt?"

"Go ahead."

"Have you heard anything from Becky this morning? The women's prison called, wondering when she was coming to pick up the witness there."

"No. I called her house this morning then went there when she didn't answer. Her patrol car was gone. I assume she's on her way to the prison."

"10-4. I just thought she'd have made it there by now. Must've got caught up in this Raleigh traffic."

In the back of the van, Harrison Tolly wore shackles with his hands cuffed to a belly chain. The Bible he'd brought with him lay open on his lap. He studied the drawn map and handwritten words in it once more and pretended not to listen.

He turned from the highway onto a narrow drive that led behind a gas station. It was the place he'd chosen after hours of scouting the route. This part of his plan, though desirable, was not necessary. Though he wanted the old man included, he now had what he needed. He would not allow a failure here to ruin the rest. The moment things appeared to be going wrong, he would simply drive away.

His excitement was stronger than the pain in his right arm. The amount of blood leaking out, however, concerned him. He walked to the back of the van and cut another cloth strip to replace the saturated one. The girl looked away while he changed his bandage. Her strength was waning. She struggled less against her sister's cuffs on her wrists and the duct tape on her ankles. He found the muffled cries that came through the tape over her mouth becoming tiresome.

"Be quiet," he told her. "Look at me. I said be quiet and look at me." He waited until her glasses and scared eyes turned to him. "It's not my plan to kill you, but I will if you continue to make sounds. Close your eyes and sleep. This will all be over soon." He found the bottle of alcohol in his supplies and poured half of it over the deep puncture wound in his arm. He clenched his teeth from the sting and looked back at the girl. "Is your sister the fighter your boyfriend was?" He wrapped his arm and snickered while she wept.

They were twenty minutes from Bolton County when the radio transmission crossed Curt's radio. "Our man in the back says he needs a bathroom break. I believe I could use one too. I'm pulling over at the next station." A minute later, Curt followed the van into the sandy lot of a Phillips 66.

"Would you mind taking him? The driver asked after they placed Harrison into his wheelchair. "I'll buy us both a drink and some snacks while you do."

There was much Curt had heard and read about Harrison "Papa" Tolly. Nearly everyone in Bolton County knew the name and the notoriety attached to it. Stories of his cruel and terrible past, both factual and embellished, had grown to myth-like proportions. For Curt, as silly as he knew it was, the simple act of guarding Tolly alone for a few minutes excited him. It would be something he could mention off-hand to the guys at the lumber plant and his girlfriend.

But Tolly's condition disappointed him. He was now only a dementia-riddled old man, more a breathing corpse than a heartless killer. Curt struggled getting him balanced and on his feet when he found the bathroom door too narrow for the wheelchair.

"Thank you," Harrison wheezed, "Could you undo these?" He held up his cuffed hands and chain.

Curt looked for the driver. "You can't manage with them on?"

"No. It's not a tinkle. I'll need to wipe." Harrison wheezed and coughed. He glanced around with lost eyes.

"Ok, but only the cuffs and belly chain. The shackles stay on." Curt found his key and unlocked them.

"Thank you. Please hold me so I don't fall." Harrison shuffled into the small bathroom with Curt's hands on his shoulders. "I'll need help with this jumpsuit also. I'm sorry. Simple things are so hard at my age. I'll sit. If you unbutton it, I can slip it down and under me."

Curt eased Harrison down and began unsnapping the buttons. As the front of the jumpsuit spread, the old man reached inside it and turned his hollow gaze. Curt followed it to the plywood wall at the back of the bathroom. Sunlight peeked through the saw marks that formed a crude square in it. Curt studied it for a moment before looking down into eyes that were now sharp and burned.

Harrison's hand brought the sharpened can lid from his jumpsuit and made a quick, backhand swipe. Just as with Bud Sweeney, it sliced straight through the carotid artery and trachea. Blood splattered the wall. Harrison listened to a wheeze and looked into widened eyes while swinging the lid once more, forward-handed this time. It sliced another deep wound, and then slipped from his fingers, leaving a bloody starburst when it struck the wall. He stood while Curt fell, locked the door, and rummaged through the dying man's keys.

CHAPTER 40

Highway 421 led Becky directly to I-40, on which she sped west, flipping on her blue light and using the shoulder of the highway when traffic became snarled. The enormity of the situation overwhelmed her thoughts. Her mistake at the old hospital still haunted her, making her self-doubt over her present actions grow with each mile. Not once, however, did she doubt that this man would follow through on his promise if she broke his rules.

But there was something even stronger that pressed her on. Her sister's pleas for help had tapped a strange emotion in Becky. Something about the accent and cadence in the voice had stirred something deep. She felt a powerful connection now with her sister and a sharing of the terror her voice had relayed. She ignored her speed, keeping her eyes on the blurred white lines and a firm grip on the wheel in the hours she drove. She made just one quick stop to ask directions before reaching Millpark and the scenic mountains surrounding it shortly before one o'clock. Then, she prayed that this was where she should be.

Cool, mountain air blew through the windows and recharged her after the long drive. An overcast day defied the weather report by turning cloudless, allowing her a clear view of the near green and distant blue ridges surrounding the town. Becky guessed, in its heyday, the simple beauty of the place would've persuaded tourists traveling through to stop and shop for a while. But things had clearly changed. She met one car on the winding mountain road that led into the vacant streets of the town. Most of the buildings were boarded with foliage overtaking them. In the center of town, past a set of traffic lights, she found an open gas station and drove in.

An aging man in a blue jumpsuit walked out. White sideburns extended from under his ball cap. He wiped his hands with a rag. "Fill it up?" he asked at the car window.

"Yes, please."

He walked to the back, hooked the nozzle to the tank, and then came back and cleaned the windshield. "Black Lake Police Department, huh?" His eyes turned down to the nameplate on Becky's uniform. "And Becky Hawk in the flesh."

She looked close at his face. "Yes. How do you know me?"

"Dan Bowman's oldest girl, right?"

"Yes."

"Heard a lot about you."

"But how do you—" She waited when the nozzle clicked, and the man walked to the back of the car. She handed him a five when he came back. "Keep the change. How do you know me?"

"Thank you." He stuck the bill into his pocket. "Well, because Dan has made real sure that I know his oldest daughter is a chief of police." He laughed. "You and Shiloh are what he talks most about. If he's not stretching the truth, I'd say you both have a right to be proud. He's been dropping in most days recently around this time to use the phone. Must've called everybody in the county looking for Shiloh. His losing his highway job and her running off has been awfully tough on him. But I suppose I'm not telling you anything you don't know. I guess you're here to help look for her." He brought his face down to the window. "Mrs. Hawk?"

Becky blinked and looked up. "Yes, I am."

"Well, I know your father appreciates it. He's having a hard time right now. He sure needs somebody to lean on. Good luck. Hope you find her soon."

"Can you tell me where he lives?"

"Yeah. Straight through the lights. Go past the school for about two miles and turn left onto Old Mill Road. It's a dirt road. Dan's house is less than a mile down on the left, up on a hill."

"Thank you."

Pastor Owens tipped his cap and watched the patrol car drive away. "I sure hope that helps some, Dan," he said to himself.

The condition of the house, with its missing shingles, peeling paint, and weedy yard didn't surprise Becky. She knocked on the door, pulling it open when nobody came.

"Dan," she called. "It's Becky." She stepped in, finding the inside as disheveled as the outside. She called again and walked through the kitchen. Dishes filled the sink. On the table were the dried crust of a sandwich and a glass with orange juice pulp in the bottom. Becky went down the adjoining hall, past a bathroom and a bedroom with girl's clothes hanging in an opened closet. She tapped on the closed, third door before opening it.

"Dan?" She stepped into an empty bedroom. Empty Ball jars covered one side of a chest of drawers. Beside them were framed pictures of two young girls, Becky and Shiloh. A life insurance policy lay unfolded on the bed. She read it and caught herself genuinely worried about the man.

Shiloh woke to the sound of tires still humming beneath the metal floor her head lay on. Sleep had given her no break from the horror of it all. Her bound arms and legs cramped, but she kept still and silent, so as not to let the old man riding in the back with her know she was awake. He and his blood-splattered, orange jumpsuit scared her even more than the man driving. The things he'd said to her were worse than his slaps to her face. The man driving hadn't stopped it. He was insane, she'd decided. The old man was simply evil. Thoughts of Chris entered her mind and crushed her again. She felt a kick.

"Stop your blubbering. I'm getting tired of it. Any more and I'll wring your scrawny neck."

"Don't touch her anymore unless I say so."

The old man looked toward the front. "How much longer? Do you really know what you're doing?"

"Not long now. And, yes, I know perfectly what I'm doing. Be patient."

"And you're sure she'll come to us?"

He smiled and wondered if Becky Hawk had solved the first part of his riddle yet. Part of him wanted her to fail so the game could continue. However, his badly punctured arm was by then making it clear that it would all have to end that day. One way or another, his secret would soon be revealed. It made him happy that there was another one in the back who could take the Chief's place if need be. He turned on his walkie again, called for her, and listened. There was still nothing. But the old man in the back needed reassurance. "She'll come," he said.

"And bring half the police in the state with her. What made you think this would ever work?" Harrison eyed Shiloh. "To hell with your plans. If I can't have her, by God, her sister will do."

Shiloh yelled into the gag when Harrison's hand tugged on her hair.

"Leave her alone." The van slowed and the Luger pointed over the driver's seat. "I make the rules. You *will* follow them. I have not underestimated Becky Hawk. She'll find us. And she'll be alone because she knows not to underestimate me. Don't you either, old man. She won't let the girl die."

Harrison seethed. "What if you're wrong about it all?"

"Then the girl will be dispensable, and you may have your way with her."

There was something about the chuckle she heard from the old man that made it all impossibly worse. Shiloh jerked against the tape and cuffs, slinging her head side-to-side until her glasses flew away. If she couldn't escape this nightmare, at least she wouldn't have to see the faces.

She felt tearing uncertainty again when she walked back to her car. One thought told her to call for help. It was the only way to give Shiloh a chance. Another told her it was the worst thing she could do. No matter what, Becky knew her decision would haunt her forever if Shiloh died. She sat and thought for a minute before turning on the walkie.

"I'm here," she said. "Me only. Do you hear me?" She listened to dead air before turning the switch off and detecting the distant hum of highway traffic. She cranked the car and drove slowly toward it, anxiety growing, her eyes concentrating on every detail of the road and surrounding area. Farther down, tire tracks showed in the dirt. They went in and out of a soggy place beside the road. She stopped and walked to it.

The tracks had deteriorated but were still clear enough for Becky to see the familiar design of rain and snow treads. She scanned the road and surrounding woods. A distance from her, a piece of cloth waved in the breeze from the broken branch of a rhododendron bush. She walked to it and removed a torn piece of print material smudged with blood.

This was indeed where the hunt had begun. But what now? What good was this without knowing more? She walked back to her car in thought. This was a game she'd never win. He'd made it that way. Because tormenting her was his only game. It was time, she decided, to call for assistance. Local law enforcement would know the area and the people. They might have an idea of where to go from here.

Her hand was on the door handle of her car when she heard and then saw a blue pickup truck speeding toward her and throwing up a dust cloud. It slowed when it approached. The dust settled, and a young man's eyes locked on her with a hard expression while he rolled past.

"At the start of the hunt, the young jackals go before the experienced lion." It came to Becky along with what Dan had said about the last person to see Shiloh. "Stop. I need to talk to you," she said, sprinting to her car when the truck accelerated. Becky flipped on her blue light, spun the car around, and sped through dust thick enough to almost cause her to crash into the back of the truck when it slowed and turned into a drive.

The young man parked the truck near the house and strode toward the front porch without looking back.

Becky threw the car door open and slid out. "Stop."

He glanced over his shoulder as he walked into the house.

Becky walked up cautiously while loud voices came from the other side of the door. She felt a shot of adrenaline and ran back to her car, taking cover, and leveling her revolver at the man who'd burst out of the house carrying a shotgun. "Drop it!" she demanded.

He spit tobacco juice. "Who are you and what the hell do you want?"

"Becky Hawk of the Black Lake Police Department. I need to speak to your son."

"Dan Bowman's girl?"

Becky kept her revolver pointed. "Yes."

He cocked his head. "You're a long way from home, aren't you? What you need with Brant?"

"Dan told me he was the last to see my sister, Shiloh. Will you tell me your name?"

"Rylie Holbrook." He propped his shotgun against the wall. "You can put that gun away."

Becky holstered her revolver but stayed behind her car. "I don't have much time, Mr. Holbrook. I need to talk to him now."

"Just a minute," Rylie said before walking inside.

Sounds of a brief argument came from the house before they both returned. Brant struck an arms-crossed pose while boring a stare at Becky. "You want to talk to me?"

"Yes. Why didn't you stop when I asked you to?"

"Because I damned well didn't feel like it."

Becky faked a smile in an effort to soften him. She walked closer to the truck and snuck a peek at the tires before looking into the bed. A genuine smile played on her lips when she looked up. "Brant, you know Shiloh Bowman, right?"

He smirked. "Well, yeah. We've been neighbors since we were born. That don't mean I keep up with what she does. I already told her old man I saw her walking down the road with a bag. That's all I know. So, I'll be seeing ya." He turned to go inside.

"I believe it's best you don't go anywhere, Brant. I found a piece of a girl's torn dress back there with blood on it. There's also snow tire tracks made by a truck or van on the side of the road. Shiloh ran through the woods that day you saw her. One way or the other, you're going to cut your bullshit and tell me who she was running from."

Brant turned with a glare.

"You listen to me," Riley said. "I don't care if you are Dan's girl. You're not coming to my house and talking to my boy that way. Now, unless you have a warrant, I believe it's time to leave."

Becky moved aside grocery bags in the truck bed to expose the sacks beneath. "Did you know that I once was a mountain girl, Mr. Holbrook? It's been awhile, but I can still remember what fine moonshine yellow dent corn makes."

Rylie scowled. "It's also used for chicken feed."

"Where's the coop? I reckon you're also going to tell me you're planning on doing a lot of baking with this case of yeast."

Rylie spit his wad of tobacco out. His face was reddening.

"I didn't come here to cause you trouble," said Becky. "All I want is the truth from your son. I suggest you persuade him to tell it, all of it. Or you can most likely expect a visit from the alcohol tax department boys today."

Rylie looked at Brant. "If you know more, I'd say you'd better tell this lady now or get ready for a hide tanning."

Brant took the time to give Becky another hard stare. "Yeah, me and some of my buddies offered her a ride that day, but she didn't want it. I guess she got a little spooked and ran off."

Becky's face deadpanned. "Spooked over what?"

"Damned if I know. It don't take much with her."

"What about the tire tracks?"

"It was a black Chevy panel van. That weird guy from the funeral home was driving it, the one who preached at Grandmaw's funeral."

"Was he following her?"

"Hell, I don't know. But he drove away in the direction she ran."

Riley's eyes narrowed. "Why didn't you tell anybody all this before? Go inside and wait for me." He watched Brant do it before looking at Becky. "Vandenberg Funeral Home in town," he said. "Two sisters run it, Ruth and Rosa. Ruth's son is the one he was talking about. He does the embalming and preaches the services. I think his name is Carl. I can take you there if you want."

"No. I really don't want to pull you away from your father and son meeting. Just tell me how to get there."

CHAPTER 41

"Vandenberg Funeral Home." The sign stood in the well cared for yard of a white-columned, Victorian style house. With its size and elegance, the place stood out amongst the other homes in the neighborhood. Becky sat in her car and looked over an empty street. She then studied the upstairs and downstairs windows of the house, half expecting to see one of the tightly drawn curtains pull back.

She drove into the driveway and circled to the back of the house, studying the windows there also. Detecting no movement or sound, she stepped out of her car and used a loading ramp to walk onto a white-painted wraparound porch. No response came when she rang the bell to the back door. As she expected, it was locked. She walked to the front.

"Nobody is home, officer," an elderly man walking his small dog called from the road.

His voice made Becky jerk away from the "Closed Until Further Notice" sign on the front door.

The man tugged the leash and made a beeline toward the porch. "They like to travel. Been away for over a week now."

Becky knew nosey neighbors gave the best information and smiled at him. "Ruth and Rosa?"

"Yes." He stood beside the porch now, pulling the leash to contain his dog. "I hope there's no emergency."

"No. I just need to speak to someone who lives here. What about Carl?"

"I haven't seen him since Friday week. It was the same day I noticed that sign on the door. He was leaving in the service van that afternoon. I waved to him, but he didn't stop to speak. That's nothing unusual, though. Kind of kept to himself, he is."

"What kind of van was he in?"

"Black, of course. One of those without back windows.

"So, you know Carl well?"

"Why, yes. Ever since he was born. He's Ruth's. A good boy, only never has much to say. A fine undertaker. Makes the deceased look very natural and at rest. If you've ever lost a loved one, you know how much that means to the family. He's a minister also. Becomes a different man when he preaches a funeral and speaks long and eloquently. He did my wife's. There's no trouble, you say?"

"Nobody around since you saw him?"

"No one except for the men who cut the grass and trim the shrubbery." He stumbled when the dog jerked on the leash.

"Thank you," said Becky. "There's no trouble. It looks like your friend is ready to go." She waved as the dog more than less pulled the man away. She waited until they were far down the street before she walked to the back again, lifted a metal doorstop, and punched it through one of the three small windows on the door. She reached through the curtain and turned the door lock.

"*...where two sows lay.*"

That feeling of nervous dread Becky got when she knew she was about to discover something awful hit her. She held her revolver in front of her when she entered the house. "Police," she announced, peeping past another doorway that led to a hall. The sunlight that filtered through the curtains was enough for her to see the parlor at the other end of the house. She walked toward it, shifting her eyes to the doors she approached.

A chemical smell hovered in the air when she came to the first door. Becky pushed the door open and peered into an embalming room. She pinched her nose when the smell hit her full force. The room was ransacked. A brown glass jug with skull and crossbones on the label lay broken on the floor, its contents spread over the tile. Embalming fluid was Becky's guess. Drawers and cabinets stood open with mortician supplies on the floor. Makeup jars and wigs lay on the slab.

She opened the doors of the other rooms and looked inside each while carefully moving down the hallway. All appeared in order in those. But, past a curving staircase, she found a thoroughly ransacked office. Inside it, a pastoral painting lay on the floor beneath an open safe. Black and white photographs hung on the wall behind a desk that was disarranged with papers and files. Becky pointed her revolver toward the parlor and walked, again announcing her presence.

Finding the parlor untouched, she turned back with the intention of checking the upstairs rooms, but an unmistakable stench swept over her when she moved to the other side of the room. She turned and walked toward a soft light coming from a viewing room to her left. A funeral guest registration book on a podium had been placed in the hall outside. The one name in it was in bold, red letters: "*KAGE.*"

She pulled a breath and peeked inside the room before entering. A floor lamp with a pink shade glowed between two caskets. A single mum lay on the lid of each. She swatted at the flies hovering around her.

One hand held her revolver and the other pinched her nose. The smell and the flies left no doubt that she'd found where the "two sows" lay. There would be no need to look more—unless a clue as to where the "praying man" could be found was inside. She holstered her revolver while walking closer and then traced her hand around the lid of the first coffin. A latch clicked. She held her breath when she raised the lid.

Sounds of vehicles hurrying into the driveway entered the room. Becky looked toward the curtain-drawn window, and then down again at the back of a woman's swollen and discolored body. She waved at the converging swarm of flies and pinched her nose tighter while viewing a ligature mark around the woman's neck, darker than even the advanced putrefaction.

There came banging then breaking at the front door. "State Bureau of Investigation!" was shouted before the door broke open. Four agents with guns drawn entered, Aaron being the last in.

CHAPTER 42

Becky cleared access to the now needed loading ramp in back by moving her car to the front of the funeral home. She waited in the driveway with Aaron while they watched the lead agent tape a copy of his search warrant to the front door of the house. He then turned and marched straight to her with something between a frown and a snarl on his face.

"You need to be honest with this guy, Beck," Aaron whispered. "He's the no-bullshit type."

The lead agent walked up too close for Becky's comfort. "Once more, why are you here?" he asked, his red cheeks contrasting his short cropped, blonde hair.

She leaned against her car, looked at Aaron, and then back at the agent. "Would you be kind enough to give me your name?" she asked.

"Collins. Mack Collins. Now answer me. Explain why you're three hundred miles outside your jurisdiction and at a murder scene with no search warrant."

Aaron stepped forward. "Sarge, the man who did this also has committed murders in Black Lake. Chief Hawk must've had some exigent circumstances to have come here and executed her own warrantless search."

"You want to let her answer my questions, Aaron? I want to know exactly why you're here."

Becky ached to spill the truth, but her gut told her it would seal Shiloh's fate. There was much, however, she felt Collins needed to know now. "I was doing my own investigation," she said. "Aaron can tell you it's been my theory that there's a person from this town who's left those bodies on the interstate. He's the same one who murdered two women in my town and the two inside. And there's more." She pointed toward the high, jagged crests to the north. "There's more of them up there somewhere. They were his first, before the interstate gave him a bigger hunting ground. He's been killing for a long time."

"So, for God's sake, why didn't you organize it with us, lady. We have a double murder inside there and now the scene could very well be contaminated."

"I didn't touch anything other than the coffin lid and a few doorknobs."

Collins blew a breath. "You broke in without a warrant. That's a criminal act. Anything we find in there is prone to be questioned now. How do we know you didn't alter or plant something? How's a jury to know differently after we make an arrest?"

"Because her credibility has been established in her two years as a police chief," Aaron said.

"Dammit, I'm talking to her." He looked at Becky. "Do you realize how complicated you've made things now?"

"I don't blame you for being mad," Becky said. "I'm sorry."

"Sorry ain't good enough. Aaron, I want you to stay right here with her. If she tries to leave, arrest her for B&E and tampering with evidence." He walked away and looked back. "You and I are having a long talk later, lady."

Aaron stepped over. "Geeze, Becky, you've sure knocked over a hornets' nest this time. Sheriff Donaldson called, wondering if we knew where you were. Wendy and Bobby are worried out of their minds. I know you well enough to know you had a good reason for coming here. Why don't you tell me why?"

"I'm sorry I caused so many problems."

"Why are you here? Why didn't you tell anyone?"

"I'd like to know why you guys showed up first."

Aaron's face dropped. "Oh, hell. You don't know yet."

"No. Tell me."

Aaron leaned against the car with her. "Papa Tolly escaped on his way to court this morning. It was planned. Someone sawed a hole in a service station bathroom wall and left it barely in place. All Papa had to do was push it out. Curt was guarding him. His throat was cut. I'm sorry. He's dead."

Becky winced, dropped to her knees as if punched, and covered her eyes. "Holy shit!" Her wail made onlookers on the street turn. "Curt! My God! This hell doesn't end." Tears rolled from under her hands.

Aaron knelt beside her and rubbed her shoulder. "Sorry, Beck. He was a good guy. I know it's a tough blow for you." He reached into his jacket and found a cigarette pack. "Seems to get that bad smell out of my nose at scenes like this," he explained.

Becky wiped her eyes and nose. "I could use one for sure," she said with a heavy voice.

Aaron lit it for her. "Put it in the car ashtray when you're done. Let's not piss off Sarge more by leaving our butts on the crime scene." He flashed a slight grin. "Anyway, Papa had a visitor at the prison yesterday, a Reverend Carlton Marcus Vandenberg, using this address as his residence. He's Ruth Vandenberg's thirty-three year old son.

Someone reported seeing a black van speeding away in the area where Papa escaped. The tag is registered to this business. It looks like we've taken a big step toward solving a bunch of murders and preventing more. Sarge is only pissed because he doesn't want any issues after we nail Vandenberg. It would help if you'd give a good explanation as to why you came here alone."

Becky's mind began clearing from shock. "So, this Vandenberg guy was behind Papa's escape?"

"We don't know for sure, but I'll bet when we find Vandenberg we find Papa."

"Why would he help Tolly escape?" Becky asked it more to herself than Aaron. Her reddened eyes darted side to side while the reality of the situation came to her.

Aaron stood when she did. "I have no idea why he would help him escape. Any theories?" He grimaced when she tossed her cigarette.

Becky squeezed Aaron's shirt desperately. "Listen to me. With all we've been through, you trust me, don't you?" she asked.

"Yeah. You know I do."

"Then please, please don't ask me questions. Just listen. There's a good reason I came here on my own. I can't explain it to you now, but I have got to get back inside that house. Trust me, it's important. There's something there he wants only me to find."

"Who? Carl Vandenberg?"

"Probably. I'm not sure yet. But there's something inside there that I need to find and quick. You've got to work it out so I can go back in. Just tell them I want a guided tour. I promise I won't touch anything. You said you trust me."

"But I also wish you'd tell me what the hell you're talking about."

"Please, Aaron."

He nodded. "You know I'm going to get my ass chewed," he said. "But I'll see if I can clear it. Just pick up your cigarette and don't move from this spot."

From inside her car, Becky watched county deputies arrive with lights flashing. Two of them rolled crime scene tape around the yard. It drew out more onlookers to the sidewalk.

The elderly man who'd walked his dog earlier came to the car window, looking aghast. "What's happened? Are Ruth and Rosa alright?"

"I'm sorry, but I don't think so," Becky said.

"Oh, dear. Oh, dear. Was it an accident?"

"May I ask you a question?" Becky asked. "Are you sure it was Carl Vandenberg you saw leaving in the van that Friday afternoon?"

"Yes, quite sure."

"You couldn't have been mistaken?"

He rubbed his hand through his thinning gray hair. "No. I don't think so. I'd recognize Carl anywhere."

"Thank you. I'm sorry about your neighbors."

"Quite sure," he mumbled to himself while walking away. "Yes, quite sure."

Becky watched an agent with a notepad and pen approach the gathering of neighbors. She kept an eye on him while she reached down, flicked on the walkie, and extended the antenna. "I'm here," she said into it. "Give me time. Do you hear me? Give me just a little time." She heard only dead air. "Are you listening?"

A faint, staticky voice came. Becky twisted up the volume. The voice crackled again, too weak to understand. "Please," she said. "Don't hurt her. And don't let *him* hurt her. Please, don't let him near her. I'm following your rules. I swear I am. Tell me where your final clue is so I can find you. Nobody else will know."

Garbled words came through the static. "Time is waning."

Becky threw open the car door and walked to the agent taking notes. "I need to speak with Aaron right now," she said.

He didn't look up. "We're very busy. Go back to your car and wait. Someone will talk to you when we can."

Becky barely checked her anger. "Agent, in case you haven't noticed, I'm wearing a badge too. I've had two murders in my jurisdiction and lost an officer just this morning because of this man. I'd appreciate a little professional courtesy here."

He wrote a few moments more before looking at her unfazed. "Go back to your car. As soon as I'm through here, I'll see if Agent Powers has a minute."

She stood outside her car while plain clothes detectives arrived. An ambulance parked at the roadside and waited. Becky looked at her watch. It had been ten minutes since the agent walked back inside, the limit she'd decided to wait. A deputy held up his hand when she approached the crime scene tape.

"Hold on, lady," he said.

"I'm not a lady. I'm a police chief. Get out of my way."

He started to speak again, but Becky's look froze him as she strode past.

She was on the front porch when Aaron stepped out and looked exasperated. "I told you to stay in the car, for goodness' sake," he said. "They Ok'd your doing a walk-through. But only if you stay by my side and don't touch anything. Those are my orders, Beck. Please follow them and don't get me in trouble."

"Fine. Let's go."

He handed her a handkerchief. "Better hold this over your nose. It's worse in there now."

The handkerchief only helped some when they walked into the parlor. Both lids of the caskets in the viewing room stood open while detectives dusted them for prints. The flies now concentrated on two body bags on the floor. The chatter of the deputies and agents quietened when Becky and Aaron passed.

Sergeant Collins stepped up with a tightened jaw. "She's got five minutes," he told Aaron. "If she touches anything, escort her back out and detain her."

Becky saw the red in Aaron's cheeks. "Thank you, Sergeant," she said. "I promise I'll stay close to Agent Powers and not cause you any more trouble."

"He's a jerk," Aaron whispered when they stepped away.

Becky's eyes darted over every detail they passed.

"...you will be led to a praying man."

"Never mind that. Just show me around and tell me what you know about this place and these people."

"We're still piecing it together. We have a BOLO out for Carl Vandenberg and the black Chevy panel van."

Becky remembered Kage's threat to exit this world and take Shiloh with him if any other law enforcement came for him. "Tell me the rest." She walked with Aaron down the hall and listened.

"The victims are Ruth Vandenberg, fifty-six, and Rosa Vandenberg, fifty-four. Their mother died when they were young. Their father raised them in this house before it was a funeral home. They and Carl still lived upstairs. It looks like they've been dead for at least a week, probably since the morning the neighbor saw Carl leaving." He led

Becky to a kitchen in an expanded part of the house. "Ruth appears to have a single bullet wound in the back of her head. Looks like she was shot in here while she was cooking breakfast. I guess you can see why that's our theory."

Becky looked at mildewed eggs and bacon in a skillet and a blood splatter on the wall above the stove.

"So, one head shot to his own mother," Aaron said. "After that, he goes upstairs and chokes Rosa to death while she's still in bed. We found the garrote he used beside the bed. It looks like she put up a heck of a struggle. Want to go up and have a look?"

"Show me around the rest of the first floor first."

"Not much else to see down here, other than the bodies and blood smears where he drug Ruth to the casket room to prepare her and Rosa for the last service this funeral home will ever have."

They walked down the hall. "It's weird," Aaron said. "The wall safe is open and empty and the office is ransacked, kind of a mixture of robbery and passion killing MOs."

"Any life insurance policies?"

"Yeah. Big ones. Both sisters were each other's primary beneficiaries. Carl was secondary for both. That would've given him motive to have staged a robbery gone bad, but why put the bodies in coffins then take off in the van?"

"Not your normal crime," Becky said. She followed Aaron into the office area. Books and files lay strewn on a desk and floor.

Aaron led her to the pictures behind the desk. "I agree. But we're dealing with a homicidal maniac here, so nothing is going to be normal. We don't know what finally pushed him to kill his mother and aunt. The neighbors say Ruth was very controlling over Carl. Even when he was a kid, she planned on him being a part of the business. She sent him to mortuary school right after he graduated high school, and then to seminary college. She wanted him to do both the embalming and perform the services. This business and his mother and aunt became his life. They say he hardly ever dated because Ruth was so critical of any girl he met. Maybe all that together is the childhood trauma you were talking about."

Becky stepped to the desk and looked at the wall behind it. On either side of a large photograph of their mother and father, the Vandenberg sisters with pompadour hairstyles in their younger years smiled from individual, oval-shaped frames. Becky walked around for a close look at the one under these. The sisters, older then, stood and smiled in front of the funeral home with Carl, looking gloomy in his white, short-sleeve shirt and black tie, standing between them. "What else do you know about them?"

"According to what we've learned, their father was some big-time broker who moved the family here from New York. The Vandenbergs became a prominent family back in the heyday of this town. Rosa never married. Ruth married a Finnish man in the early-thirties. He left town a few years after Carl was born and never came back. Nobody we've talked to knows why. We're still trying to piece it all together."

Becky stepped closer to Carl's image. His eyes were light in the black and white photograph, but she didn't doubt the true color was icy blue. They were piercing, the same as the mime's at the festival. "Strange," she said.

"Yeah, the whole damned thing is strange."

"So, it was Ruth who was shot once in the back of the head, and Rosa who was strangled with a garrote?"

"Yes."

"How was Ruth placed in the casket?"

"Face up."

"And Rosa face down."

"Well, yeah, but I imagine he wasn't too concerned about how they were positioned. Probably just wanted to do it as fast as possible then leave."

"But he took the time to ransack the embalming room and this office. It's like there were things in particular he was looking for. Why would Carl do that? It seems he would've known where everything is."

"I don't know. But how do you explain the combination safe open and empty and Carl and the van gone? The guard at Central Prison matched the face of Papa's visitor to the picture on Carl's ID card. Don't make this complicated, Becky. Carl is Kage."

I'm just wondering why Rosa was strangled. Why did he take the time to choke her to death with a garrott when he could've just shot her like Ruth? That and the fact that he placed her face down makes me believe his anger was directed mainly on her. You guys could have this wrong."

Aaron stepped beside her. "You mean the motive?"

"I mean everything. The person who wrote the letter to me was left-handed. Take a look at Carl there. His watch is on his left wrist. It's hard to tell, but it also looks like his belt is looped from the right side. That's what you'd expect from a right-handed person."

"I'd really love to know why you think the person who wrote that letter is left-handed."

"Your wife told me. I let her read his letter. She picked it up from the handwriting." Becky glanced over the desk while Aaron stepped closer to the picture and studied it.

"EXPENSES 1965." It was written across the top of the first notebook in a pile. They lay neatly on the corner of the desk, away from the jumbled things.

"I'm an expense to this world. Always have been…"

"Look real close and see if you can tell how his belt is looped in the picture," Becky said. She flipped open the first notebook. The funeral home had paid out little in the month of January that year. Fuel oil, electricity, and water payments were there as well as a two hundred dollar payment to the Bethel Casket Company. The last payment that month was a hundred dollars to a Nellie Hager. She peeked at Aaron and flipped to the February page. Nellie Hager's name was the last there too, as well as March, April, and May. Becky slipped her hand away when Aaron turned.

"Yeah, it does look like it's looped from the right," he said. "But that doesn't mean anything. There's lots of people who write left-handed and do other things right-handed. And, who knows why he shot Ruth and strangled Rosa. We can't get inside the mind of a crazy man."

Becky smiled. "Yeah, you're right. Sorry. I *am* making it more complicated than it is. Thanks for letting me look around."

"I thought you said he'd left something for you. Would you mind telling me what?"

"I guess I was wrong. I believe I'll step outside now. This smell is getting to me."

"Yeah, sure. We'll talk more when we're done here. I'll call Wendy so she and Bobby will know you're alright."

Becky walked toward the door. "Hey, Aaron," she said over her shoulder. "Make sure you tell them I love them. There's letters for you guys back home." She trotted to her car and sped away with Aaron waving her back in the rearview mirror.

Far up the street, a black van slipped away from behind a vacant house.

CHAPTER 43

Dan felt a pulsing pain in his head when he woke. That, and a rising burn in his belly prevented him from sleeping more. He flinched at the sunlight when he opened his eyes and sat up. It took him a few moments to remember where he was and why he'd woken so extraordinarily sick. The pint jars, one empty, one on its side with the remaining liquor dripping out, reminded him. He reached into his bag, found the canteen of water he'd brought, and turned it back to relieve his dry mouth. He then rolled over and retched.

A breeze had broken the heat that day. The sky was cloudless. There was a time when he'd loved days like this, the days spent on secret trout streams known to only him and a few school buddies. They'd stand in the cool water and leave their hooks in even when the fish weren't biting. They talked about everything. Dan had learned his friends' dreams and ambitions early. Few of them would be realized, but it didn't matter then. Life was young. Anything was possible.

The memory made him sad. He wiped his mouth, picked up the empty jar, and scowled at it. With a frustrated yell, his arm swung, and the jar sailed over the rocks of the cliff. He staggered to his feet and paced around until his legs steadied him. His belly squeezed again, forcing him to bend over and dry heave. When the convulsions stopped, he stood with defeat in his reddened eyes.

But determination was there too as he walked toward the giant rocks of Overlook Hang. He took a few deep breaths, feeling his stomach rise with his steps out onto the rocks. He stopped to balance himself and looked to the sky.

"I tried," he said. "But I'm tired now. I'm so very tired. You know… some things can't be changed. Some of us aren't strong. I hope you understand. Please do."

He took five more hesitant steps out and felt the downward pull. Three more took him past the trees and bushes around him. His feet slid toward the steepest part of the slope, but he managed to catch his balance for a moment to look at an unobstructed view, glorious enough for him to stand there and take it in. On that clear day, the panorama of mountain ridges appeared to roll forever. Details far away came sharp enough to amaze even a man who'd spent his entire life in the mountains. It was *his* view, he realized. Nobody else would've ever had the courage to stand there. He felt thankful for this final gift.

One more step, he thought. One more, before a short slide. It'll be quick. Then—rest. He looked at the view once more, and his hand came up to shade his eyes.

In his life, Dan had worked many manual labor jobs. One of the first had been with a logging company. The job had given him a detailed knowledge of the surrounding mountain terrain. He recognized the trail that he saw on the next ridge as one he'd once driven teams of mules on. They'd been used to drag the logs down, because the grade was too steep for trucks. That's why his concentration stayed locked on a black van attempting the impossible climb. He stepped back and watched longer.

The van crept higher. It spun side to side as the driver attempted to find traction for the tires. Dust clouds rose each time the van rolled backward and lurched forward less than the distance it had lost. It did this several times before sliding one last time and stopping at an angle on the trail.

Dan squinted when the backdoor of the van opened. A man exited with someone in his arms, a girl wearing a familiar dress. He saw she was tied. She fought with the man when he slung her over his shoulder and carried her up the trail.

"Holy hell," Dan said.

The man and girl disappeared from the view of the cliff when they moved amongst the trees. But Dan didn't see that. He was crawling as fast as he could back up the rocks.

CHAPTER 44

The postmaster in Millpark had been reluctant to give Becky the information she'd asked for, but her uniform and badge, along with the advice "You really don't want to piss me off," had persuaded him.

Her search for the address he'd given her on route three took her outside the town limits and onto a narrow road that wound over and around a fast-flowing, whitewater river. Homes and small farms dotted the wilderness area she found herself in. Becky slowed in front of each one she passed, looking for box one-eleven. Finding it was proving more difficult than the postmaster's directions had seemed. The road twisted up a mountain. Homes became even fewer and the terrain more rugged. She wondered if she'd missed a turn after the road narrowed more and turned from asphalt to dirt with deep erosion.

She tightened her grip on the wheel when a rolling view of Millpark and all the valley it rested in opened to the left of the road. Conspicuously absent were guardrails for vehicles that veered more than the few feet the shoulder allowed. Certain now that she'd misdirected onto something more a trail than a road, Becky mumbled tight curses while searching for some turnaround room and receiving none from a rocky wall to her right and the dropoff to her left. It was more than a mile farther when the road leveled but with an impossibly steep climb looming ahead.

A rusty mailbox before the hill with "111" painted crudely on it seemed out of place enough to remind Becky of a *Twilight Zone* episode. The erosion of the road compared nothing to that of the driveway she turned onto. A cracked oil pan seemed more likely than not while the car bounced up the drive.

Hound dogs ran up to meet her, howling in their deep way, at the small, clapboard-sided house she arrived at. Two dilapidated buildings, overgrown with briar vines and honeysuckle, crumpled at the edge of the yard. There was a chicken coop with a dust covered pickup truck parked amongst the trees behind it. A woman with an apron and gray hair in a scarf stopped gathering clothes from a line and gawked.

Becky stepped from her car with her palms sweaty from the drive. "Ma'am?"

With that word, the woman jerked the remaining clothes from the line and strode toward the house.

"I'm Becky Hawk, chief of police from Black Lake. I need to talk to you." Becky stamped her foot at one of the hounds when a growl rolled from him.

"I don't know you," the woman said, not slowing down.

"I know that, but we've got to talk." Becky shooed the dogs back again and kept a watch on them while jogging after the woman.

"I don't like folks just showing up here," the woman said over her shoulder. "Especially ones in uniforms from places I don't know about."

"You're Nellie Hager, right?"

She turned with a scowl at the front door steps. "How do you know me?"

"Your name was written in a notebook inside Vandenberg Funeral Home. I need to know why they were paying you a hundred dollars a month."

The scowl dropped to a startled stare. Nellie's eyes darted around before she turned and finished her walk up the steps, closing the door behind her. Becky shoved it open while Nellie was trying to lock it.

Nellie dropped the clothes basket and backed up. "What is this all about?" she asked, more fear than anger flashing in her eyes.

Becky stepped in and bent down. She lifted a pair of men's jeans from the basket then dropped them back. "You know what it's about, Nellie. But, maybe you don't know that Ruth and Rosa Vandenberg were found dead today. He murdered them. Very soon, he'll kill my little sister too if I don't stop him. He knows his time is short now. I expect it won't be long before he comes for you too. So, you're going to tell me who he is and where I can find him."

Nellie's face had paled. She stood silent with every bit of the whites of her eyes showing. Becky knew for certain then that the story she needed to know was behind those eyes.

"Are you telling the truth?" Nellie asked. "He killed them both?"

"Yes. Why were they paying you?"

Nellie rubbed her hand over her mouth and turned away. "I don't know," she muttered. "I shouldn't... I really shouldn't."

"Tell me, Nellie."

She turned back to Becky and in a loud, scared voice, "What are you going to do if I don't tell you?"

"As I said, my sister will die if you don't. So, take a guess."

Nellie walked to a worn out, blanket-covered sofa, shooed a cat away, and sat down. She stared past Becky in thought. A tremble came to her. "Did he kill Carl too?"

Becky shut the door behind her. She took a glance at the hall to her left and the kitchen to her right. Her hand rested on the butt of her revolver. "I don't know. Probably. Who is he?" She waited. "Nellie?"

Nellie pulled a breath. Her hands played with the clothes pins in her apron. She started to speak twice. Then, in a voice deep and trembling: "He never had a given name. My grandpa used to call him Johnny. We took him in just after he was born. He's Rosa's."

"I'm guessing she had him out of wedlock." Becky kept a close eye on the hallway.

"Don't worry, he's not here," Nellie said. "I haven't seen him in over a week." She sighed. "Yes, it was out of wedlock, only worse. That's why they paid me to take him."

Becky felt confident in her suspicion and wanted to make it easier for Nellie. "Ruth's husband was the father. Am I right?"

Nellie nodded without eye contact. "Yes. His name was Edvin. From Finland, I heard. Handsome with the lightest blue eyes you'll ever see, the same as with Carl and the other boy. Both boys are nearly like twins. Ruth kicked Edvin out when she found out. It took her years, but she finally forgave Rosa."

"How did you get involved?"

"I went to school with them—graduated with Rosa. I guess it was because my grandpa and I lived so far away from town, or maybe they just knew I would keep their secret. They offered to pay me to keep him. I just had to promise to never tell anyone. The Vandenbergs were always the most well-to-do family around here. It would've been too much a stain on their name. Rosa never left the house after she began showing. She even tried killing him while he was in her womb, and almost killed herself doing it. They called me to the house to take him the minute he was born. There never was a birth certificate. Grandpa lived here with us until he died. Believe me, we tried raising that boy right. We really did. Grandpa taught him to read and write and did things with him. But he was just bad, just bad. I saw it early on."

"When did he start killing people?"

"I never knew about that for sure," Nellie said. "But I surely suspected it. After Grandpa died and the boy became old enough to start wondering, he started asking questions—who I was and why he was with me. I couldn't tell him a lie that he'd believe, so I finally broke down and just told him the truth. That's when he went from bad to horrible. I'd find my dogs and chickens killed. I won't tell you the things he did to them, but it showed me just how wicked he was. He'd get mad and scream at me. He even choked me with his hands once until I passed out. The strange thing was, I think he enjoyed it. He'd disappear into the mountains for days or weeks. I was glad when he did. There's caves up there. The dirt and clay on his clothes when he came back told me that's where he'd likely been staying. Later on, he taught himself to drive Grandpa's old pickup. He'd come by and take it, sometimes for a day or two. Sometimes I'd find pieces of women's jewelry or clothes in his room after he came back. I never asked questions. I was afraid to. I really didn't want to know no way."

"Where is he now?"

"I don't know."

"Where do you think he is?"

"If he brought your sister here alive, I reckon he took her up to the high woods. But you'll never find him there. There's so many caves and other hiding places he knows of."

"He wants me to find him," Becky said. "He told me a praying man would lead me to him. Who would he mean by that?"

Nellie looked genuinely confused. "I don't know. Maybe he meant Ruth's son, Carl. He's the only preacher I know. There's one church left in Millpark, but I've never been to it."

Becky looked at her watch and tugged her ponytail. "Please, think hard. There's a reason he wanted me to find you."

Nellie shook her head. "I don't know. I just don't…" She looked up before standing. "Wait. Come with me."

Becky followed her down the hall and stopped at the darkened bedroom Nellie entered. She stepped in when a light came on. The smell reminded her of trash cans in the summer. Blankets cloaked the windows. Clothes hung from opened dresser drawers. Some of the many books there lay haphazardly on shelves. The rest lay strewn over the floor amongst a maze of newspapers piled halfway up the walls.

"This is his room when he's here," said Nellie. "Only Carl visits him. He brings him the books and newspapers and sometimes a little money. When it's cold out, he'll stay here with the door closed for weeks, reading and not coming out except to walk around some and use the bathroom. I'll leave his food outside the room but never bother him. He'll leave without speaking and use Grandpa's truck without asking." She moved aside a pile of books blocking the wall on top of the dresser. "Could this be what he meant?"

Becky knew instantly it was.

The photograph hanging in a frame showed a man with white hair and a beard giving thanks over a loaf of bread, bowl, and Bible. Becky had seen it before. Her mother had kept a print of Eric Enstrom's "Grace," on her dining room wall.

Becky didn't wait for Nellie to give her permission to walk over and remove the picture from the wall. She reached into a tear in the brown paper on the back and pulled out folded notepaper. Nellie moved close when Becky opened it and read:

> *Respectful greetings.*
>
> *You must be a remarkable individual. As I write this, I wonder if you exist or not. If you do, I wish I could see your face and know about you now. If you are reading this, it means I've found you and discovered you to be unique and worthy enough to participate in my final endeavor. It also probably means that I'm in possession of someone of great importance to you, someone you are willing to give your life for. I'm sure that you understand by now that is what you must do. But don't fret. We're only spirits drifting through this world anyway. Now our names together will be synonymous with virtue and darkness. I'm happy they'll be mentioned in the same breath. But you must feel hurried now. So go to Wildcat Trail, just up the road from where you are. As I'm sure I've already instructed you, come alone or the tragedy you fear will become reality.*
>
> *See you soon—*
>
> *Kage.*

Nellie looked up. "It's an old logging trail, about half a mile up the road on the left. You'll have to walk it."

Becky dropped the note. "Thank you."

"Kill him," Nellie said. "Kill him. Please."

CHAPTER 45

He waited in concealment and watched with a pair of the Vandenberg's binoculars. Blood dripped from his bandage again. His struggles taking the girl and the old man into the cave had aggravated his wound and further weakened him, but he felt the energy renewed when he saw Becky Hawk laboring up the old logging road. She carried the walkie. Her sidearm came out when she approached and inspected the van. He roamed the binoculars farther down the road and felt satisfied that she was alone.

He savored the feel of it all coming together. Chance no longer played a part in his plans. The satisfaction of being in total control now surpassed all the other times. He was glad it would end this way for him. He'd do it where his bones wouldn't be found. He'd escape the world while leaving behind uncertainty and fear. The name Kage would haunt the mountains forever.

He crouched down more between the rocks and watched her approach the trail, waiting until she was there before lifting his walkie. "You'll need to toss the gun, Chief," he said and smiled when her head jerked upward.

The clarity of his transmission told her he was close. She took cover behind a tree and pointed her revolver up the trail. The walkie crackled again.

"Step out where I can see you. Follow my instructions precisely or your precious sister will die."

"Ok," she said, carefully stepping out and looking up the trail in hopes to get a good enough view of him to snap off a shot. "Do you see me?" she asked into the walkie.

"Yes. Now, about your gun."

Becky bent to lay it down.

"No. Toss it into the gully to your right. I want to be sure you don't make the mistake of coming back for it."

A colder fear gripped Becky while she kept searching for him.

"Now, Chief Hawk."

She threw her revolver and heard it crash into brush.

"Very good. You may proceed now. The walk here takes five minutes. That's what you have."

The trail narrowed and became a steep and difficult climb. Becky grabbed saplings and vines to pull her way along. She realized fully the desperation of her situation. Her mind scrambled. She wondered if Shiloh was even still alive. If so, would he keep his word and release her. A numbing fright settled on her when the trail leveled and she came upon a clearing at the base of an even steeper hill. A chalk scribbling over a crevice between rocks invited her to *"Come Inside."*

Becky looked around. "Where are you?" she asked into the walkie. Blood drops trailed up sloping rocks to the crevice. She climbed there and looked into the darkness. Cool air emitted. She racked her brain for a plan, but there was none. Her five minutes were up.

Against every survival instinct, every fear within her, she dropped the walkie, pushed herself between the rocks, and crawled. For a moment, she became lodged and thought it was one of his evil tricks to trap her there for eternity. She managed to move some and pushed on. The space soon widened, and she crawled out into a cooler place where the only light came from the opening behind her.

The cave was deep. She knew that from the sounds of water dripping near and far. "I'm here," she said.

"Glad you made it." The proximity of the voice startled her. "Walk toward us now." A light began weak and brightened.

Becky heard weeping as she walked. She detected two figures ahead. A lantern lay beside them. She stopped to allow her eyes to adjust. As details focused, she saw a young face that evoked memories of her younger years, the years before she'd met Ed and had been uncertain of her future. The man sneering a smile behind that fear-stricken face bore striking similarities to the picture of Carl Vandenbreg.

"Outstanding job, Chief," Kage said. "I knew you had it in you. It's so good to finally meet you face to face." He pulled Shiloh close and brushed her hair with the pistol while smiling at Becky. "This has been a most trying experience for her. I believe you'd agree that she appears more than ready to part my company."

Becky walked closer. "Are you hurt?"

Shiloh shook her head.

"Ok, I'm here," Becky told him. "Just like you wanted. Now let her go."

"Just as soon as you do me a small favor." He reached into his pocket and tossed Becky's handcuffs. They clattered beside her feet. "Thanks for letting me borrow them. Please pick them up and secure your hands behind your back."

"I'm not doing anything until you let her go." She saw the icy eyes flash with a grin under them.

"Then, I suppose you made your long trip for nothing."

Shiloh whimpered when he pressed the silencer tight against her left temple.

"Wait," Becky said. She bent down and picked up the cuffs.

"Very good. Now, do as I said."

Becky clicked a cuff onto her left wrist, leaving it as loose as possible. She placed her hands behind her back and clicked on the right in the same manner. "Let her leave," she said, nearly certain both she and Shiloh were about to die.

Kage nodded. "Tighten them first. Let me hear the clicks."

Becky locked her eyes on him with a look of disdain. She worked her hands and squeezed the cuffs down.

"Excellent," he said, lowering the pistol. He shoved Shiloh forward. "Now, walk toward me, Chief. This young lady will take a step with each one you make. Once you're to me. She is free to go her merry way." He raised the pistol again. "But if my instructions aren't followed, I will fire a round into the back of her head."

They both walked. Shiloh's eyes appeared lost, darting around while not focusing on anything. Becky remembered the missing glasses.

"Becky?" Shiloh said when they met.

Becky took a moment to look at her young sister's face. "Run straight ahead, Shiloh," she said. "When you see sunlight, go to it. The place in the rocks is narrow, but you can crawl through. Turn to your right when you get out and go down the trail. You'll find a road. Run down it. Someone will find you."

Shiloh hitched a breath. "No. I don't want to leave you here."

Becky took another step. "Go," she said. "Do it now."

The lantern made tears in Shiloh's eyes shine while she took steps. "Becky, I—"

"Run!" Becky said, moving herself directly in front of the pistol.

Kage smiled. "Yes, Run. Run and tell them about me. Tell them all about Kage. Send them here to see for themselves."

Becky listened to the echo of Shiloh's feet falling as she stared at the silencer and walked forward. She noticed that the gun was a Luger. She also noticed the blood leaking bandage. "That's a bad wound," she said. "You won't last long bleeding that way. The real hell will begin when gangrene sets in. End this silly game now. I'll get you help while you can still be helped." She saw by his expression that her attempt had failed.

"Remember my second letter to you?" he asked. "I used the word respectfully when I signed it. I still mean it. So, I'll see that this goes quickly and painlessly." He picked up the lantern and stepped aside. "After you. There's someone you know waiting all in a twitter to see you."

Becky walked down the slick, steep slope of the cave. She tugged on the cuffs and, finding them too tight to slip, fought against growing panic. Ahead, to her left, she saw a glow coming from the cave wall and felt the silencer press between her shoulders.

"Keep walking. Turn where the light is." It was a hiss in her ear.

Becky did as he said and stepped into the space. She smelled decomposition again. Her eyes were drawn to a part of the cave room blazing with light. She froze and gasped, knowing she'd found the others.

An ensemble of skeletonized remains, at least double the number of missing Aaron had told her about, dangled in poses on an elevated platform of limestone. Cords tied to shining stalactites above held them like puppets in a macabre show. Lanterns burning at full flame surrounded their stage and cast their shadows on the wall behind them. They stared at her with dark eye orifices. Stained garments hung on some, only shards of cloth on others. There were vases of dried mums around them. Carl Vandenberg was there too. He sat tilted forward on the edge with a dark hole on his forehead. On the wall above it all, in letters the same color as Carl's wound, *"KAGE'S HELL"* was written.

Becky turned. "And this is what you want them to find. This is how you want to be remembered. For the love of God, how did you become this sick?"

"Love is something I know nothing about," he said. "I was born an abomination, so I chose to live as an abomination. This world gets what it gives." He took her arm and turned her.

On the darker side of the alcove, his jumpsuit smeared with clay and sprayed with Curt's blood, Papa Tolly sat atop another rock slab. A press of the Luger against the back of her head directed Becky toward him. Closer, the glow of the lanterns and Papa's sneer intensified his deep wrinkles.

"Kneel," Kage told her.

She looked at the man who'd killed her husband and felt her hatred of him return fully. "No," she said, and then fought against the hands on her shoulders before falling to her knees.

The sneer spread wider, showing stumps of browned teeth. Papa's eyes glinted while he looked down at her. Becky jerked back when he spit on her.

"You have no idea," he said, "how often I've wished for this." His words came slow and euphorically. "You could never imagine the things I've done to you in my dreams. I couldn't possibly describe them all. Just let me say, it will be a joy blowing your brains out—just as I did your husband's." He reached and took the pistol Kage handed to him.

CHAPTER 46

His lungs burned. His legs refused to move anymore without rest. Dan fell to his knees on the forest floor, heaving for air. It was his fifth stop, and it angered him that his body tired so quickly. He spat phlegm and looked for the old logging road. He wondered if his sense of direction had been thrown off during his descent from the mountain and run across the gorge. Once he could've navigated to any spot in the hills without thinking, but that had been decades ago. He felt no confidence now, only desperation. When his legs felt like they could carry him again, he was up walking and grabbing trees for balance while he slogged up another hill.

The landscape leveled with soft grass underfoot. Somewhere near, a grouse broke cover and took flight. It blurred past him. Wondering what had flushed it, he turned and heard her feet running before he saw her. She screeched when she neared him and turned direction.

"Shiloh," he yelled, chasing her. He saw she was panicked, and her pace was too fast for him. He yelled her name again. "It's me— Daddy."

She stopped and turned. Apprehension showed on her face while he walked to her.

"It's me," he said again, forgetting the circumstances, only relishing the pure joy of seeing her face again. He embraced her and felt her trembling while she cried against his chest. His hand stroked her hair. He didn't want to let go but realized there was something he had to do. He pulled back and looked into her face. "Where is he?" he asked.

"One shot between the eyes," Kage told Papa. "I promised her it would be quick." He stepped back to enjoy this final destiny he'd created, happy he felt so powerful on his last day.

"I don't care what she was promised," said Papa. "If I was able anymore," he told Becky, "I would—"

"One shot," Kage said. "She upheld her end. I will mine."

Becky tugged her hands on the cuffs again, this time digging the metal into her flesh. No use. They were too tight. She was out of ideas. A look at Kage and Papa told her their minds couldn't be changed. She glanced around the cave and toward the previous victims seemingly watching the show by the flickering light. Such a terrible place to die, she thought, far below ground and at *their* hands. She wondered if she would be found. If so, it would undoubtedly be in a pose to Kage's liking as the latest addition in the display of his hell, just another detail to help drive Bobby to his next mental breakdown, just another horrible experience to undo all the young man had overcome. With that thought, one last idea flickered in her mind. She looked up at Papa savoring the moment. If this didn't work, she decided, a quick death would be better than seeing his disgusting smile a minute longer.

"You'd better pray there's more than one bullet in that," she said.

He snorted and smirked. "I'm old," he said. "But one is all I'll need, bitch." He aimed the pistol.

"What about the one for yourself? Or have you even thought about his plans for you?" She attempted a confident tone while speaking fast. "What's it like being in the dark alone, waiting for death?" She saw his finger wrap around the trigger. The emaciated muscles in his arm twitched. "What's it like being buried alive, Harrison?"

A reaction came to his face. "How do you—"

"It doesn't matter how I know. This time, nobody will be coming to dig you up. This time, there'll be enough air to draw it out for a long time. I'm betting the sound of that dripping water itself will drive you mad within a day."

"She's playing you," Kage said in a tighter tone than Becky had heard from him.

"No, he's playing you, Harrison. He only wants his name remembered. Look over there. That's the sick monument he wants to leave behind. He wants me to be a part of it, but not only me. He's been playing you from the beginning. What makes you think he ever cared about your revenge."

"Shoot her," Kage said. "Do it now."

Papa's smirk quivered and fell. His eyes dimmed and froze. He no longer looked like a monster, just a very old man with a dreadful memory playing in his head.

"You know as well as I do that you can't trust him," Becky said. "He's a psychopath. He shows mercy to no one, including you. I think it was his plan all along to leave you down here to die and rot. He calls this his hell for a reason. I wonder how long it will last. Days? A week? There's one thing I do know, if that wasn't his plan before, it damned sure is now. It may be a prison cell you go back to, but I'll get you out of here. He won't." She held her breath and set her eyes on the muzzle pointed at her, hoping its shaking wasn't just from Papa's old age. Slowly, it began turning toward Kage.

The instant Kage charged Papa, Becky was on her feet. She ran toward the hole of the alcove and dove through it, hardly feeling the jagged stone scrape over her skin. She jerked on the ground until she planted a foot, pushed up, and ran clumsily up the slope with her arms wriggling behind her back. Her shoe struck a rock, and her crash against the limestone coincided with the pop of a round fired. A death groan wavered from the alcove. If it were Papa's, she knew she had only moments to regain her footing. Precious seconds passed while she fought to stand. She rose and ran blindly up the dark slope.

"You won't make it, Chief."

The voice was Kage's, a short distance behind her. She forced her feet to move faster. They struck more rocks in the darkness, causing her to stumble more while she ran. She heard his feet falling behind her and his echoing laugh. But she felt a sliver of hope when the ground leveled. A little farther ahead, sunlight showed her the exit. Becky continued her wobbly sprint toward it. She was wondering how she would crawl through the narrow hole when his hand gripped the back of her shirt. He spun her around and slung her to the ground. She fell hard, hitting her head on the limestone floor and seeing white flashes behind her eyes. Dazed, she huffed while she looked up at him walking between her and the way out. He moved lethargically while breathing hard too. Blood leaked freely from his arm. Becky watched him tear away his soaked bandage. He wrapped each end of it around his hands.

"I'll give you credit," he said. "You tried." He wound the cloth tighter around his hands. "Was no easy task convincing that old devil not to kill you." He came to her with the blood-dripping cloth held out. "So now it's only us, Becky. I enjoyed our game. You've been a worthy opponent."

Becky saw the light behind him dim. "I understand your anger," she said, crawling backward, trying to buy time. "Anybody would understand. They treated you terribly. But you got your revenge." She watched the hole behind him. "They're dead. Killing me isn't important."

"Wrong," he said. "You're Becky Hawk. You're the one I chose, the special one. Killing you means everything." He moved closer with the cloth. "I'm sorry, but I'm not feeling as generous as before. This may not go quickly and painlessly." He hovered over her, peering down at her, and then he unwound the cloth from his left hand. "You are resourceful," he said, "but your face is much too readable." He removed the pistol from his waistband, turned, and fired.

Becky's wail echoed through the cave when a red hole erupted on Dan's shirt. Blood spread over his chest even before he fell. "You son of a bitch!" she screamed, lunging forward.

Kage pushed her back down and returned the pistol to his waistband. His hand wound the cloth around it again while he straddled her. "No truer words have ever been spoken." He leaned down. The bloody cloth went around her neck.

The first jerk of pressure cut off Becky's cry. His weight pressed down on her. His eyes locked on hers. She felt her throat burn. Primal fear sprang deep inside her. She kicked and thrashed with all she had, only to feel herself fading. Her sight dimmed and her movements slowed. His eyes staring into hers were the only thing she saw.

"This is our moment," she heard him breathe. "Soon, our spirits will be bonded forever. It's meant to be, Becky. Accept your fate. I'll be following you soon into eternity."

Then came darkness. She heard herself gag, but it sounded distant. So this is how it ends, she thought. There was silence. She stopped struggling and had one last thought: *How nice it will be to see Ed again.*

A trace of light flashed. The pressure on her neck tightened, eased, and tightened again. She saw him through tunneled vision. She wanted to reach for him. She wanted to go to him. But the pressure eased once more, and soon she realized it wasn't Ed she saw. Her brain resurged. Sounds returned. Kage no longer looked down at her. His head was turned back with a facial contortion. A haggard, sun-scarred arm was wrapped around his neck.

Blood rolled from the corner of Dan's mouth. His face cringed in his effort to apply more strength. Becky felt the squeeze on her neck again. Her sight faded once more then returned. "Hold him, Dad," she spluttered. She watched him fight to keep his arm locked. Veins bulged in his neck. His arm trembled while he maintained his grip. Kage bucked against the pressure with his eyes wide and his face turning color. Blood streamed from his open knife wound and down his arm. His movements slowed. Becky felt the pressure he was applying reduce to a weak tug. He gagged saliva onto his lips while his eyes lost focus, and then he fell when Becky rolled herself from under him.

Dan labored with his breaths. He leaned toward Becky just before he fell seated and rolled over onto the limestone floor.

Movement at the cave entrance switched Becky's focus. Shiloh crawled through. She paused just inside while her eyes strained at her blurred images.

"I'm here." The shout scorched Becky's throat. Her vision spun as she worked her way to her knees then her feet. "Come to me." She heard a cough and saw movement from Kage. His eyes opened some. His hand roamed for the Luger. Becky staggered within kicking distance and summoned all her strength into it. Her foot slammed under his chin, throwing his head back and making his teeth clack together before he crumpled.

"Daddy?" Shiloh's head turned side-to-side as she walked into the cave. She gasped and jerked back when Becky approached her.

"It's me," Becky said. "No one is going to hurt you now. You're safe."

Shiloh's eyes remained unsettled. "Where's Daddy? Is he all right?"

"Just a minute and we'll see him. I need a favor from you first. Look down and take the keys from my belt. Find the little, thin one. I need you to unlock my hands." Becky turned and watched Kage while her sister leaned in close, found and removed the keys. She could feel her fumbling with the cuffs. "The small hole," Becky said, trying to sound patient. "Fit the small key in it and turn. You only need to unlock one. Hurry, Shiloh." She heard the click and pulled her arm free. She saw Kage stirring again while she took the key from Shiloh and unlocked her other arm.

Kage was still dazed when Becky got to him. She jerked the Luger from his waistband and placed it in her holster. Seconds later, she had his left wrist locked in a cuff. He fought with her then. Becky felt no regrets in twisting his injured arm hard and making him screech while she brought it behind his back. The sound of the second cuff clicking on his wrist sent him into a wild struggle on the ground. Becky stood up and watched him jerk against the cuffs until he tired.

"Kill me," he begged. His voice had changed entirely. It sounded like that of a scared child. "Shoot me, Chief. Please, kill me. No one will ever know."

Becky knelt over him with her hand reaching for her duty belt. She removed her key again and, this time, used it to double lock each cuff. She felt a brief flash of pity when she heard him whimper. "Sorry, Johnny," she said. "That's one fate you don't get to decide." She turned toward Shiloh's cry and walked to her.

The young girl knelt over her father, holding his hand and begging him not to die. "We have to get him help," she said.

Becky knelt beside them and pulled open Dan's shirt. She placed her hand over his wound and applied some pressure. "Thank you," she said. "Hang in there."

He squeezed Shiloh's hand, removed Becky's from his chest, and squeezed it too. There came a smile and a glint in his eyes while he looked at them both. "My girls," he said, and then faded.

CHAPTER 47

"Take care of yourself, Cynthia," Becky said into the phone. She hung up and walked to the window Wendy stood at. It was the end of a long day. Neither woman had taken the time yet to change her dress.

"Do you think she'll ever get over it?" Wendy asked.

Becky looked across the lawn at Bobby and Shiloh sitting at the end of the pier. They were dangling their feet in the water. "Bobby did. She will eventually. But whoever this boy was, he must've been really special to her."

Wendy nodded. "He sure must've been. Young love. Who was yours?"

"You know it was Ed."

Wendy patted Becky's back. "Then maybe you're the one who should talk to her. How are you by the way?"

Becky nodded. "Good. I really am."

"Did you read the letter she wrote to him?"

"Yes. All fifteen pages. I feel like I know him now."

Wendy smiled. "Well, with the hell you've been through, I'm glad you have that now. Tell you what, how about I drive to Jabber's and get some barbecue plates. We can just start over. Only no chicken piccata dinner this time."

Becky broke a laugh. "I'll never have an appetite for it again anyway. Need some money for the barbecue?"

"Nah. It's on me. Go talk to her. I'll be back in a flash."

Sheriff Donaldson and Aaron arrived just after Wendy left. Becky joined them on the back deck.

"Any luck?" she asked. Their faces answered it.

"No," Donaldson said. "We didn't send a man down to look for him. It's just too dangerous. The lodge could collapse at any time. That sinkhole under it is the biggest I've ever seen. The Lord only knows how deep it is. The fall itself probably killed him. He could've been washed out into the lake. If so, we'll find his body eventually. But it's impossible that he survived."

"On a better note," Aaron said, "we saw Detective Evans today. He's doing a lot better. He said he understands your confusion in the old hospital, because he was a hair away from pulling the trigger too. He wanted us to tell you congratulations on a hell of a fine job putting the Interstate Killer behind bars. He thinks you may see a change in attitude from the deputies toward you now."

"Sheriff Newton too?"

"Some things never change, Becky," said Donaldson.

"You're right, Sheriff," she said. "But enough does if you keep giving a damn, right? I suppose I should go tell her."

"Want me to help?" Donaldson asked.

"No. I believe this should be between me and her."

"Did they let you talk to Aunt Cynthia?" Bobby asked when Becky joined him and Shiloh on the pier.

"Yes." Becky removed her shoes, sat between them, and put her feet in the water also. "I told her that I forgive her."

Bobby smiled. "Sure, is better when you learn which wolf to feed, isn't it?"

"It sure is. I wish I'd learned it sooner."

Bobby slipped on his shoes. "I believe I'll visit with Aaron and the sheriff for a while."

"Thank you, Bobby," Becky said. She waited until he was gone before turning to Shiloh. "Pastor Owens preached a nice service today, don't you think?"

Shiloh kept her eyes on the lake. "Yes. Daddy would've liked it." Her feet swept through the water. "They didn't find him, did they?"

"No. I'm so sorry. He must've been a great guy."

Shiloh nodded and wiped her finger under her glasses. "Yeah. He was. He made me feel like nobody else has. He made me feel special. He had so many dreams. I wish he could've had a chance for them to come true."

"I think at least one of them did," Becky said. "You know, I don't like telling people that I understand what they're feeling. But I believe I can in your case."

"Does the pain get better?"

"Yes. You'll have good days and bad ones. There will be setbacks, but in time, the good days will come more. When I think of Ed now, I remember the joy he gave me. I smile instead of crying. It helps when you have people who love you around. I'd like for you to stay with us until you know what you want to do. It can be for as long as you like. Will you at least think about it?"

"Yeah, I'll think about it. Thanks, Becky."

Bacon fried in a skillet the next morning when Wendy walked in from the guesthouse wearing her robe.

"Good morning, Beck."

"You're up early," Becky said, pouring pancake batter into a hot pan. "I thought you might sleep in."

Wendy poured herself a glass of milk. "Junior is kicking again. I guess the smell of bacon frying is having its effect. He or she is saying "feed me.""

Becky forked the bacon onto paper towels. "What are you guys doing today?"

Wendy snatched a piece. "I don't know. How about just hanging around here and resting? I think we all could use it, especially you."

"Wish I could," said Becky. "But I need to go to work. There's reports to follow up on. I need to visit Curt's family too."

"I'm very sorry about him," Wendy said. "From what I heard, he was a hell of a guy."

"One of the best." Becky tried keeping her smile while her throat tightened. "Anyway, breakfast is about done. Why don't you go get Aaron? I'll wake up Bobby and Shiloh."

Becky walked down the hall. She called for Bobby, and then knocked on the next bedroom door, waited, and knocked again. "Shiloh, are you awake yet? Breakfast is ready." She turned the doorknob. "Shiloh?" she said while walking in. "Oh, no!"

Wendy stopped at the back door when she heard it. She hurried to the bedroom, where Becky stood at an opened window. "What happened?"

Becky looked at the screen on the ground below. "The latches were pulled up," she said. "Looks like the screen was removed from the inside."

"Good grief. She's run away again?" Wendy looked around the room and went to what she saw on the nightstand."

Becky studied the window. "It's a pretty good jump to the ground. I just wonder why she didn't go out the backdoor."

Wendy handed over the note she'd found. "Maybe someone came to the window and helped her down."

Becky read it: "Becky, please don't look for us. We'll be Ok. Thanks so much for everything. Proud to call you Big Sis. Love always, Shiloh." The S swept around the other letters of the signature.

Wendy raised her eyebrows and grinned. "Well, are you going to look for them?"

Becky folded the note, slipped it into her pocket, and looked out over the lake. She thought of Ed and smiled. "One day," she said. "But not now."

About the Author

Robbie Lanier is a retired, thirty-year law enforcement officer living in Lexington, NC. He wrote short stories for most of his life, mainly for his own entertainment and his family's. The year after he retired from law enforcement, he began writing *Black Lake: A Becky Hawk Murder Mystery,* his first novel published in 2023. Along the way, he decided Becky Hawk and the other characters might work in a book series. *Kage* is his second novel in the series.

When not writing, Robbie enjoys traveling to the beaches and mountains of the Tarheel state, fishing, and bow-making. But his biggest enjoyment is spending time with his wife (Sherri), Son (Jerry), daughter-in-law (Sarah), and grandson (Oliver).

ANOTHER BOOK
BY ROBBIE LANIER

Black Lake: A Becky Hawk Murder Mystery

In the small, timbering town of Black Lake, North Carolina, life seemingly consists of only honest, hard work. But that's before newcomer Ed Hawk becomes the town's lone police officer and is found murdered on Halloween night, 1963.

While a manhunt closes in on the suspect, the grieving widow discovers evidence of her husband's last investigation and begins having questions. Is it possible that Ed stumbled onto a dark town secret before his death? Who in town can she trust?

With the help of her quirky schoolteacher friend, Wendy, and rookie deputy sheriff, Aaron, Becky Hawk walks the thin line between finding her answers and avoiding the same fate as her husband. Her search for justice takes her from the mountains to the coast of the state... But there could be one answer she doesn't wish to know.

This is the first book of the Becky Hawk Mystery Series.

TESSELLATA

"The law of evolution is that the strongest survives.
Yes, and the strongest, in the existence of any social
species, are those who are most social. In human terms,
most ethical... There is no strength to be gained from
hurting one another.
Only weakness."

Ursula K. Le Guin